ANDREW C.F. WHITEHEAD

OUT OF THE
DIGITAL
ETHER

A young man travels back in time to help a noble
family face a terrible enemy

ANDREW C.F. WHITEHEAD

OUT OF THE DIGITAL ETHER

A young man travels back in time to help a noble
family face a terrible enemy

MEREO
Cirencester

Mereo Books

1A The Wool Market Dyer Street Cirencester Gloucestershire GL7 2PR
An imprint of Memoirs Publishing www.mereobooks.com

Out of the Digital Ether: 978-1-86151-855-2

First published in Great Britain in 2014
by Mereo Books, an imprint of Memoirs Publishing

The address for Memoirs Publishing Group Limited can be found at
www.memoirspublishing.com

The Memoirs Publishing Group Ltd Reg. No. 7834348

The Memoirs Publishing Group supports both The Forest Stewardship Council® (FSC®) and the PEFC® leading international forest-certification organisations. Our books carrying both the FSC label and the PEFC® and are printed on FSC®-certified paper. FSC® is the only forest-certification scheme supported by the leading environmental organisations including Greenpeace. Our paper procurement policy can be found at
www.memoirspublishing.com/environment

Typeset in 12/18pt Plantin
by Wiltshire Associates Publisher Services Ltd. Printed and bound in Great Britain by Printondemand-Worldwide, Peterborough PE2 6XD

ABOUT THE AUTHOR

Andrew C.F. Whitehead was born in the seaside resort of Brighton, England in 1951. He left school at the age of 15 having been an academic failure (he is a little dyslexic.) He remained in Brighton, working locally and attending the town Technical College, until he went to the University of East Anglia in 1974 at the age of 23.

Having qualified as a teacher in 1979, he taught in what is now the Bucks New University and various school in Buckinghamshire before moving to West Oxfordshire in 2007. Here, he began looking into the history of his new home and began to write his first book, Into the Ether, which is largely set in the West Oxfordshire area but in two time periods – the 21st century and the 14th.

This book is dedicated to MY Megan – the world's most reluctant muse.

CONTENTS

CHAPTER ONE

SORCERY

"Captain, they have disappeared!" the lead Gloucester Cathedral guard exclaimed to his captain, who was bringing up the rear.

"Don't be ridiculous, man. Look for them!" replied Captain Scarlett, who had not properly seen the disappearance of Edmund and Sir Henry.

"But sir, they were both sitting on the ground, and then they weren't." The other three guards mumbled their concurrence.

"Look for them!" shouted the captain, and the four guards began to spread out among the stubby bushes to begin their vain search. Their search got wider and wider as the captain continued to insist, "They must be here somewhere." After about 10 minutes, this began to gently morph into "Sorcery! The work of the Devil! He has made them invisible to protect his own!" He directed his men to continue their search wider and wider afield.

"Sir, there are horsemen approaching!' shouted the guard furthest from the point of disappearance and closest to Burford.

"Cease the search and form a defensive line in front of me," commanded the captain, aware that the approaching horsemen were probably Burford's men.

The four guards lined up in front of their captain with their swords drawn and raised towards the approaching horsemen, who were galloping towards the Bishop's men. In the lead of the eight horsemen was Knut, closely followed by Alfred, with six other men behind them. Knut reined in his horse a few feet in front of the swords pointed in his direction. Ostentatiously he did not draw his sword, and nor did any of Lord Burford's other men. There would be no point in attacking the Bishop's men, and the lack of swords indicated confidence in Lord Burford's men's sense of numerical and moral superiority.

There was silence as Knut assessed the situation, and then he asked, "Where are Sir Henry and Sir Edmund?"

There was no answer, as the Bishop's men had none.

"Where are Sir Henry and Sir Edmund?" repeated Knut more forcefully. "What have you done with them?"

Silence. The Bishop's captain opened his mouth and closed it again. Knut stared into Captain Scarlett's eyes, finally eliciting a statement of the blindingly obvious.

"They are not here," said the captain.

Now it was Knut's turn to be dumbfounded. He took a deep breath and responded, "Don't be ridiculous, man! They came this way and you were close behind."

The captain took a moment to gather his thoughts, and hoping not to sound as ridiculous as Knut had said he was, replied, "We pursued the heretics to this point and they simply disappeared."

Knut looked around, looked at the captain, pursed his lips and emitted a dismissive "Pouff!"

"It is true. They just disappeared into thin air."

Knut looked at the captain again and expressed the obvious. "That is impossible."

The Bishop's captain now felt more confident and sneeringly enquired, "Do you think we have them in our saddlebags? Or do you think we killed them and buried them before you arrived?" His men were now feeling more confident as well, and sniggered at their captain's wit.

Knut was clearly getting nowhere with this line of enquiry and he turned to Alfred, saying, "Take three men and search the surroundings."

"Yes, sir," replied Alfred and directed three men to join him in a repeat of what the Bishop's men had been through just before Lord Burford's men arrived. As they spread out, Knut fixed his eyes on the captain once more and said, "Tell your men to lower their swords, captain, there will be no bloodletting here today."

"Indeed, there will not – and that includes the blood of the heretics. Sheath your weapons, men."

The guards did as they were ordered and there was a long period of silence as the surrounding bushes were searched for any sign of Edmund and Henry. As Alfred and his comrades got further and further from the circle, a serene smile came across the face of the Bishop's captain. Knut could see that one of his men had hold of a riderless horse, and when it became clear that the men were not finding the two escapees, Knut called, "Return, men!"

On returning to the group Alfred said to Knut, "Sir, we could find nothing except this one horse. Another was sighted but could not be caught. We have found only light hoof prints starting from this point, which we assume were the hooves of the Bishop's horses looking for Sir Henry and Sir Edmund. There is no sign of the two horses having galloped onwards, sir."

"Told you so!" the captain said triumphantly.

"Aha! So, if they are not here, clearly you have not got what you want," Knut responded, trying to put the captain in his place. "I believe you tricked your way into Burford by telling the men on the gate that you had the Bishop's business to discuss with Father Mackenzie."

"We *are* on the Bishop's business," retorted the captain sarcastically. Knut ignored the captain and went on, "So, let me make it clear, you are not to try to enter Burford again without..."

"Oooh, made you Lord have they?" interjected the captain sarcastically.

Knut ignored this once more and went on, saying, "Without the express permission of Lord Burford. I shall inform the men on the gate. Now you can go back to Gloucester and inform the Bishop."

"Oh, I am sure he will be very impressed with the words of a *servant,*" the last word being emphasised in further sarcasm. "But there can now be no doubt that these two are agents of the Devil. How else would they have simply disappeared into thin air?"

At that, Knut turned his horse and trotted away with the other men following him. The Bishop's men went along the hillside at an angle, heading to pick up the Gloucester road a little further west, the other side of Burford. When Knut reached the crest of the hill, all the horsemen stopped and watched as the Bishop's men reached the road and galloped off into the distance.

From the makeshift gate at the top of the hill going out of Burford, Knut and the other men could be clearly seen in the light of the rising three-quarter moon, as could the Bishop's men disappearing into the distance. There was much commotion and discussion about whether or not more men should be sent out in support of Knut and the others. With nobody left 'in charge' it was difficult for any decisions to be made.

As the discussion continued, Knut and his men began to trot towards the Burford gate. The trot soon developed into a canter and it was not long before they reached it. A cheer and words of encouragement erupted as they arrived and Knut shouted, "I have told the Bishop's men they are not to return without the express permission of Lord Burford, so, if they arrive, you know what to do."

Another cheer went up and Knut turned to Alfred and the others, saying, "Sir Henry and Sir Edmund are safe and gone for now, so you men get on with your duties. I must report to the Lady." With that he trotted down the hill towards Burford House, leaving the others to disperse as their duties required.

Of course, only half of what he had told the men was true – they had gone, but were they safe? And it would not be long before the other men told the story of the disappearing young men, but he really hadn't got the time, or the inclination, to explain now. Anyway, what could he say? If he were honest he would have to say that he was as confused as Captain Scarlett. The only difference was that he was more concerned as to the fate of the men, particularly Sir Henry, than was the captain, who only wanted to take the two as prisoners to the Bishop of Gloucester, to be tried for blasphemy and heresy at the least. This was before the crime of sorcery was added in, as the only possible explanation of their disappearance. Knut was pretty low down the feudal pecking order, and the fact that he had played such an important and confident part in the interdiction of the

Bishop's men made the other lower orders feel good. He was one of their own.

As Knut approached the door of Burford House it was opened by Peter, who called, "The Lady is waiting to see you, Knut".

"And I wish to see her," replied Knut as he dismounted. As Peter rushed in, followed by Knut, they passed various members of the Burford household, including the four remaining Burford children, Stephen, Anne, Marion and Joan, plus Cook and Megan. Knut had not yet decided how to approach the explanation of the disappearance of Sir Henry and Sir Edmund, and the problem was still running through his head as Peter knocked on the door.

"Come," came the voice of Lady Burford from within the room. Peter opened the door and ushered Knut into the room where Lady Burford was seated. She was waiting to hear about the Bishop's men, but most of all about her son, Henry. If the events sounded implausible to those who had been directly looking for the two, how much more implausible would they sound being told to a third party?

As Knut entered, his eyes caught those of Lady Burford and he immediately looked down in deference and stood to attention. "My lady," he said, genuflecting automatically.

"You do not have Sir Henry with you, Knut," said Lady Burford with a clear sense of apprehension and disappointment in her voice.

"No, my lady," replied Knut, irrationally feeling responsible and guilty for the absence of her son.

"Tell me what has happened, Knut," demanded the wife of the Lord. She was the only person with any real authority in her husband's absence.

"Well, my lady..." Knut began to relate how, after Lady Burford had called for Knut, when it became clear that the two young men had slipped out the back of the house and the Bishop's men left in pursuit, he had organised a pursuit party that had been a few minutes behind the Bishop's men. He told how he and his men had arrived at the point where the Bishop's men were looking for their quarry and how they could be found nowhere by either search party. This factual account left Lady Burford to draw her own conclusions as to the reason for her son's disappearance. Having described the disappearance of the two, Knut stood in silence, leaving this news to sink in.

"Go on, Knut," said the Lady. She wanted to know more and was hoping for some clue as to the fate of her son and his friend.

Knut took a deep breath. "Of course, Captain Scarlett made use of their disappearance, saying it was sorcery and that it proved they were agents of the Devil," he said. He had thought of leaving out this bit of bad news, but had decided that the Lady needed to know the full truth of the danger that her son, and the Lord's heir, was now in.

The Lady's demeanour became more despondent and she waved her hand slightly to indicate to Knut that he should go on with his story. This he did, telling her that after the search was given up, he had told Captain Scarlett to go back to Gloucester and not return to Burford without the express permission of the Lord. He did not add that the captain had mocked him for his presumption of the Lord's authority. Knut himself had been very reluctant to tell the Lady he had taken it upon himself to issue this command and was afraid of what the Lady, let alone the Lord, would make of it.

"And?" was the only response from Lady Burford, so Knut concluded the story by telling how he and his men had watched as the Bishop's men rode towards Gloucester, and then they had returned to the gate at the entrance to Burford and instructed the men there not to let any of the Bishop's men back again without the express permission of the Lord. Once more the Lady remained silent and Knut was left wondering how his actions were being judged.

Lady Burford sat in silence and then jumped up, startling Knut. "I shall write a letter to Lord Burford explaining the situation. It must be conveyed to Lord Burford immediately, but not by you, Knut, as I shall need you here. Who do you suggest should go?"

Knut thought and then said, "Arthur is a strong rower, my lady, and capable of carrying out any instructions given to him."

"Rower?" responded Lady Burford. "Would it not be quicker across country than down the river, as he will have no luggage to convey?" Knut felt awkward again as he was only used to following instructions, not giving his opinion on what should be done. He gathered his thoughts and replied, "From my experiences as we rowed to Windsor and back again, there is much fear abroad and there may not be inns and liveries willing to supply horses to strangers crossing country. Also, many roads are closed and he may not get through and might get lost."

"I see," mused the Lady as she gave his words thought. Then she decisively commanded, "Arthur is to come here as soon as possible to collect a letter I shall write to the Lord. You shall tell the kitchen to provide food and anything else he may need. The stables will know which is the best horse to get him to Tadpole. Were they still functioning at Tadpole when you returned from Windsor?"

"Yes, my lady, they were," Knut reassured her.

"Then off you go, Knut, and I shall write the letter for Lord Burford."

"Yes, my lady," responded Knut. He left the room feeling very relieved that although Lady Burford had not passed comment on his actions, neither had she expressed her displeasure at his presumptuous behaviour.

It was the middle of the night when Captain Scarlett and his men arrived back at Gloucester Cathedral, and far too late to report to the Bishop, so the captain dismissed his men and took to his own bed. A few hours later he was at the Bishop's palace requesting an audience with the Bishop. His request was conveyed to the Bishop and he was immediately ushered in.

"Ah, Scarlet, what news of the heretics?"

"The Devil has taken his own, Your Grace, and they are nowhere to be found."

"Nowhere to be found?" responded the Bishop, "Tell me all!"

The captain explained the situation in great detail, ending with the obvious conclusion that the Devil must have taken them away to protect them. He did not really embellish the story, not so much out of honesty and integrity but because he was pretty sure that blaming the disappearance on the Devil would absolve him from the responsibility of not having found the two young men.

"A clear case of sorcery," observed the Bishop. "Mmmm! But how did the heretics know you and your men were coming to get them?"

The captain had given no thought to this question. He stammered, "I... I... I do not know, Your Grace." He paused and added in self-justification, "When we arrived at the church of Saint John the Baptist, which was at night, we stayed hidden with Father Mackenzie until word reached us that the two had returned. Then we went to arrest them, but as we searched the house it became clear they had gone out the back and taken to two horses. A stable lad told us they had ridden towards Shilton and then up over the hill towards Black Bourton, so we pursued them to the spot I have told you about, Your Grace."

"Mmmm! It would seem someone had warned them."

"Perhaps the Devil himself, Your Grace?" suggested the captain helpfully.

"Or a more temporal informant," said the Bishop dismissively. He was not entirely content with the easy explanation that it was the Devil's work.

The captain concluded his saga, relating how Knut had acted as the Lord's agent and told them never to return to Burford without the express permission of Lord Burford.

"Did he indeed! A mere villein giving orders in the name of the Lord to prevent the lawful work of God," the Bishop said indignantly. "We shall see about Knut when we do return to Burford. But for now, there is little to be done. Lord Burford will eventually return to Burford and be informed that his heretic son, and his Devil's agent friend, have disappeared and are under the protection of the Devil himself. Let's see how unpious and mighty he is then! I am sure Father Mackenzie will, with God's help, find a way of informing me of the Lord's return." The Bishop then added as an afterthought, "Or if anyone else should return!"

"Yes, Your Grace," concurred Captain Scarlett.

"Off you go, Scarlett. I shall call you when God sees fit to require us in his work. Again."

"Thank you, Your Grace." With that Captain Scarlett withdrew, feeling happy that he would not be held responsible for the failure to capture his quarry.

CHAPTER TWO

HOME AND AWAY

Bdumff! I landed and slid down the back of the settee just in time to hear an "Ow!" from Henry as he landed hard and fell over on his back. I had arrived a little too far back on the settee and he had arrived a foot higher than he had left the 14th century. I took a deep breath as the mist cleared and realised we had *both* got back to the 21st century, and then realised that Henry had not 'got back' as he had been brought forward.

As I sat there breathing hard, Henry quickly leaned forward and grabbed hold of the laptop once more. I realised why and calmly said, "It's all right, Henry, you can let go now." He did so and began to look around, bewildered. I clicked 'shut down' and closed down the laptop before picking up the nearby mains lead and plugging it in.

Henry quickly leaned forward and grabbed hold of the laptop once more. I realised why and calmly said, "It's all right, Henry, you can let go now." He began to look around, bewildered, as I clicked 'shut down' and closed down the laptop before picking up the nearby mains lead and plugging it into it.

As I jumped up, Henry was sitting on the floor. In a weak voice he asked, "Where are we?"

"Home," I replied perfunctorily. I quickly walked towards the landline and pressed the messages button on the base.

"No we're not!" observed Henry in a slightly less weak but more confused voice.

"Yes, we are, but it's my home, not yours, Henry."

"Your home?" he questioned as the first message began to play on the answer phone. "Hello, Edmund. How are you?" came Mum's voice. I needed to hear no more, so I switched it off.

"What was that?" asked Henry, now sounding more like himself.

"My mum."

I picked up the piece of paper left by the phone with my family's Australian number on it. Henry was looking around and becoming more and more bemused. As I started to dial the number on the landline (I certainly wasn't going to use my mobile to call Australia) he asked, "What's a mum?"

"My mum. Mother." I answered factually once more and probably no more enlightening for poor Henry, who was obviously in a state of real confusion and getting worse by the second. I finished dialling and looked at the clock on the DVD recorder. 9:17pm. It was getting dark outside, as it had been when we had left the 14th century, but it seemed a little darker here as we were indoors.

Henry opened his mouth again to speak and I said, "Stay quiet please while I talk to my mum." Henry's mouth closed again as I heard the phone ringing the other end. Henry looked around and out of the window onto the driveway where my Mini and my dad's car were. My family had driven to the airport in mum's car. It must be morning in Australia, so I was hoping they would be there to talk to me.

"Hello?" said a woman's voice in an Australian accent.

"Oh, hello. Is that Karen?" I asked, hoping I had correctly remembered the name of the friend in Australia they were staying with.

"Yes, it is. That must be Edmund. Your family will be glad to hear from you. Your mum's standing here. I'll pass you over."

"Edmund!" exclaimed my mum. "Where have you been?"

"I have been to see a friend of mine in Cornwall and there was no signal," I answered. It was a prepared lie. Well, I could hardly tell her the truth.

"But we've been calling you for days, Edmund. We've been so worried."

"Yes, I'm sorry mum. Anyway, I'm back now. How have you all been?" I asked, trying to move the conversation on.

"Oh, we're fine and all having a wonderful time and I'm so much happier now we are talking to you."

"What have you been doing in Australia?" I asked, making it clear the previous subject was finished with.

"We've been doing the tourist things, going to the local town, to the beach, swimming in Karen's pool, even though it is winter here, she lives in the Northern Territory so it's warmer in their winter than it is in our summer," she told me, seemingly happy with the explanation of my silence.

"Oh, that sounds great, Mum. Almost wish I were with you." I spoke only half-untruthfully as I was still not sure my trip into the past had been a good idea.

"Yes, and tomorrow we're starting our trip to the Outback, so you might not hear from *us* for a while."

I could see Henry hopping from foot to foot and looking at me more and more confused as I continued to talk to myself. Then he realised there was a voice at the other end and seemed even more confused. Not surprising really. How could he have any concept of a telephone?

"Look, mum, I have only just got back and I have a million and one things to do, so I can't chat now," I told her, feeling the need to calm down poor Henry.

"All right, Edmund," she said. "Your brother and sister are playing in the pool, at the end of a very long garden, but your dad's here, so I'll pass you over. Bye, Edmund, we'll talk to you soon and I'm so much happier now I know you're okay. I'll put your dad on."

"Bye mum."

"Bye, my darling boy. Here's dad."

I looked at Henry again. He seemed to be even more stressed and was running around me trying to put his ear near to mine. His breathing was short and I knew I couldn't leave him much longer.

"Hello, Edmund. Where have you been, son?"

"Oh, I have explained all that to mum and I'm sure she will tell you," I told him, trying to make the conversation as short as possible.

"Ah, okay. Well, as long as you're okay."

"Yes, I am, Dad, and Mum tells me you're off to the Outback tomorrow so you will be away for a few days."

"Yes, we are, but I'm sure we will find a phone at some time. Things have changed since the 19th century."

Not nearly as much as since the 14th century, I thought, but I certainly wasn't going to start on that one.

"Okay, great to talk to you both, dad, and don't bust a gut trying to call me, I probably won't be in much."

"All right, son. Have a good day. Bye for now."

"Yes, bye, dad," I replied.

"Bye, Edmund!" shouted Mum in the background.

"Yes, bye, Mum." I clicked the red button, pleased to get back to the highly-exercised Henry before he had a nervous breakdown. He looked at me, but seemed lost for words. It was very hot and dry in the house, as I had been away for a few days leaving the doors and windows closed, so I walked over and threw open a window and felt the fresh, clear air flood in. It reminded me of when the window had been opened in the nuns' sick room.

Once more I turned to look at Henry, whose jaw seemed to be attached to a yoyo. Eventually words emerged.

"Where are we?" he asked very reasonably, but I could not tell him the full truth immediately, so I started with what I had said before.

"This is my home. I live here." I left that to sink in for while and indicated to him to sit down. This he did and then enquired, "Are we in Saxony?"

I had not thought of this and simply replied, "No."

This didn't seem to help him and he asked the next obvious question. "But how did we get here?"

I had thought about this while I was talking to Mum and Dad and all I could come up with was,

"The laptop we held onto brought us here. That's why I told you to hold on and not let go."

Once more I left this to sink in, hoping he would not ask me the question I simply could not answer – "How?" As he was thinking I leaned over, without giving it any thought, and switched on the table lamp. Immediately the gloom was illuminated by the increasing glow of the bulb. Henry jumped up and shouted, "What's that?"

"It's all right! It's all right," I tried to reassure him, while thinking that this was the least of the technology shocks he was going to get. "It's a sort of candle but a lot easier to use and much brighter. Look!" I leaned over again and switched the lamp off, then switched it on again. After a pause, Henry's hand tentatively went towards the switch.

"Yes, you do it, Henry," I said.

He clicked the light off and then after about ten seconds, during which he seemed to be plucking up courage, he switched it on again, jumping slightly as it lit up once more.

"Sit down, Henry, and don't worry about anything. Nothing is going to harm you."

He sat down again, looked at me and asked, "Where are the Bishop's men?"

"We left them where we were. They can't follow us here, so there's nothing to worry about." I was still trying to make him relax.

Suddenly, the next thought tumbled out of his mouth. "Who were you talking to?"

There was no need to avoid the truth here, so I said, "To my mum and dad... my mother and father."

"How?"

I sat motionless for a while and then picked up the phone hand set and crouched next to him, saying, "Hold this." He took it gently and I walked to my mobile, which I had left on charge all the time I was away, thinking how Dad would have had a go at me for being wasteful and damaging the environment. I picked up the mobile, unplugged it and went through to my contacts until I found 'Home'. I touched 'Call' and waited with the phone at my ear, looking at Henry. A few seconds later the handset rang in Henry's hand and he immediately dropped it. I leaned down, picked it up and pressed the green button, handed it to Henry and said, "Put it next to your ear."

"Hello, Henry", I said sitting down opposite him again.

He flinched but replied, "Good day, Edmund."

"See, easy, isn't it? And it doesn't hurt." I switched off and took the handset from him, replacing it on its base. Henry looked bemused but seemed less stressed, which was a step forward. It made me feel Henry was beginning to settle into the 21st century.

I didn't want to have to be too delicate towards Henry, or to have to tread on eggshells until I got him back to the 14th century (whenever/if ever that would be) and was determined to press on with 'normal' 21st century life. He would simply have to deal with it as I had to deal with 14th century life. Accordingly I said, "I'm going to put some music on," and picked up the television remote control and clicked on.

"Put some music on? You mean you are going to play some music?"

"No, I mean I am going to put some music on," I said. At this point the TV jumped into life with the music radio channel I had left it on last time I had used it. A hundred decibels of electronic music and vocals shot out of the speakers either side of the room. The screen on the wall remained blank and Henry took a step back.

"What's that?" he gasped.

"Music" I replied, and turned down the volume on the remote control so we could at least hear each other talk. Once more Henry's expression was fearful.

"It is going away!" Henry observed.

"No, I have just turned it down." I handed him the remote and pointed to the volume button, saying, "Press that."

Tentatively, Henry pressed the volume button and the music got a little quieter.

"Press again and hold it down" I instructed him. This he did and the music disappeared completely.

"Now press and hold that one," I told him. This he did, and the music reappeared at deafening volume.

"Wow! Wow! Turn it down again," I said, sounding like my parents.

With a bit of fumbling he did so and asked, "Music?"

"Yes, music," I replied. At this point the track came to an end and the DJ started to talk. Once more Henry's jaw dropped and he asked, "Who is that?"

"The DJ," I replied, not very helpfully.

With the remote in his hand he walked forward and stood between the speakers. "But where is he?" Henry enquired as another song started.

"He is a long way from here. You see these two boxes?" I asked, pointing to the speakers on either side of the wall screen. "Well, that is where his voice is coming from."

Henry walked up to one speaker and said, "Good day to you."

"No, Henry, he cannot hear you. It's not like a telephone," I said pointing to the telephone, now on its base.

"Telephone?"

"Yes, a telephone."

"Distant sound," Henry explained in translation from the Greek, more to himself than to me.

"Correct!"

He stood listening for a while and then observed, "But I can hear the instruments on either side of the room."

I didn't think this was the time to go into the details of digital recording and stereo and simply replied, "Yes."

He stood there listening for another minute, then looked at

the remote in his hand and pressed a button. I closed my eyes and cringed. A couple of seconds later the channel changed and the screen sprang into life.

"Holy Mother of God!" exclaimed Henry, and he crossed himself.

On the screen were two people sitting at a table talking. Henry slowly and gently moved towards the screen and, turning his head to one side as if to face someone on screen, said, "Good day to you."

"No, they can't hear you either. It is not like a telephone."

He slowly raised his hand and carefully touched the screen. Of course, nothing happened. Then he stood by the side of the wall screen and tried to look behind the back of it. Of course, he couldn't see anything. After a while he said, "They speak strangely."

"Yes," I replied, pleased that he had brought up the subject of language. "It is a form of English we speak here. You must learn to speak like that until you go back home."

This was greeted with silence and then he expressed what must have been a very deep need: "I want to go home now."

"Well, you can't go home now, Henry," I replied.

"Why not?"

"Because we must wait for the Bishop's men to go away. Maybe even wait until your father returns from Windsor."

Henry stood watching the screen as he thought about what I had said, and became more and more wide-eyed as the scene changed. Eventually he asked, "What if they follow us here?"

"I promise you they cannot follow us here, Henry."

"Why not?" he asked, quite reasonably.

"Because they do not have one of these," I told him, pointing to the laptop.

Another silence ensued and he asked, "But where are we?"

What could I do except to answer honestly and say, "Not far from Burford". I gently took the remote control from his hand and changed back to a music channel, as I thought he would see too much on screen for someone who was nearly 700 years ahead of his time. I thought that this must be even more difficult for him than it was for me in the 14st century. At least I knew from history roughly what to expect; he would have no idea at all. I was now home and quite comfortable, but he was away and well outside of his comfort zone.

I went to open the door to the kitchen, and as I did so, a very loud roar came through the open window. Henry stepped towards the window and looked out.

"Look, there's a giant bird screaming across the sky!" he shouted above the noise.

"Yes, it's a Tornado, and if you think that's loud you should have been here when they still flew VC10s. Or when the Vulcan used to visit sometimes. But at least that was a beautiful aircraft."

Henry stood looking through the open window and added, "It is on fire".

"Sort of. What's more, it is a lot cleaner than the VC10s were."

"But where has it come from?"

"The airbase just across the road, but it's not a bird. It has people inside it."

"People in it?" he asked, seeming even more confused. I ignored this and continued into the kitchen. Henry was now leaning out of the window and craning his neck to see the plane disappearing.

"It's gone!" he said as I walked into the kitchen.

By now I was very hungry and determined to have

something to eat, so I walked to the kettle and picked it up to fill it, only to find myself nearly bumping into Henry as I turned around.

"What is this room?" he asked, looking around.

"It's the kitchen."

"Kitchen?"

I tried to ignore him, finding it a little difficult answering so many questions.

"So where is the fire?" he asked.

"Look, Henry," I said rather exasperated, "you must simply accept things are not the same here as where you come from."

He stood in silence open-mouthed, so I decided to pre-empt the questions by giving him a tour of the kitchen.

"Okay, this is a kettle," I said, "and this is the tap I get water out of." I turned the tap and let the water flow into the kettle. "Now I put it on here and wait for it to heat up." Placing the kettle on its base I moved to my right, gently pushing Henry out of my way. I continued to assess Henry's state of mind by watching his face. It seemed more interested than frightened, which pleased me.

"This is a cooker, or a stove. We boil pots on top," I said, turning the four knobs and pressing the ignition, causing the gas rings to ignite. "And down here are the two ovens."

Henry's eyes bulged at the sight of the instant flames. "But it's so small!"

I thought, if that was his main concern we were making rapid progress. But I did not respond. I moved on and reached up, saying, "These are cupboards." I opened and closed them. "And these are drawers," I added, opening and closing the drawers below. I was sure these did not present any technical shock and moved on to the wall light switch.

"Here is our candle system," I said, flicking the switch on, and immediately the halogen floodlights filled the room with light. It was fortunate that Henry had seen the lamp in the other room, because the bulbs in the kitchen were not low energy and made the kitchen instantly brighter than daylight. Even though he had seen electric light before, he cowered and shaded his eyes from its brilliance.

I crossed the room and edged behind the kitchen table, pointing to the white box under the work serface. "This is a washing machine," I said.

"A what?" asked Henry.

"A washing machine," I answered and Henry looked blank. "A machine for washing clothes."

Henry continued to look blank. "Washing, yes, but what's a 'machine'?"

"A machine. A machine!" I told him, but I was clearly not making things clearer. "A machine is something that does things for you." Henry seemed no more enlightened. Then his face brightened and he said, "Oh, an engine."

"Well, yes, but it's not going anywhere!" I added, not very helpfully, as I realised 'machine' was not a 14th century word or concept. I pointed to the white box next to it, saying, "This is a tumble dryer." Henry shrugged, which was quite pleasing, as it showed he was now a little more relaxed.

"When we take the damp clothes out of the washing machine we can put them in here to dry them," I explained. I avoided talking about washing lines and the cost of electricity.

"This is the heating cupboard," I added, and pre empted Henry by adding, "It is where we get hot water from and it heats the house in winter." Henry was gently shaking his head. He didn't seem too disturbed by his whistle-stop tour of a 21st century kitchen.

"This tall, white box is a fridge on top and a freezer below."

"A fridge?" He asked raising his eyebrows.

"Yes, a fridge," I answered, opening the door to reveal the usual things to be found in a fridge. Henry looked in and said, "Another candle!"

I did a double take and said, "No, that's not the point". I took his hand and put his fingers on a tub of cream. Two seconds later, "It's cold!" Henry exclaimed, pulling his hand back.

"Yes, and I hope it's cold enough to keep that cream fresh after all this time." Henry's jaw had dropped again. I leaned down and opened the freezer. "Yes, and this is a freezer. It's much colder." I pulled open one of the drawers and started to look for something quick we could eat.

"Snow! Henry exclaimed, as I pulled out a couple of microwave curry and rice packs.

"Yes, snow. That means it needs defrosting."

I was just about to close the drawer when Henry's hand lowered towards the 'snow'. He gently touched it and withdrew his finger an inch before lowering it again and scratching it with his nail. As he raised the ice to his mouth I closed the drawer and turned to the dishwasher. Having tasted the 'snow', he exclaimed, "Oh, a fridge, like a Roman frigidarium!"

"I suppose so, yes," I responded and moved on to explain, "This white box under here is called a dishwasher. It washes plates, cups and dishes for us." I opened the door and immediately closed it again because of the smell emanating from it after days of having been left half full.

"And last, but not least... *Da-da-da-da-da-doo-da!,*" doing my best impression of a fanfare, "The microwave oven!" I pressed the door button and added, "No, not another candle but a method for cooking food very quickly."

I turned my back on Henry to leave him to absorb all he had seen and read the heating instructions on the curry packs. Having removed the outer packaging, I turned to get a fork out of a drawer to pierce the film covering. Out of the corner of my eye I could see Henry looking around with a perplexed expression on his face. As I put the first packet in the microwave, I heard him grunt. I said nothing, pressed the timer and began to lay the table with mats and cutlery. Henry watched my every move and as I placed the cutlery on the table he picked up a table fork and asked, "What's this?"

"A fork," I replied and suddenly realised I had never seen a fork in the 14th century. "It's useful for eating with." As I said this, the kettle clicked and Henry looked at the steam emanating from the spout. I asked, "Tea or coffee?"

"Eh?"

"Would you like to drink tea or coffee?" There was silence as I stood there trying not to show my lack of patience.

"You have coffee?" Henry asked.

"Yes." I took that as a decision, taking the instant coffee jar out of the cupboard and mixing two strong coffees.

"Sugar?" I asked.

"Sugar? You have sugar! I have tasted sugar."

I was beginning to get tired of this and continued to make the coffee as I would drink it. Having got the milk out of the fridge, I poured it into the cups and placed the milk bottle on the side. Henry picked it up, looked at it and asked,

"What's this?"

"Milk."

"Milk?" he said and held it up to the light. "This isn't milk. You could read a book through this."

"It's skimmed milk. The fat's been taken out of it," I explained.

"Fat?" he asked.

"The cream has been removed," I explained calmly.

"What for?"

"Good question," I replied. I couldn't be bothered to discuss cholesterol and health issues.

The microwave pinged, and as I was swapping the packets there was another roar through the open window in the other room. Henry rushed to look and shouted, "It's another Tornado!"

I followed him through, looked out and said, "No, that's an Airbus 400, I think. They're a lot quieter than the Tornados." I was fully aware Henry would have no idea what I was talking about.

"I thought you said they were Tornados?"

"No, they are all called aeroplanes, or aircraft. The first one was a Tornado but that one's an Airbus 400, which is a transport aircraft. The Tornados are fighter aircraft. Or maybe they're fighter bombers? I'm not too sure."

I returned to the kitchen, taking my mobile with me. As I waited for the microwave to finish I called Josh. Henry continued to watch out of the window.

"Hello, Josh."

"Oh, hello, Edmund. Where have you been?"

"I've been with a friend in Cornwall," I said, deciding to stick to the same excuse. "Are you doing anything tonight?"

"Yes, Mario and I are going to Triumph's."

"Oh, great! I'll see you there later."

"Okay, Edmund."

"Bye, then, Josh." I switched off to find Henry at my side trying to listen again.

"Was that your mother again?" he asked.

"No, that was my friend, Josh. We will probably meet him later."

"So, it's not just your mother you can speak to with that?" he enquired.

"No, I spoke to you didn't I? I can speak to anyone I want with one of these as long as the other person has one as well."

The microwave pinged again. "Come on, let's eat," I said, and began to serve the food onto plates. I put them both on the table and said, "Sit down." Henry did so and looked at the steaming plate and then at me. Looking down at his plate again he observed, "It's hot!"

"Yes, it's hot. Did you think I would give you cold curry? Curries are meant to be hot in more ways than one."

"But I saw you getting it out of that white ice box."

"Yes, but then I put it in the microwave oven and that made it hot. Eat up before it gets cold." I didn't want to spend all evening discussing how the 21st century works.

Henry looked at me again as I picked up the knife and fork. I realised he was watching to see what I did with this strange implement. I began to eat and Henry did the same, loading a large portion onto his fork and putting it into his mouth. He chewed and then gulped, coughed and nearly spat out his food before swallowing.

"Eerrr! Aahh! What is it?" he gasped, taking gulps of air.

"Oh, I am sorry, Henry. Have you never had curry before? I'll get you some water." Quickly I grabbed a glass and filled it from the tap, then put it in front of Henry before filling one for myself. Henry drank quickly, and I took some bread out of the fridge and put some on a plate. "Eat that as you eat the curry," I said Henry's face was a little red, but he was able to eat again now.

"I'm sorry, Henry, I didn't think before I gave it to you," I said to excuse myself. The curry wasn't very hot, but then he had never eaten one before.

"What is it?" Henry asked again.

"It's curry. A spicy Indian dish."

"Indian spices. Yes, I have had spices before, but none like this."

"Curry is very popular here," I said, and then realised I was once more raising the question of where 'here' was. I quickly added, "Eat it with the bread". Henry took a small mouthful of food and tried to cut the bread with his blunt knife. I remembered what he had told me while we ate in Burford House, that only base animals tear off food with their teeth, so I jumped up and grabbed two small, sharp knifes from the drawer and put them on the table.

Then I saw Henry holding his glass of water up to the light. I looked at him and he asked, "This is water?"

I anticipated what was coming and told him, "Yes, it's water, and it's perfectly safe to drink it." To emphasise the point, I picked up my glass and took a large gulp. It tasted refreshing and very cool, even though it was straight from the tap, and I realised this was the first water I had drunk since leaving the 21st century. I drained the glass and returned to the tap for a refill.

Henry cautiously took a sip and asked, "How much of that water do you have?"

I was confused by the question for a while, but then realised what he meant and told him, "Er, this tap" (I tapped it in a pointless word game) "has an endless supply of clean, fresh and very healthy water." Then I found the little gremlin was back on my shoulder and added rather mischievously, "Some people do think bottled water is better for you, but I think they are Evian backwards."

Henry looked perplexed and simply asked, "How?"

This was a question to which I had to find an answer that would not take too long, so I took a deep breath and said, "Henry, there will be many things that confuse you and you will have many questions, but I cannot answer them all in detail, so you will have to just accept some of the things I say and you will probably understand later."

Henry looked more worried, but carried on eating more carefully, mixing the curry with bread and increasingly larger sips of water. As he munched the curry and bread he observed, "This is very light bread. It must be highly leavened."

"Oh, yes," I replied, not wanting to go into the details of modern bread making and aware it was a little stale now after so long in the bread crock. We both ate in virtual silence as Henry was bravely struggling with the mild curry and I hoped the process was a distraction for Henry from the shock of the 21st century.

Suddenly, Henry asked, "Where are your servants, Edmund?"

"We don't have any," I answered.

Another silence followed, then Henry asked, "Are they all dead from the pestilence?"

"No, we just don't have any. Never have. Oh no, I tell a lie, we did used to have a cleaner but my dad kept complaining she moved things." Henry was clearly biting his tongue in a state of yet more confusion.

Towards the end of the meal, Henry asked, "How did that white box cook this food?"

"With microwaves," I answered, truthfully but probably not very helpfully. Henry thought about this, then said, "But I could see no water in the box."

That confused me again, and then I clicked. "No, no. Not that sort of wave. A wave of photons. They agitate the molecules in the food and they have to move apart, which makes them hot. Or something like that." Henry seemed none the wiser so I added, "I think microwaves are about half way between radio waves and gamma rays." He continued to look blank, so I continued to talk this nonsense to him. "It's radio waves, then microwaves, then infra-red, then visible light, that's how we see things, then ultra violet, with x-rays and gamma at the top of the scale – as far as I remember."

I knew Henry had no idea of what I was talking about, and I wasn't too sure myself, but although it was a bit cruel, I had to admit I was enjoying myself. He continued to look at me between mouthfuls of food then asked, "How do these microwaves get there?"

"Well, they're everywhere, but I think those ones are agitated by electricity."

"Electricity?"

"Yes, it's the same thing that operates the lights, or candles, and the television, but I think that works on high frequency radio waves radio, even though it's not a radio. And, of course, a radio operates on radio waves but at a lower frequency – I think."

"Telly vision?" Henry enquired this time.

"Yes. Television."

"Tele being Greek for distant, and vision, being Latin for

seeing," Henry explained, as didactically as I was being.

"Is it," I asked rhetorically, not expecting an answer.

"Yes. Don't you speak Latin and Greek?" he asked, sounding rather critical.

"I have enough difficulty with two forms of English, let alone any dead languages," I answered, more honestly than I could have done when we had been in the 14th century.

The meal was finished and Henry drank his coffee. "Mmmm! This tastes good. As sweet as honey and as bitter as vinegar."

A strange combination, I thought, and realised he was swilling the coffee around his mouth. Almost immediately he began to babble about nothing very much and he gave me no chance to answer his question. I was taken aback at first and then realised this must be because of the caffeine in the coffee, which he wouldn't be used to. I tried to ignore most of his prattle and managed to get in, "Henry, you know you lent me these clothes I'm wearing?"

"Yes?"

"Well, I must change them for clothes suitable for my homeland. I will lend you some clothes to wear so you'll fit in."

"Fit in?" he enquired.

"Yes, it is important you fit in here and don't mention your home to other people, as it will raise so many questions you – or I – cannot answer."

"Why?" he asked rather indignantly.

"For the same reason I did not mention this home when I was in your homeland."

Henry, shrugged and I said, "Come on, I'll show you the clothes". I picked up the plates and put them in the dishwasher, getting a dishwasher cube and popping it in as I closed the door and switched it on with the other hand, before walking towards the kitchen door. As the dirty dishes had been sitting there for days I was pleased to think we were going to get rid of the rancid smell. It then occurred to me that the smells in the 14th century had been far worse, yet I had quickly got used to them. Also, I had quickly got used to the general level of dirt and the practice of eating food without giving too much thought as to what conditions it was prepared in.

Henry had been continually sniffing throughout the meal as a result of the chilli in the curry. I was sniffing a little too and told him, "We both need to blow our noses."

"Coughs and sneezes spread diseases! Coughs and sneezes spread diseases!" he said in his first light-hearted moment since we arrived in the 21st century.

"Come with me" I said and walked out of the kitchen and across the corridor towards the loo. I opened the door, aware that Henry had not yet seen the rest of the house. I opened the toilet door and pulled some loo paper off the roll and handed it to Henry, who took it. He pointed to the toilet pan and said "What's this?"

"It's a privy", I said and blew my nose on some more bog paper, depositing it in the pan. Henry looked at the paper and seemed more interested in studying it than using it. I stood and looked at him, realising what his thoughts were. "It's paper," I said.

"Paper?"

"Yes, paper. You blow your nose on it and then just pop it into the pan. Oh, but not if you're in Greece," I added as an afterthought, in memory of my holiday in Greece.

Henry shook his head and said, "You blow your nose on *paper?*"

I just looked at him, and he blew his nose and popped it into the pan and I flushed it. Henry's expression of amazement returned. I rinsed my hands, as I had told him people should always wash their hands when they have blown their noses, and dried them on the towel.

As I walked out past him he asked, "Where is the water coming from for the privy?" He followed my example and rinsed his hands and dried them.

"That white box on top," I said, pointing to the cistern. There was a silent pause. I added, "It then fills up ready for the next time".

Henry just looked at the loo, so I lifted the lid of the cistern to show him the workings and how it was refilling. I lifted the ball cock a couple of times to show how the flow stopped when it was full, and Henry's hand went towards it to do the same. In fact, he seemed more curious about how the loo worked than he had been about how the television worked. I suppose when something has moving parts it is more understandable than microchips and electricity which you can't see.

He seemed happy with how it worked, so I walked out of the loo and up the stairs. Henry followed close behind, rather like a puppy dog.

Opening the door to the spare room, I said, "You can sleep here." Henry looked at the bed and around the little room. "Thank you," he said.

"Come on," I said and walked to my room, where I opened a cupboard, selected some clothes for myself and said, "Help yourself." He looked into the cupboard and after a few seconds said, "The colours!"

I couldn't stand there forever, so I left him there and went to have a quick shower. As I was standing under the flow of warm water the door opened and Henry's voice said,

"What are you doing?"

"Having a shower. What's it look like?" I turned to see him standing dressed in a strange collection of clothes and colours. Oh well, it was his choice, and at least he looked 21st century.

"That water's hot!" he said, once more stating the obvious.

"Yes, and when I've finished you can have one. Though you could use the shower in my parents' room," I said through the shower door, feeling a little uncomfortable to be watched having a shower, though he didn't seem at all embarrassed. I began to shampoo my hair and Henry continued to watch me like a child. Eventually, I pushed open the shower door, which made Henry step back out of the bathroom, and lied, "Your clothes look good, but go and take them off to have a shower yourself." He disappeared and I closed the door, relieved to have some privacy to dry myself.

When I was half dressed, Henry reappeared, stark naked. This sort of behaviour I accepted blithely in the 14th century but it seemed a lot more difficult in the 21st century. I ushered him into the shower and showed him how the taps worked. He jumped as the hot water streamed onto him, but seemed to be enjoying the experience. Shower gel and shampoo were new experiences too, and he was clearly enjoying himself as I dressed and picked up my electric shaver. Immediately I put it down again as I knew that if I used it, Henry would want to use it as well. Finding the disposable razors and shaving foam, I began to cover my face in the spray foam.

"What are you doing?"

Oh dear, here we go again. I thought and answered, "Shaving". Henry watched me again as he carried on shampooing his hair much longer than necessary. Shaving a few days' growth was a little painful, but I was pleased to feel clean and back in the 21st century again. I finished and washed my face before looking in a mirror again, realising I had not done so since I had left my own century.

"Come on, that'll do," I told Henry and he turned off the tap and hopped out of the shower as I handed him a towel. "When you've finished dressing I'll show you how to use a safety razor," I said, and went out of the bathroom to finish getting ready to go out.

"I'm ready!" Henry's voice came across the landing, like a child playing a game of hide and seek.

"Okay," I answered and returned to give him the disposable razor and can of shaving foam.

"What is this made of?" Henry asked, studying the razor.

"It's plastic."

"No it's not," Henry said, trying to bend the handle. "It's not plastic at all."

"Yes, it is," I insisted and took his hand to spray some foam onto. He shrugged and then asked, "What is that made from?" He was pointing to the shaving foam can.

"I think it's made from tin. Or maybe it's aluminium? Or perhaps tin lined with aluminium."

"Aluminium?" he enquired, and once more an explanation simply led to more questions.

"Yes, it's derived from bauxite and is, apparently, very common in the world, so it's not about to run out." I knew Henry would have no idea what bauxite was, but fortunately, he could not question every word I spoke. I watched him rub the foam on his face and take the first stroke with the blade. I then turned to leave him to it saying, "I'm going to phone my girlfriend and I want to speak to her privately, so please don't follow me to listen in."

"Girlfriend?" Henry enquired yet again, but I really could not be bothered to explain and walked out.

I went into my bedroom and closed the door, then called Serene on her mobile, and was pleased to find it was back online. She answered, sounding excited to hear from me again. I gave her the same lie about being with a friend in Cornwall and told her the truth about why I couldn't see her straight away: that I had a friend staying with me and I couldn't really leave him alone. I did feel really bad about lying to her, but I simply could not tell her the truth.

Suddenly she mentioned what I had said to her just before 'travelling'; about her not worrying if I disappeared, and was that why I hadn't been around? I had not prepared for this and was completely speechless for a few seconds. Eventually, I mumbled that we could discuss it when I saw her again. She asked when that would be and I promised I would call her again tomorrow once I had sorted things out.

When I switched the phone off I was shaking, taken aback by the fact this had disturbed me more than all my experiences in the 14th century. I felt selfish that I was having a night out and not going to see Serene, but I couldn't leave Henry on his own in these circumstances, and I certainly didn't want to take him with me.

As I emerged from my room Henry was standing outside the door. I felt immediately annoyed he was listening in, but then I consoled myself that it must be out amazement at the concept of a telephone and not out of some prurient interest.

"So, you use the word 'phone' when you are using a tele*phone*?" Henry asked, as if the previous conversation was just carrying on.

"Yes, we use it as a short form of the noun 'telephone' and we also use it as a verb when we make a call," I explained rather didactically.

"Mmmm!"

Once more this was a verb/noun problem and it reminded me of the modern English problem. I said, "Look, Henry, it's important that you talk in the form of English we use here, or people will not understand you and it will raise so many questions as to where you came from."

"Why can't I just tell them I come from Burford?" he asked innocently.

"Because..." I stumbled, as I had no real answer for him. "Please, Henry, just try to speak as I speak. I will translate any words you have difficulty with, but please try to talk how I talk and if other people ask you where you come from, tell them you come from Bulgaria."

"Bulgaria? Why Bulgaria? Where is Bulgaria?" he asked, quite reasonably.

"It's on the Black Sea I think and..." Henry looked blank again. "Near Turkey, and no one knows how they speak there so they will think it is your Bulgarian accent if they have difficulty with your English. Please, Henry, just accept what I say for now. I can explain a lot more later but for now please just do as I ask?" I requested rather exasperatedly.

"Okay", he said smiling at his use of 'my' sort of English. "I will try to use your dialect of English."

I was just about to say it wasn't a dialect, but I really couldn't be bothered and it would just open up more questions, so I held out his hand, with the toothbrush in it, and squeezed a small knob of toothpaste onto it.

"Now put it in your mouth and slide the button up," I said,

putting his thumb on the toothbrush button. This he did, and the brush started to vibrate. Immediately he took the brush out of his mouth saying, "Eeaah!" Of course the toothbrush continued to vibrate and toothpaste went flying everywhere.

"Turn it off!" I shouted, and grabbed the toothbrush to turn it off. Too late. Toothpaste was everywhere. "Oh no, Henry, you must keep it in your mouth," I said and began to sponge the streaks of toothpaste from all over his 21st century clothing.

"Oh, sorry," he said trying not to laugh. At least he was laughing rather than feeling stressed in this strange environment. I finished cleaning him up as much as I could, putting more paste on his brush and telling him to try again. This he did, and it was much more successful this time.

"Right, keep it in your mouth until it sort of switches off and starts again after a couple of minutes. Move it around your teeth as you did with the toothbrush you used when we were in Windsor." While he was doing this I cleaned up some more of the toothpaste which had been scattered all over the bathroom. The toothbrush stuttered and I said, "Okay, slide that button over again and rinse your mouth out." I really had not got the time, or the patience, to go through flossing and mouthwash, so I walked out of the bathroom. Henry followed like a puppy dog.

In the kitchen, I picked up a couple of bananas that were starting to turn and tossed one to Henry, saying, "Catch!"

"What's this?" he enquired as I went for my shoes.

"It's a banana," I said. "They taste good."

As I was putting on my shoes I heard him say, "Eerrrah!" Oh, what now? I thought. I looked up to see Henry had bitten into the side of the banana and through the skin.

"No, no, Henry. Like this." I showed him how to peel a

banana by peeling mine.

"Oh!" he said and bit off the end as I had done with mine. "Mmmm. That is good," he said through a mouthful. "So sweet."

"I'm glad you like it, Henry. Now, we are going out to a bar – a hostelry, and we'll meet a group of my friends so I will simply introduce you as Henry from Bulgaria. Okay?"

"Okay", he agreed. I picked up my dad's car keys and we left the house.

CHAPTER THREE

LADY BURFORD

Lady Burford sat at her desk writing to her husband. She was not sure how to express her thoughts. Should she tell him the full details or simply ask him to return as soon as possible without needlessly frightening him with the full enormity of the situation?

After three lines she changed her mind and discarded what she had written. As she was halfway down the page on her second attempt she changed her mind again and discarded this letter as well. At the third attempt her thoughts were much clearer. As she was finishing telling her Lord that his son and heir was missing and in much danger, there was a knock at the door.

"Come!" she called and Megan entered the room, curtseyed and said, "Alfred is here to see you, my lady."

"Tell him to wait outside the door and I will call when I want him."

"Yes, my lady," replied Megan and she turned to leave.

"Oh, and Megan, when Alfred leaves, come back again. I have some questions to ask you."

"Yes, my lady," Megan repeated and hurried out of the room.

Lady Burford returned to writing her letter. Finally she signed it, "Your loving and obedient wife, Mary." She waved it in the air to help dry the ink and then carefully folded it and picked up the candle she had been using to cast light on her task. With her other hand she held some sealing wax and used the candle to melt some onto the letter join. Then she pressed the Burford family seal into the hot wax.

"Alfred!" she called, more loudly than necessary, and the door opened.

"my lady," Alfred said with a bow and stopped just inside the door, keeping his eyes low, not being used to speaking directly to either Lord or Lady Burford. He was a stocky man and looked as if Knut had chosen him well for a fast dash to Windsor.

"Ah! Alfred. Come closer, man," she commanded. Alfred tentatively approached the Lady. "Has Knut told you what is expected of you, Alfred?"

He paused, swallowed hard and said, "I have been told you wish me to go to Windsor as fast as possible and deliver a letter to Lord Burford, my lady."

"Yes, Alfred, so take this letter and ensure it is kept safe and *dry* on the journey," instructed Lady Burford. She held the letter at arm's length, as Alfred was still some distance from her.

"I will, my lady," Alfred replied, trying to sound both obedient and as capable as possible.

"And if they question who you are at the castle, then you must show them the seal on the letter, but you *must not* part with the letter to anyone except Lord Burford. Do you understand, Alfred?"

"I do, my lady," he said, still trying not to make eye contact with his superior.

"Then, go now, Alfred. God speed and watch over you."

"Yes, my lady." He turned and scurried out of the room as fast as he could.

When Alfred had left, Lady Burford sat with her thoughts for a while. She was used to giving orders around the house, and even in the town, but she had never been alone in such a perilous situation without Lord Burford, who was the real source of authority behind any commands she may give. Add this to the fear of her son's fate and she was in much inner turmoil. She knew she must not show her fears to any of the household, or to those in the town.

As she was gathering her inner strength, there was a gentle knock at the door.

"Come!" Lady Burford commanded. The door opened slowly and Megan entered, but without her usual air of confidence. She stood with her hands clasped in front of her and curtseyed.

"Megan, come and sit down here," said Lady Burford, indicating a chair next to her. Megan was not used to being told to sit with her Lady, and this added to her trepidation, as she had some idea of what was coming.

Lady Burford looked straight at Megan, who had the strength of character to return her gaze. The Lady of the Manor had no time for niceties and went straight to the point.

"Now, Megan, what do you know about why Sir Henry and his friend have disappeared?" Megan looked for a second and then took a deep breath. "Ooh, my Lady, I don't really know what I can tell you."

Lady Burford looked at her sternly and said, "Now, Megan, I can tell you know something about this, so just tell me everything you know."

Megan felt in a terrible position. She was sure she had done nothing wrong, but she wanted to protect her friend, the altar boy, who had told her about the arrival of the Bishop's men. If Father Mackenzie, or even the Bishop, should hear that he had told Megan who had warned Sir Henry and Edmund that the Bishop's men were here to arrest them, then his fate would be unimaginable. But what could she do? She knew she could not lie to Lady Burford. She could only tell her the truth and hope her Lady would protect her friend.

"Oh, er, my Lady..." Megan stammered, panting anxiously.

"Megan, we have not got time for this," said Lady Burford. "You must tell me everything so I can decide what to do."

Megan held her breath and let her shoulders drop. Her Lady and Lord had always been kind to her, and in fact, she owed her life to them, so she could only trust Lady Burford to do what was best. She gathered her thoughts and began, "I was talking to my friend, David, you know, the altar boy?"

"Yes, Megan, go on," Lady Burford said, more kindly.

"Well, I was talking to him this morning and he told me how the Bishop had sent men to arrest Sir Edmund and Sir Henry on charges of... of... heresy and blasphemy...b ecause... because... they were helping the sick and saying their sickness was not God's punishment for their sins."

Lady Burford caught her breath and gave a little encouraging smile to Megan, saying simply, "Uh huh."

"Well, my Lady, I was so worried for Sir Henry and Sir Edmund, but I didn't know what to do, so..." Megan looked at Lady Burford, trying to assess whether or not what she was saying would get her into trouble. "So, when I heard the two gentlemen ride into the courtyard I waited where I hoped I'd be able to talk to them alone." Once more she looked at Lady Burford for approval.

"Go on, Megan, you are doing very well."

"Well, my Lady, I waited at the top of the stairs, and when I heard them starting up the stairs I called, 'Sir! Sirs, you must go out immediately'. Of course, they didn't know what I was talking about, so I quickly explained that the Bishop's men were waiting to arrest them for blasphemy and heresy." Thinking her story was over, Megan heaved a sigh of relief and looked at her Lady.

Lady Burford thought for a moment and then asked, "And what did Sir Henry say?"

"Well, my Lady, he didn't say anything but he looked very frightened, but Sir Edmund just sort of laughed."

"Mmmm, go on, Megan."

"Well, my Lady... eventually Sir Edmund said he knew a place he could go to but said he couldn't take Sir Henry, and he asked why not, and eventually Sir Edmund said Sir Henry could go with him, and by then the Bishop's men were knocking at the door so Sir Henry and Sir Edmund went out of the back of the house and that was the last I saw of them, my lady."

Lady Burford sat in silence for a while and Megan, knowing her place, remained equally silent. Eventually Lady Burford said, "You have done well, Megan."

Megan sighed audibly, physically relaxed, and then expressed her deepest concern. "But my lady, what about David?"

Lady Burford thought for a moment and then told Megan, "I am sure that when Lord Burford returns he will understand that you and David have done all you can to help Sir Henry and his friend." She paused for a while and Megan let a smile drift across her face. Lady Burford went on, "It seems the actions of you, and David, *may* have saved Sir Henry and Sir Edmund. But we do not know where they are, and until they are home and safe we cannot be sure."

Megan looked down, having been brought back to earth with the realisation that the fate of Henry and Edmund was still unknown. She replied with the simple, "Yes, my lady."

"Tell me Megan, David, like you, has Welsh parents. Correct?"

Megan answered quickly, "Yes, but he *is* loyal to Lord Burford."

"It is clear that he is, Megan, and, as I have said, Lord Burford will be made aware of that when he returns."

"Thank you, my lady." Megan hoped that she had not betrayed her friend. She wanted to ask a lot of questions, but knew it was not her place to do so.

Lady Burford brought the interrogation to a close by saying, "Now, Megan, go and get on with your duties. The Lord will return and he will instruct what is to be done."

"Thank you, my lady." Megan rose and left the room quickly, pleased the ordeal was over and reassured that her position was secure and her friend would be safe.

When Megan had left, Lady Burford moved to a more comfortable chair and tried to assess the situation she and her family were in. Thoughts raced through her head: where was her son? What would happen when he returned? Would he ever return? How could Lord Burford help when he returned? How could she, or even her husband, challenge the Church? As she thought, the stress of the situation got the better of her and she drifted off to sleep.

Some time later she was awoken by a knock at the door. "Er, who... come!" The door opened and in came Peter.

"Excuse me, my lady, but Father Mackenzie is here to see you."

"Really?" She looked out of the window to see that it was completely dark. "What could he want at this late hour, Peter?" she asked in her waking confusion.

"I know not, my lady."

"Oh well, send him in."

Peter left and Lady Burford wondered why the troublesome priest would want to speak to her at such a late hour. A minute later there was a forceful knock at the door. "Come!" Lady Burford commanded, and the door opened to reveal Father Mackenzie with an obsequious smile on his face.

"My lady," he said with a bow.

"Yes, Father, what is it I can do for you at this late hour?"

Father Mackenzie's smile turned from obsequious to simpering and he said, "I thought my lady would need to know that Sister Cecilia has, unfortunately, gone to our Father in heaven."

Lady Burford was shocked that one of the sick nuns had died, and realised what Father Mackenzie was revelling in this turn of events.

"Oh, may God have mercy on her soul," she replied.

"I'm sure he will," said Father Mackenzie, maintaining his benign smile, and then got to the point of his late night visit. "It seems that despite the, er, *efforts* of Sir Henry's young friend, the good Lord has called Sister Cecilia to his side." He paused and looked at Lady Burford with his fixed smile.

After a long silence she realised there was nothing to be gained from entertaining Father MacKenzie any longer than necessary. "Thank you for bringing me this sad news, Father Mackenzie, I am sure the whole town will pray for her soul."

"Yes, my lady, and I'm sure you will agree that the will of God cannot be subverted by any, er, questionable and questioning ideas."

Lady Burford looked at Father Mackenzie and chose her words carefully. "Thank you once more, Father Mackenzie, and may God guide us all in these difficult times. Good morrow to you, Father." With this she picked up the small bell on the desk and shook it. Almost immediately the door opened and Peter appeared in the doorway. "Ah, Peter, kindly show Father Mackenzie out." With this she turned to Father Mackenzie and repeated, "Good morrow, Father."

He continued his simpering smile, bowed slightly, and walked through the door. Peter closed it behind him and Lady Burford was left once more with her thoughts. The situation now seemed even more grim. Her Lord was away, and it was not known when he would return. Her son was still missing and she did not know whether he was alive or dead. And now Father MacKenzie was carping over the death of Sister Cecilia, proving that the work of her son's new friend had been in vain. She was beginning to think that the arrival of Edmund had not brought any good upon her family and the people of Burford.

CHAPTER FOUR

NIGHT OUT

We walked down the path towards the two cars waiting on the driveway; Mum's car was not there, as it was the one my family drove to the airport. Proud as I am of my little Mini, I did want to play 21st century gadget games with Henry, and dad's car was much better for that.

Out of the corner of my eye, I could see Henry stopping to look back at my house, and I guessed he was thinking how small it was in comparison to his Burford home. Yet it had five bedrooms and was a lot bigger than most houses. Plus it was off the road in its own grounds. But then he still thought Edmund was Sir Edmund de Covney, a knight of the realm.

As we approached Dad's car I pressed the key and the indicators flashed, and there was a clunk to indicate an unlocking. Henry slightly paused in his step but said nothing. There were so many surprising things for Henry to assimilate, and this was just one more.

"Go around the other side," I commanded as I opened the driver's side door. This Henry did and got into the car next to me.

"What's this? Some form of carriage?"

"Exactly right, Henry," I answered. Now for the real fun!

I pressed the start button and silently the electric engine started. Two seconds later, "I'm all lost in supermarket. I can no long shop happily. I came in here for..." boomed out of the speakers.

Henry jumped a bit and asked, "Another ghost wall?"

"Ghost wall? What are you talking about?" I asked, having had the tables turned on me.

"Like the ghost wall in your house."

"Eh?" I was none the wiser.

"Where the singing comes out and the ghosts move about on the wall?"

"Oh no. This just plays music, there are no pictures. It's not a television. This is my dad's car and it's his music disc (dad still uses discs) in the player. Not my choice." I pressed the eject button on the CD player and the music immediately stopped and the disc popped out. I picked it up and said, "The music is all on this piece of plastic". I waved the disc in his face. Then I put it in again and of course a different song played. I'm not a particular Clash fan, but it was as good as any other disc my dad would have in his car.

"If it's not a ghost wall, then what's that candle light there?" Henry said pointing to the illuminated panel.

"Ah, that tells me what disc is playing, what track and how long it has been playing," I said, pointing to each piece of information. I turned the key another click and the dashboard illuminated. "This tells me how fast I'm going. This tells me how far I've been and this tells me how many revolutions the engine is doing," I told him, pointing to each display in turn. Henry just looked bemused, but no longer fearfully stressed, as he had been when he had arrived in the 21st century. This reminded me that we had not yet touched on the fact that Henry was now in a different time but he, as yet, had no idea of that. I continued to look at him and he just shrugged, so I said, "Put your seat belt on please." Knowing he had no idea what I was talking about, I reached over, pulled the seatbelt round him and plugged it in. I expect he was confused by this as well, but by now he was way past the point of asking questions on every minor thing.

Now for the real fun. I put the car into gear, clicked on the headlights and the driveway was illuminated ahead as I let the clutch out and we slipped down the drive towards the road.

Henry gripped his seat and said, "Whoa! What's happening?"

"The carriage is moving," I responded, stating the obvious.

"How? There are no horses!"

"Oh, I think the engine has quite a few horsepower," I replied, playing games again. We stopped at the edge of the main road and Henry asked, "Where is the light coming from?"

"The front of the car, but even when we are moving forward the light is still travelling at about 186,000 miles per second," I told him , teasing again. "Relatively speaking, of course!" Probably not the best time for discussing Albert Einstein's ideas. Henry said nothing, but he must have been thinking all sorts of things.

We reached the road and as nothing was coming, I turned and accelerated along the street. I glanced at Henry and could see he was grasping his seat even tighter and his face was becoming drained of blood.

"All these lights in the sky!" he said, looking up.

"Not quite in the sky. They are all on poles and they are called street lights."

Another car came around the corner and its lights shone upon us. I slowed down and Henry gasped, "What's that?"

"It's another car. No problem." As the car passed us Henry observed, "So, this isn't the only carriage car!"

"No, there are hundreds, thousands, millions of them."

"How can we be going so fast?" He asked with bated breath.

"Fast? We're only doing 30 miles an hour. I've just set the cruise control."

As we came towards Brize Norton the car headlights lit up the 13th century church and I made my first attempt to broach the subject of what century I had brought Henry to.

"Do you recognise that church, Henry?" I asked him.

"No," was the simple reply as we passed. Well, it was dark and we passed it quite quickly. I'm sure he had much else to think about as well. More cars passed on the other side of the road and I had to slow down for one in front. Out of the village we drove and I accelerated to 60 miles an hour.

"Whoa!" Henry exclaimed again.

"Relax and enjoy it, there's no problem."

This seemed to have some effect. His body fell back into the seat and a little smile crept across his face. Good. This was not meant to be some sort of punishment for him. As we entered Witney, Henry again observed, "More sky lights. Street lights," he added, correcting himself to 21st century terminology. More and more cars were around us and I pulled into the car park near to Triumph's.

"There are hundreds of carriage cars here," said Henry, looking around.

"I told you. This is called a 'car park'. A place to leave, or park, your car. That's why there are so many cars here," I informed him.

We sat in the car as Henry looked around and I showed him how to undo his seat belt. "Now listen," I said. "Remember what I said. Try to talk the way I, and everyone else here, talks. And if anyone asks, you come from Bulgaria."

"Bulgaria," he repeated.

I opened the door to get out and realised Henry had no idea how to open a car door. Well, why would he? So I showed him, and we stepped into the cool night air and began to walk towards the entrance of Triumph's. As we entered the precinct Henry made another time shift observation, "It's as bright as daylight here! How can there be so many candles here?"

"They are not candles. Though they may be many candlepower," I told him.

As we approached the door, Henry stopped dead and stared. "All the gay girls are half naked!" he said in amazement.

"That's just how they dress," I told him. "And try not to stare please." I walked forward and eventually Henry followed, but he seemed deeply shocked by what he had seen. I remembered from my first time in 14th century Burford that all boys and girls were called girls, and girls were called gay girls. 'Boy' was a term reserved for a servant of some sort.

Outside I gave him some money and told him that if someone bought him a drink he should later buy them one in return. We entered Triumph's and I introduced Henry to a few people as my friend from Bulgaria, then I began to mingle and soon lost sight of him. To be honest I was happy to do so, as I needed a little 'normal' time in my own century. There was no one I could share things with and I really needed a bit of time away from any association with the 14th century.

After a while, and a couple of halves, I had almost forgotten Henry was with me. I felt rather bad because of this, but realised it meant he was probably enjoying himself. I was chatting with old friends, and giving the same old excuse about having been in Devon, to excuse my absence over the last few days.

As I was chatting, a friend of mine, Julian came up to me and said, "Your friend... he's bit weird. Says he's from Bulgaria, but he needs a visit from the fashion police."

I simply said, "Yeah!" It seemed the easiest way to deal with it.

The night passed quite quickly with a few more similar comments, but it seemed Henry was happy dealing with the 21st century on his own. This made me feel less guilty about not 'holding his hand' all night. At one point he found me and started to gabble about nothing at all, and I realised he was drunk and wondered how he could get so pissed so quickly. Then I remembered that in the 14th century, small beer was less than a quarter the alcoholic content of strong lager in the 21st century. Oh well, at least he was enjoying himself.

Before chucking out time I was getting bored as, once again, I was about the only sober person in the bar, so I sought out Henry and told him we were going to leave soon. I may as well have been talking in a foreign language, which I virtually was, given the vast difference between modern English and Chaucerian English, because he was so drunk.

Eventually, I physically dragged him out of Triumph's towards the car. Immediately we were outside he seemed to sober up, but he continued to prattle about nothing at all. As we were walking through the precinct, a few yards in front of us we saw an argument taking place. As we got closer it turned into fisticuffs and a crowd began to gather. The precinct was just far enough away from Triumph's for the bouncers not to get involved. There was lots of shoving and shouting with drunken swinging of fists, but then suddenly one of the men had a knife in his hand and lunged at the other man, who backed off and tried to avoid being stabbed or slashed.

There was a collective intake of breath from the crowd as they as they backed away from the danger. Then there was more lunging and slashing as the unarmed man was pursued backwards towards us. I too was frozen and backed off. But then, before I knew what was happening, there was a flash of bright clothing and the assailant was on his back and pinned to the floor with his own knife at his throat. There was an even bigger intake of breath from the crowd, and then silence fell again. The man on his back was motionless – frozen in fear.

And then I realised that the man on top was Henry. Oh Christ! I thought, as I became aware of what was happening. Then I was struck by the thought that the police would soon be here and, although Henry was not the aggressor, quite the opposite, far too many questions would be asked.

I stepped forward and tapped Henry on his shoulder. "Leave it, Henry. Just get off him now." Henry looked back at me and just laughed. "No, I'm serious, Henry. *Please* get off him!"

He gave a disdainful look at the man on floor and began to get up. As he did so he held out his hand with the long kitchen knife in it. I instinctively went to take it from him, but fortunately, I stopped myself.

"Just drop the knife and let's leave," I told him. The knife fell to the floor and I pulled Henry away from the crowd. I was relieved I had not put my fingerprints or DNA on the knife, though it didn't matter for Henry. There was no chance the police would be looking for the prints or the DNA of a man from the 14th century.

As I was getting Henry to realise we had to leave, my ears

were filled comments such as, "Well done!" "Good man!" "What a hero!" "How impressive!" "You're a legend!" from those in the crowd, who were now slapping Henry on the back and treating him as a 'have a go hero'.

I dragged Henry towards the car as fast as I could, trying to explain that the police would ask too many awkward questions. His only response was, "Who are the police?"

This was just too much to enter into and I said, "Just let's go," and bundled him into the car. I drove off as fast as I could and Henry asked, "Why was he using a knife when he obviously doesn't know how to use it?"

"Not everyone here has had lessons in swordsmanship."

Henry said nothing. In fact he said nothing much more on the drive back, which seemed so much longer than our journey to Witney, but my head was filled with fears. What if someone gave my name to the police as having been with the man who had disarmed the knife man?

As we approached my house I became aware that Henry was gently snoring, probably because of the alcohol. I couldn't help but think how fast he had thought, and moved, to disarm the knife man, given that he was so drunk. I turned into the drive and parked the car, feeling relieved that we were off the road and somewhat hidden from view. I shook Henry and he came back to life, getting out of the other side of the car and following me into the house.

I closed the door and locked it, pathetically thinking this would protect us from any pursuing police.

"Right, Henry, I'm going to the privy."

"Me too," he responded, so I said, "Okay, you use this one, I'm going to the one upstairs. Follow me up when you've finished."

As I was emerging from the upstairs loo Henry was coming up the stairs. "Come on, this way, mate," I said, guiding his tumbling frame into his bedroom and turning on the light.

"Oh kay," he replied in his best modern English.

"If you need the loo during the night, there is no pot under the bed, so you'll have to walk to the one outside the room."

"Errr, ummm, mmmmm," was his only response so I added,

"Do you understand, Henry?"

"Yeah, I do," he slurred and fell back onto the bed. I wasn't going to undress him, so I left him to sort himself out. I realised I had left the light on and he probably would not know how to turn it off, but I couldn't be bothered to go back again. I went to my own room, undressed quickly and got into bed. For a while I lay there thinking about the knife fight and wondering if the police would come around, and that's the last I remembered.

CHAPTER FIVE

A TIME OF WORRY

Before dawn, Arthur was awoken by a loud knock on his door and he began to prepare for his urgent race to Windsor. He had gone to bed as soon as he had spoken to Lady Burford, and now Peter had come from Burford House to wake him and to provide food and anything else he might need for the journey. Arthur had been chosen for his strength and rowing skills, despite the fact he was pretty low down the medieval pecking order. In truth, the usual, trusted servants were either in Windsor, hence Arthur's journey to bring them back, or could not be spared. This was Arthur's opportunity to prove himself as a capable and loyal servant to Lady Burford, and thereby, to Lord Burford.

Arthur's wife, Jennifer, was also woken by the knock, and as Arthur was washing and dressing, she opened the door. She found a large bag on the doorstep, which she brought in and put on the kitchen table. Then she began to prepare her husband's breakfast as quietly as possible in an effort not to wake the children, who were still asleep in the same room. In fact, the house consisted of no more than one room with part sectioned off as a sleeping area.

Jennifer, too, was aware of the family's lowly position and the honour of her husband being asked to carry out such a vital task for the Lady of the Manor. She placed a bowl of hot gruel on their small table and looked at the bag of provisions that Peter had left on the doorstep to sustain Arthur as he rowed. As her husband shaved, not an everyday occurrence, she could not resist peeking into the bag to see what he had been given. A feast fit for a king greeted her eyes. Well, for a lord at least. There were many boiled eggs (hens, ducks, and even two goose eggs), different sorts of meat, various breads, all of a quality the family usually only dreamed of, a large flagon of small beer and even some preserves. She gasped in amazement at this fare her husband had been given to sustain him, but at the same time the family's poverty was brought home to her.

Arthur saw her looking as he dried his face on the dirty cloth the family used for a towel. He sat at the table and quickly ate his bowl of gruel while thinking of the day, week and month ahead. Who knew how long he would be away? As he had never left the manor before, he had no real idea of how far Windsor was or how to get there. Knut had told him to ride to Beamtoon, a place he knew, and to then go around to the left of the town, because he would not be allowed in, towards the rising sun and pick up the road again for another three miles till he reached the river. There he would find boats; he was to tell the boatmen that Lord Burford would pay later.

He finished his meal and wiped his mouth on his sleeve. He stood up, towering over his wife, and had to stoop to avoid the ceiling in their little hovel. He walked to the other side of the room and kissed his three children one by one, hoping not to wake them. Returning to the small table, he picked up the last loaf of bread the family had and put it next to the bag of provisions he had been left by Peter, from the Burford House kitchen.

Jennifer looked at her husband, a little confused, and then Arthur removed a loaf of good bread from the bag, three hens' eggs, a duck egg and goose egg and put them on the table. He then put the family loaf into his provisions bag. Then he spoke, for the first time that morning. He said to his wife, "Give one hen's egg each to the children, you eat the duck egg and you all share the goose egg and bread."

"Oh no, you need that for your journey!"

"There is plenty here for me if I take our loaf, so do not argue with me, wife."

"Thank you, husband. The children will be so pleased and it will help to make up for them waking up to find their father has gone away for a few days."

Arthur popped the vital letter into the bag of provisions, then kissed and squeezed his wife before walking out of his home and down the hill towards the bridge. The town was empty and completely silent except for the echo of his footsteps.

It was just beginning to get light as he walked over the bridge. As he did so he saw a stable lad waiting at the entrance to Burford House. They exchanged greetings and Arthur was led around to the back of the house and into the stable yard. There was a horse, tethered next to a mounting block. The stable lad took the bag of provisions from Arthur as he mounted the horse. Having settled into the saddle, the lad attached the bag across the back of the saddle and untied the horse, passing Arthur the reins. Arthur squeezed his knees and the horse moved off and out of the yard towards Swinbrook.

Before long he found himself approaching Beamtoon. It was clear outsiders were not welcome to enter the town, as he had been told, and it was not difficult to find the way around the town as it was now well trodden with footprints and horses' hooves. Then he picked up the road again and kicked his horse into a gallop. The countryside around the road was flat and it was not long before he could see the river ahead. As he approached the river he could see there was no one awaiting him. What should he do now? He was nervously pacing up and down the riverbank on his horse when he heard a galloping sound behind. Turning his horse around, he saw a rider approaching.

"Here I am, sir," said the rider. He slowed to a halt next to Arthur and said, "My wife heard you ride past Chimney and woke me. I'm Ned. How can I help you?"

"Ah, I'm Arthur and I am here to get a boat to take an urgent journey to Windsor to get Lord Burford to come back as soon as possible. Lady Burford said to say Lord Burford would pay you later."

"Oh yes, I have provided many services for Lord Burford. If there is only one of you, you will only need a small boat and it will be quicker. Take that one there." He pointed to a small boat by the river bank. Arthur got off his horse, and Ned unfastened Arthur's bag and held it while his new customer got into the boat. He handed Arthur his bag and watched as he pushed off from the bank and began rowing upstream. "No, no, no! It's that way, Arthur. Downstream!" he called. Arthur waved and turned the boat around, trying not to look at Ned because he felt a little embarrassed.

Lady Burford arose early, having had a restless night worrying about her son and her husband. Her main thought had been that if Henry did not return and something happened to her husband, that would make her second son, Stephen, the heir to the Burford estate and the title. But he was still too young to take on the mantle of Lord of the Manor. Furthermore, he had not been groomed for the position. The only thought that consoled her was that at least she and Lord Burford did have a spare.

The rising sun seemed to make the world a better place, and Lady Burford resolved to do her best, as she believed her lord and husband would want, to manage Burford in this time of great distress that was now becoming all too personal. For now the bishop's men had gone, but she had little doubt they would be back at some point. The town could be defended against those trying to enter for sanctuary from the plague, but what if the Bishop should send an armed force? The men of Burford had shown their loyalty to Lord Burford, but what if Father MacKenzie and the bishop told them their mortal souls were in danger if they did not hand over Sir Henry and Sir Edmund – should they ever return?

As she breakfasted she planned her day and knew her first duty was to visit the Abbey to give her condolences for the loss of Sister Cecelia. There was a knock at the door and Lady Burford said, "Come." The door opened to reveal Megan with an empty tray.

"Ah Megan, yes I have finished so you may clear. Do you know where Knut is?"

"I believe he is around the house somewhere, my lady."

"Tell him to come and see me."

"Yes, my lady.", and she left the room.

Two minutes later there was another knock at the door. It opened and Knut entered with a little bow.

"Ah, Knut!"

"My lady."

"Sit down. I need to talk to you."

Knut sat and awaited his orders. But this was not just a meeting for him to be given instructions. Lady Burford talked in some detail about the situation she, her children, the absent lord and the whole of Burford were in. She encouraged Knut to express his views, not something he was used to, even if he was one of Lord Burford's trusted right-hand men. She was also trying to assess his loyalty, for she knew he would be torn between his lord and the Church. One had command over his body in this life, but the other had command over his soul in the afterlife. Lady Burford knew Knut was a popular and influential man in the town and he could influence the battle of hearts and minds that probably lay ahead.

After a long and probing talk she was assured he could be trusted and ordered him to do whatever was necessary to help defend the town should the Bishop's men return with a large force.

"Go now, Knut and keep me informed of anything you think I need to know."

"Yes, my lady." He rose and left the room.

Before long Lady Burford was walking through the town, escorted by Peter, towards the abbey. By now the market was in full swing and the town was bustling. Not as much as it would have been before the sickness, but still busy, and the people of Burford parted as their lady made her way towards the abbey.

On arrival at the door Peter knocked hard and it was opened almost immediately. "my lady," said the sister, curtseying.

"I wish to speak to the Abbess."

"Yes, my lady." She turned back into the abbey. Neither side expected the two visitors to be invited into the house of death, as only those as foolish as Sir Henry, Sir Edmund, Scabbard and Megan would enter the abbey.

Soon the Mother Superior arrived and the formalities were gone through. Before Lady Burford said, "I have come to give my condolences for the passing of Sister Cecelia."

"Thank you, Lady Burford."

"What is to be done with her body?"

"That has already been dealt with. She was interred in her waiting grave early this morning with a blessing by Father MacKenzie, my lady."

"Oh, I see!"

"And Father MacKenzie will hold a Mass for the repose of her soul this evening. I am sure that all the town will be there."

"Of course. How is Sister Florence?"

"She is battling bravely but much distressed by the loss of Sister Cecelia. With God's grace she will live."

"We must all pray for that, Mother Superior." With that Lady Burford turned away, followed by Peter, and the door of the abbey closed behind her.

Later in the day, having eaten and tried to get some more sleep to make up for her restless night, Lady Burford resolved to face her next difficult task. She picked up the little bell and shook it. A few moments later there was a knock at the door. "Come." The door opened and Megan walked in.

"My lady," she said with a little curtsey.

"Yes, Megan. Gather the children and bring them to me."

"Yes, my lady," and Megan left. A few minutes later there was another knock and she reappeared with the children, Marion, John, Stephen and Anne.

"Please sit down, children. I wish to talk to you all," said Lady Burford.

"Yes, mother," chorused the children.

"Stephen, John, Anne and Marion," she addressed them in order of inheritance, and therefore, importance. "No doubt you have all heard the stories of the disappearance of your brother, Henry, and his friend, Edmund."

"Yes, mother."

"Well it seems to be true, and I have no idea where they are any more than, it seems, anyone else does. However, if the Bishop's men had found them we would have heard, so that is a good thing." Lady Burford remained silent for a while to let this sink in.

"Mother?"

"Yes, Anne?"

"But why would the Bishop's men want Henry and his friend, Edmund?"

Lady Burford breathed in and held her breath for a few moments.

"Because they think, erroneously I believe, that the attempts of Edmund and Henry to save Burford from the sickness and to save the lives of the two sick nuns is the work of the Devil because it goes against God's will."

There were many sharp intakes of breath followed by a long silence.

"But, mother, why would this be?" implored Anne. "Henry and Edmund were only trying to help, to do God's work."

"I do not know either," answered her mother, "but that is the way the Church thinks, and we must deal with the world the way it is and not as we would wish it to be." Lady Burford quickly moved the conversation on, not wishing to dwell on the thinking of the Church. "Until Henry returns, we must carry on." The children mumbled. "Your father will be back from Windsor, and the King, in a few days and by then I expect Henry to have long since returned."

The children expressed their joy at this, but Lady Burford was aware it could all be wishful thinking.

"Mother, has Arthur gone for Father?" asked Marion.

"Yes, I have sent Arthur to Windsor to ask your father to return as soon as possible," she assured her young daughter.

"Mother?"

"Yes, Stephen?"

"In the absence of Henry I believe that makes me heir apparent, mother."

"Yes, Stephen, you are right, but you are only 17, and I expect Henry back at any moment."

"But, Mother..."

"Yes, Stephen, I know you are growing fast, and a very capable young man, and I can assure you I will ask as soon I need your valuable help." Lady Burford's tone of voice told Stephen that this was the end of the discussion. "Yes, mother," he replied.

"Now go, and do not worry about your brother. No news is good news. Your father will be home soon." The four children went out of the room, leaving their mother to her thoughts.

SIX

BURFORD

I was awoken by the sound of a flushing toilet, and it greatly startled me as I had completely forgotten I was not alone. I jumped out of bed and ran, in my underpants, onto the landing, where I found the toilet door open and Henry watching the water flow down the pan. Clearly he was still fascinated by the workings of Thomas Crapper's idea.

"Oh, Henry, you might at least close the door," I said. "It stinks! Open the window please."

Henry turned around and I thought, I'm going to have to show him how to open a window now. But, no, a latch and retaining bar seemed to be no problem for him. Then I felt guilty for snapping at him and asked gently, "Have you got a hangover?"

"A what?"

"A hangover. Do you feel ill from the beer last night?"

"No. Why, do you?" he asked.

"No, but I hardly had anything to drink," I explained.

"Didn't you, why not?" Henry asked innocently. But I really didn't have the time, or the inclination, to explain about drink driving laws, breathalysers and the police again, so I just shrugged.

I dressed quickly and went downstairs to get breakfast. A couple of minutes later Henry appeared in the same garb as last night and I told him to sit down before putting a bowl of frosted flakes in front of him, as I really couldn't be bothered to ask him what he wanted and then explain about breakfast cereals. He looked around and picked up his spoon and began to eat the flakes – dry.

"No, Henry, you're meant to put milk on them," I said, picking up the bottle and pouring some into his bowl. He returned to his eating.

"Mmm, nice. But they were nice before you put the milk in. What are these made from?"

"Corn," I replied. He probably thought I meant corn as in wheat, not corn as in sweetcorn. I finished eating before he did and jumped up to put some toast on. Two minutes later I put a piece of toast in front of Henry and indicated the butter and marmalade. Once more Henry asked the obvious.

"How did you make this hot? Was it done in the microwave?"

"Good God, no. That would just make it warm and soggy." I didn't go on to explain about electric toasters. I ate my toast and then said, "I'll just unload the dishwasher and then we can go out."

Henry said nothing and watched as I opened the dishwasher, which I had switched on before going out last night. As I was putting things away he asked, "Did a servant come in during the night to wash those?"

"No, that's what this machine is for. It washes crockery and cutlery".

"Is that why you don't have servants, because you have a machine for doing what servants do?"

"That is exactly right, Henry. You're learning." I hadn't got time to go into the subject of rising wages for the workers, so few people could afford servants any more. Silence returned, but as I was putting away the cutlery he asked, "All those people we were with last night, were they all gentry?"

"No!" I exclaimed rather unguardedly, not immediately realising Henry would wonder why we were socialising with the working classes.

"So, who were they?"

"Just friends and other people in the bar."

More thinking by Henry, then in a confused tone he asked, "So, if they were not gentry what was their social position?"

I realised we were on dangerous ground and decided to answer honestly. "They are just workers and students."

"Workers?" he asked inquisitively.

"Yes, workers. Working-class people who have to work for a living, not rich, not gentry."

"Working class? Do you mean the lower orders, peasants, serfs?"

This was getting far too complicated. "Well, sort of, but we don't have lower orders, peasants and serfs any more. I mean, over here." I corrected myself quickly, realising I was giving away the time thing. Henry just looked confused but asked no more and I said, "Come on, I'll give you some other clothes and shoes to wear, we're going shopping."

"Shopping?"

"Yes, to the shops to buy some food."

Having sorted out Henry's clothing I took his 14th Century

clothes and some of mine and stuffed them into the washing machine.

"Is that another dishwasher?" Henry enquired.

"No, it's a washing machine, but the principle's the same," I told him and ushered him out of the door. This time we were using my little Mini.

"Is this another carriage?" was the obvious question from Henry.

"Yes, this one's mine, the other's my dad's," I explained. I turned the key and immediately the radio blasted out. Henry jumped and I turned it down, but not off. I pointed to the seat belt and said, "Same as last night," and put mine around me.

"But why?" he asked as he obeyed my request.

"To stop you going through the windscreen if we hit anything." Henry just resignedly complied. We moved off gently down the drive and at the road it was clear, so I accelerated.

"Whoaaah!" Henry said, gripping his seat as he had done last night. I sped out of town towards Brize Norton and Henry observed, "It's even faster than the other carriage." It wasn't, but the Mini is lower, smaller and makes much more noise than my Dad's electric car, so it seems to be faster. I wasn't going to disabuse him, as that made up for the lack of dials and other 'go faster' goodies.

After a couple of miles we reached Brize Norton and I stopped the car outside the church and got out. Henry got out too and I stood with him at the roadside and looked at the church. All the memories of how a few days ago I had stood in the same place slowly realising where, and when, I was came flooding in. Of course, Henry looked at the church too.

"Do you recognise this church?" I asked him.

He looked quizzically and then smiled and said, "It looks like St. Peter's at Brize Norton."

"St. Britius, actually, but it is the same building."

There was no response from Henry, so I got back into the car and Henry followed suit. He asked no questions as to why we had stopped and made no comment on the church. Oh well, I felt we were getting somewhere as I gently eased him into realising where, and when, he was.

We moved off again and Henry was clearly enjoying the ride. When I say "enjoying," I mean in the same way as a child enjoys the roller coaster at the funfair. As we drove along Henry kept turning around to look at cars passing the other way.

Eventually we arrived at the biggest supermarket in the area. I parked and Henry jumped out and ran around the cars, looking at the different models. I walked towards the door and called him to follow, picking up a shopping trolley on the way. He arrived at my side just in time for me to ostentatiously point at the automatic doors as we approached. Of course, the doors immediately opened as I pointed and Henry made a little jump, asking, "How did you do that? More magic?"

I just smiled and walked through the doors. Just another little game of mine, but I was pleased to see that Henry was not frightened of all these new experiences. I may have been playing games, but it was not my intention to upset him.

I approached the store aisles and realised Henry was not at my side. I turned around and there he was, standing open-mouthed. "Come on," I called to him and slowly he came to me.

"What is this place?" Henry asked looking all around.

"It's a supermarket. A very large shop."

"Large!" was his only response.

I pushed the trolley down the first aisle, just looking at the goods on the shelves. In truth I was giving him a tour of 21st Century consumer society. There was very little I was likely to need in most of the aisles, but I enjoyed showing Henry and seeing his open mouth. I had to keep going because if I stopped every time Henry did, we would never have got around.

Of course he kept asking questions about all sorts of things. "What's that? How come? How much? What's a pound? How many? What's a kilo?" And so many other enquiries. What seemed to fascinate him most of all was why the carrots were so straight and so large. I told him it must be an EU ruling and he seemed to accept that. He was also amazed at how big all the vegetables and fruits were.

The section for potatoes brought lots of questions. I told him it wasn't actually Sir Walter Raleigh who had brought the potato to Europe, because the Spanish had them long before they came to England, and that the Spanish Armada had left some on the Irish coast when their ships were wrecked after the failed invasion of the Armada in 1588. Now I really was playing silly games with the poor man! What concept could he possibly have of something happening 250 years after he was born?

Eventually I had all I needed and pushed my half-full trolley to the checkout. Fortunately the queue was quite short and I was soon filling a couple of bags before using my debit card to pay. Henry stood in virtual silence, still looking around at all a supermarket had to offer. As I carried the bags out he followed me and asked, "Do you not have to pay money for all those things?"

"Yes, that's what I was doing with the card in the reader." Henry said nothing.

Once outside we were soon loaded and into the car. I had

decided that since the church in Brize Norton had not made him realise where and when he was, I would have to be more obvious, so when I got onto the A40 I sped past the turning for Carterton (Henry said nothing) and on towards Burford. In fact, Henry said little on the way except to ask about the road signs; why were they there and what did they mean?

As we were going along the ridge, with Stonelands on our left and Swinbrook on our right, I noticed Henry was staring more intently at the surrounding countryside. Was he recognising things? After all, we had been here together just yesterday, though separated by nearly seven centuries.

As we approached the roundabout at the top of the Burford hill we drove past a sign and Henry read it out aloud. "Burford, Medieval Market Town."

"Yes," I answered matter of factly as we entered the roundabout. Henry began to swing in his seat looking left and right as he seemed to recognise his home town. We turned right at the roundabout and entered the town. Immediately Henry began to twitch in his chair and then exclaim, "It's Burford!"

"Well, sort of," I responded immediately. As we were moving down the hill, and I was looking for a place to stop, Henry was repeating, "It's Burford! No it's not. Yes it is! It's the same but not the same!"

By now I had stopped the car; not properly parked but just to the side of the road, near to the top of the hill so that Henry could get a good view of this Burford. He went on, "It is exactly the same, but the buildings are different and there are lots of these carriage cars around."

"Yeees," I said, like a wise old man.

After a moment's silence Henry asked, "But why? Why are things different?"

"Well, it is Burford but not the Burford you know."

He went silent again while he thought this one over. He'd had a lot of culture shocks over the last couple of day,s but this was the biggest. His mouth opened – and closed again. Eventually he said, "If it's not the one I know why is it different? Is it another Burford but somewhere else?"

I thought and then replied, "No, it's not in a parallel universe. We are not in a Philip Pullman book," then I realised that meant nothing to him, so I said, "It's not so much a different place as a different time."

This didn't seem to have any effect on his thinking. He asked, "Is my home, Burford House, here?"

"No," was my simple reply. "But we could go and look."

"Yes, let's," Henry responded eagerly.

"OK," I said and looked into my mirrors before moving off slowly down the street, giving him time to take in his surroundings. Then it occurred to me to open the windows so he could sample the sounds and smells of the 21st century – or lack of them. I moved down the hill as slowly as I could, given that there were cars behind me, so that Henry could take in as much of his new surroundings as possible. Henry seemed stunned into silence, but then as we reached the bottom of the hill he said, "That's St. Johns!"

"Yes it is, but some parts have been added on since you lived here."

I said this partly to encourage him to think of this Burford as being the same as his but much later on, so things had changed. I turned right to go towards the car park and drove past the side of the church as Henry continued to twist and turn. Into the car park and I quickly slipped into a vacant space facing the river Windrush. Henry sat in silence and looked across the river, making no move to get out of the car. I noticed that he seemed to be breathing rather heavily, which I put down to the stress of the situation he was in.

Finally, he quietly observed, "Burford House should be over there."

"Yes it was, but not any more," I said, stating the blindingly obvious.

"But why not? What happened to it?"

"I don't know," was my honest answer. "Perhaps it fell into disrepair or had some sort of accident like a lightning strike. But it was a very long time ago," I added cautiously. I let this sink in and then, after at least a minute, came the obvious question I had been wondering how to deal with,

"How long?"

"A very long time," was my immediate and not very helpful answer. I didn't want to tell him it was seven centuries, as that just seemed too much for him to cope with. After all, I would have no concept of what the 28th century would be like. Partly to avoid having to give a precise time, I said, "Come on, let's wander around the town."

We both got out and walked towards the town over the little bridge. Suddenly, Henry blurted out, "This bridge shouldn't be here! And all the fields surrounding the river should be full of water!"

"Well, the bridge is new and I expect the river has been channelled to avoid flooding." I then remembered that the fields had flooded in recent years, but didn't want to complicate the issue by telling Henry. We walked on and without saying anything to me Henry turned off the road and walked towards the church and straight in, as he would have done seven centuries earlier. Inside he walked around as if he owned the place (his father almost did) and studied the parts that had not been there in his time. There were other people in the church, but because tourists would walk around and study things his behaviour did not seem out of place. Eventually, I encouraged him out of the church and we went towards the High Street. As we left the church and walked along the side, Henry noticed a plaque built in to the wall about three soldiers who had been hanged there. Of course, Henry asked about the circumstances and I, fortunately, did know a little about it.

"I believe they were hanged by Cromwell for rebellion during the Civil War," I said. Henry looked questioningly and I added, "It was a civil war between the King and Parliament and Oliver Cromwell was an MP and its military leader."

"Oh, like Simon de Montfort?"

"Er, yes, I think so. Was he the man who established Parliament?"

"Yes, the 6th Earl of Leicester. But who won the Civil War?"

"The Parliamentary forces, but Cromwell was no democrat."

Henry grunted and we moved onto the High Street. We walked slowly, looking at all the shops and other buildings as Henry commented on what should have been there. When we were about halfway up the hill we came to the Burford House Hotel and Henry exclaimed, "Burford House?" I explained that it was a hotel and Henry asked, "A hotel? What, like the French big hall?"

I realised that to him the word "hotel" would only have its original French meaning, not that it was a building in which you can stay to be looked after.

On up the hill we strolled and Henry asked, "Why are there so many people here?"

I wondered what he meant at first and then worked out that

the pavement and road were full of more people than could possibly live here.

"Oh, most of them are tourists," I said, not thinking how many more questions that would produce.

"Tourists?"

"Yes, people who do not live here but just come here to look at the town."

"Why?"

Oh dear! What could I say to that? I tried to explain that people like to just come to Burford to see what it's like.

"What, like we have, from a previous year?"

"No no no! Not from the past, just from another part of the country. Actually, from anywhere in the world."

Henry thought about this for a while and then asked, "But why would they come to look at Burford?"
"One might well ask," was all I could think to say.

He was quiet for a while, then observed, "There are many eastern-looking people."

"Eastern? What do you mean?" Henry put his fingers on his temples and pulled his eyes back. "Oh, eastern! Oriental you mean. Chinese. Yes, there are lots who come to Burford."

"But why?"

"Why do they come to Burford? I don't really know."

"But where do they come from?"

"Eh? China, of course. Where else would Chinese people come from?"

"But... How can so many people get here? All this way?"

At this point I thought about when Marco Polo went to China. It had been a lifelong trip.

"I don't really know," I mumbled. I really couldn't start to explain. Even though he had seen aeroplanes and had been in a couple of cars, he had no idea of people being able to fly around the world in a day.

Eventually we reached the top of the hill and paused to look down on the town and the surrounding countryside. He was almost silent for many minutes and I tried to stay quiet to let him cogitate on the whole idea. It wasn't an idea I really understood myself, so I could not fully explain to Henry what was happening. He made various comments and then asked, "Where is the wood?" He pointed into the distance.

"Well, there on top of that hill in the distance."

Henry stood looking into the distance. "But it should spread all over all those hills."

Ah, I thought. Hence Shipton-Under-Wychwood, Milton-Under-Wychwood, Ascott-Under-Wychwood. Perhaps the wood once stretched as far as Witney and that was why the Wychwood brewery was there. As I was thinking, Henry asked, "What happened to all the trees?"

"I assume they have all been cut down except for that token clump left on top of the hill."

"Not just cut down but assarted, I hope."

"Assarted?" Now it was my turn to ask questions.

"Yes, you know, assarted."

I looked at Henry for further information but got none so I said, "No, I don't know."

Henry looked at me as if I was thick and said, "You know, not just cut down but the roots got out, so the tree cannot grow again or break a plough share when it hits it under the soil."

"Oh, thank you," I said and suddenly realised there was a village not far from there called Field Assarts. That must be where the name comes from. These days we call getting the roots out "grubbing up", but I suppose "assarting" sounds more technical and it would have been a very big deal without power-driven machinery.

Henry continued to look into the distance at the now much-reduced wood. "Why are some fields bright yellow?"

"Oh those are fields of rape."

"Rape?"

"Yes, it produces lots of seeds that are crushed to produce oil for cooking. It does look beautiful at this time of year, but it is impossible to walk through."

Henry continued to look at the different, but not greatly different, town and landscape around him and then quietly observed, "It is good the wood has been cut down and assarted."

I thought of the environmental consequence of what he was saying and countered this by thinking how people had been starving, literally, and needed every inch of land to grow food on. Even so I asked him, "Why good?"

"Well," he replied tentatively, "because woods are a waste of land, except for hunting, and because the spirits will be driven out."

"Spirits? What spirits?"

A look of bemusement came across Henry's face and he said, "The spirits of the forest, of course."

"Eh?"

"The spirits, evil spirits that live in the forest," was his matter of fact reply. I couldn't really believe what I was hearing. Here was my friend Henry, whom I thought I had got to know quite well, who was clearly sceptical of the Medieval Church, yet he believed there were spirits in the forest. This sounded more Voodoo "scarum" nonsense than Christian "scarum" nonsense.

There was no helpful response I could give, so I stayed quiet and encouraged Henry to come back down the hill with me. The journey down was a lot quicker than the journey up, but he made many more comments and asked more questions, most of which I could not answer.

Finally, we reached my old Mini and began the journey home. As we were driving back through Burford, Henry was doing his twitching thing all the way as he took in his old/new town. He was quiet all the way back, and when we arrived home he sat in a chair and just stared into space. I just felt pleased he had not asked me for an exact date for when he was now.

SEVEN

PREPARATIONS

Alfred was rowing as fast as he could, and he was thankful he was going downstream with the help of the current rather than upstream, as when he had gone the wrong way. As he rounded a bend in the river he came to a long, straight stretch. Up ahead he could see another boat heading towards him upstream. This was not the first fellow traveller he had met, though the river traffic was a lot lighter than normal, but he decided to ask this one how far Windsor was. He was hoping to lose as little speed as possible while asking the question as he passed the other boat. But just as he was about to shout, "How far is Windsor?" he recognised the man in the other boat, and instead of asking his question he exclaimed, "Scabbard!"

"Alfred!" came the shrill reply.

The two men knew what to do without telling each other and each raised his oar for the other to grab. They held on tight as the two boats slowed and began to circle as the forward motion energy of both boats was dispersed in all directions. The two men were pleased to see each other. Scabbard told Arthur how Lord Burford had sent him back because he would be of more use in Burford than in the Court of King Edward III. It was also to assure Lady Burford, and the whole town, that the Lord would be home within a couple of days. Not only would his wife and family be very concerned in these difficult times, it was also important that the town should not feel their Lord had left them to fend for themselves while he hid himself from the world to avoid any infection.

When Scabbard had finished explaining why he was returning without Lord Burford, Alfred asked, "How much further is Windsor?"

"Windsor?" came Scabbard's reply. "You haven't yet reached Oxford. Windsor will be a couple of days away."

"Oh," replied Alfred, a little embarrassed to have asked. He remembered now that the distance had been explained to him, but there was so much to take in that he had forgotten most of it. Before today he had never really been out of the town, and he had little concept of where places were or how long it would take to get to them.

"You will know when you have got there because it's the only very big castle on the river and it is where the river becomes very wide and slow flowing."

"Oh, thanks," said Arthur, and the two men parted as they went in their respective directions.

Father MacKenzie finished the Mass and turned to face the congregation to bless them. There was a quiet chorus of "The Father, Son and Holy Ghost," as the congregation, which amounted to virtually the whole town, crossed themselves. Then they all waited as Lady Burford, Ann, Marion, John and Stephen made their way out of the church first. Lady Burford walked through the town with her head filled with worries. Still she had to acknowledge the townsfolk, though she was wanting to get home as quickly as possible.

As she approached the house Peter caught up with the family but kept his respectful position behind them until they reached the house. Then he stepped forward to open the door for the Lady, and she stepped into the house to be greeted by the sight of Scabbard standing in the hallway waiting for their return.

"Scabbard!"

"My lady," replied Scabbard with a bow.

"We were not expecting you so soon. But where is Lord Burford?"

"He is not with me, my lady, but do not be concerned."

At the news that her Lord had not returned her demeanour changed and her shoulders dropped. "Where is he? Why is he not with you? When?" came the questions to Scabbard.

"He is still in Windsor with the king, but he tells me he will be back within a couple of days."

Lady Burford regained her composure and asked, "Do you have any other news to tell me?"

"Not really, my lady. The Lord did not instruct me other than to return and help you in the town."

There was a silence as Lady Burford dealt with her disappointment, and nervously Scabbard quickly said, "I did meet Alfred on the river," as if this were some form of consolation to his Lady.

"Oh, so you know about Henry and Edmund?"

There was no answer. Scabbard's face showed he had no idea what she was talking about.

"About Henry and Sir Edmund's disappearance?" she added in clarification.

"Er, no, my lady. Alfred did not mention it." They both knew that this was probably because Alfred did not see it as his place to tell anybody except Lord Burford. She now knew there was much to discuss with Scabbard, so she ushered him into a room and told him to sit. First, she asked what had happened in Windsor with the king and her family. She heard how the Lord had spoken to the king about the ideas of Sir Edmund regarding the pestilence and how the king seemed to be interested so he had asked to speak to Sir Edmund, but that it was only a brief conversation. Scabbard also told of the badger fight that Edmund was too unwell to attend and of their time in the hostelries of Windsor.

When it became clear that Scabbard had nothing of significance to tell her, Lady Burford began to relate how Edmund and Henry had returned from Windsor and had immediately left again, pursued by the Bishop's men. She left out the fact that Megan had warned them to get out because the fewer people who knew, the less chance Father MacKenzie would have of finding out about the role of Megan and her friend, David, in the church. As she got to how Knut and his men had reached the Bishop's men after the two young men had disappeared, she paused. She was wondering how to describe what had happened without giving credence to the view that this was sorcery, as the Bishop's men termed it. Scabbard was left with the impression that the Bishop's men simply could not find their quarry, which was how he would put about the story within the town.

When each had put the other in the picture, Lady Burford went on to tell Scabbard how he would have to assist her until Lord Burford returned. By now Scabbard was struggling to keep his eyes open, and Lady Burford realised there was no further point in talking that night, so she dismissed him to get his much deserved sleep.

The Bishop of Gloucester rapped his fingers on his desk as he waited for the knock at the door. He had spent his time in much prayer since his men had returned without catching the two heretics. He had discussed his thoughts with God and prayed for guidance as to what he should do. Should he let the matter drop? Wait for a convenient time to pick up the two young men? Or immediately dispatch a company of men if word reached him that they had returned to Burford? To let the matter drop would make the Church look weak and would encourage other heretical thoughts or, even worse, make it appear the two had disappeared thanks to the Devil looking after his own and, thereby, getting one over on God. This, the Bishop was sure, would be the worst option and could be easily dismissed. A convenient time might never come, so that left the possibility of getting hold of Henry and Edmund as soon as possible, preferably before Lord Burford returned from Windsor. He was sure they would return before long because they had nowhere else to stay and as a man of God, he did not believe in sorcery or that men could simply disappear into thin air. Such thoughts were for the uneducated lower orders, those who unquestioningly accepted the teachings of the Church.

There was a respectful knock at the door and the Bishop responded, "Come in". Immediately the door opened and the Bishop, God's most powerful man in the west of England said, "Ah, Scarlett".

"Your Grace."

"Sit yourself down, Scarlett, we have much to arrange." Captain Scarlett sat on a hard, cushionless seat. His Grace lounged in his Bishop's throne. The Bishop began, "I have considered our options to arrest the two heretics" (although he did not believe in sorcery, he did believe in heresy) "and, after much prayer, I have decided to send you and your men to Burford as soon as we hear the young Henry Burford and his errant friend have returned."

There was a pause and as the Bishop took a breath to go on, Captain Scarlett said, "Your Grace, but how will we know they have returned with Burford tightly sealed against the plague?"

The Bishop smiled benignly as if talking to a child. "Father MacKenzie is a resourceful man and I am sure he will find a way to get a message out. There are many good people in Burford who will do all they can to assist us in doing God's work and, of course, it will gain them Grace with God in his heaven." His benign smile slowly morphed into a sinister sneer.

Captain Scarlett, who had thought the two lads had disappeared forever, swallowed hard and asked, "But what if they do not return?"

The smile disappeared from the Bishop's face. "God has assured me the men will return before too long," he snapped. Captain Scarlett looked chastened and the Bishop added, "And then I will instruct you and your men what to do".

"Yes, your Grace." With that a clerical hand was waved and Captain Scarlett rose from his chair, bowed, said, "Your Grace," turned and left the room.

EIGHT

THE MUSIC ROOM

I put the radio on, partly to try to distract Henry but also to try to lift my mood. He remained seated, staring into space, as I made us something simple to eat – toast.

"What do you want on your toast?" I shouted through to Henry. As I was saying it I realised this would probably raise more questions than it answered. There was no reply, then Henry appeared in the doorway. "What would you like on your toast?" I repeated. Still there was no reply so I added, "Well, you're getting peanut butter."

"What is this stuff on top?" Henry asked through a mouthful of toast.

"Peanut butter," I replied as a matter of fact.

"Peanut butter?"

"Yes. Butter made from peanuts. Except it is a misnomer. They're not really nuts, as I think they grow underground. "

Henry continued to eat and then asked, "But how did you make the toast without any fire?"

"Good question! I used a toaster. If you want some more you may make it yourself and put something else on it".

"Thank you," said Henry. The look on his face said he did

want some more, so as I was getting up I said,

"Come on, I'll show you." We walked to the toaster on the work top and I showed him how to pop the bread in and push it down. "Push it down again if you want it done a little more."

"Who cut the bread for you?" seemed to be his greatest concern.

"No one, it comes like that. Some people think it's the best thing since sliced bread." I tapped a cupboard door and told him, "There are plenty of jams and spreads in here. Use what you want."

I went into another room to look for a large travel bag in the cupboard. I was getting out all the bags and cases when I suddenly realised I had left my backpack in Burford in the 14th century. If I didn't bring that back, there were going to be a lot of very confused archaeologists one day. Even Tony Robinson wouldn't be able to work that one out.

Suddenly there was a fast, high-pitched bleeping as the smoke alarm went off. I ran out of the room and into a smoke-filled kitchen and waved a magazine under the smoke alarm. "You've burnt the toast!" I told him in exasperation. The bleeping stopped and I asked, "What happened?" Henry's expression of fear turned to one of confusion and he raised both arms saying, "You told me to push it down again."

"Oh yes. My fault. I didn't show you how to pop it up again." I opened the back door to let out the smoke, took the burnt bread out of the toaster, threw it in the bin and put some more bread into the toaster, then said, "If you want to push it down again, press this button after a short while." I then pressed the eject button and the toast flew out of the toaster and into the air. I ostentatiously caught it in mid-air and Henry laughed, stepping forward to take over. I went to get on with what I was doing.

I found what I wanted and popped in to see Henry sitting in a chair listening to the radio. "Do you like the music?" I asked him.

"Err...yes, but it is all very strange and they all have the same *dum* dum dum dum, *dum* dum dum dum, *dum* dum dum dum rhythm."

"Oh well, if you want variety in time signature try this one." I then looked through my mum's music and put on my favourite classical piece – the 1812 Overture. As I was putting it on Henry asked, "Those people hopping about to the music. What where they doing?"

"Eh, what do you mean what were they doing? Dancing of course."

"No, they weren't dancing, except like St Vitas."

"That's what is called dancing."

"Dancing? It had no form, no structure, no style, no elegance, it was just..."

There was no point in continuing this, but the music brought the conversation to a halt. The piece starts very quietly, so I wound up the volume, knowing full well that when the cannons came it would shake the windows. As the first notes played quietly Henry settled in to respectfully listening to the music. It made me realise that before we had music everywhere, and all the time, that people would either carefully listen to music or join in, as we had at the party at Burford House. Now it is there all the time, we take it for granted and hardly notice it. Supermarket music. I am not sure if that is good or bad. I believe my parents' generation used to save up to buy records and played the same one again and again.

I went back into the other room to sort out some clothing and other things as Henry listened. About half way through the overture (I knew it lasted 18 minutes) I popped my head around the door to see Henry's face and body quite animated with the music. He wasn't actually "conducting" but was clearly really into it. I returned to sorting out various things and soon heard the cannons so once more I looked in to see him smiling in wonderment. As I could hear the piece coming to an end, I went in again to see an expression of ecstasy on Henry's face. "That's it," I said so he knew it had finished. He looked at me and smiled broadly. He then joyfully jumped up and asked if he could have some more toast. "Yes, sure. Make it yourself," I said.

After a short while Henry joined me, still eating toast. I was pleased that he seemed to have calmed down and was beginning to look after himself, as I was getting fed up waiting on him hand and foot as he was used to at home.

"What did you think of the music?" I asked.

"Wonderful! So many instruments, many of which I didn't recognise, and different parts to it. What is it called?"

"The 1812 Overture," I told him.

"Mmm, strange name." I was pleased he didn't ask why it was called that. I think the passage of seven centuries is best glossed over. To get off the subject of the year 1812 I threw in, "My mum says Roy Wood nicked the *d d d d, d d d d, d d d d, d d d* for *Night of Fear*."

"Who is Roy Wood?"

"No idea."'

He stood behind me and asked, "What's that?"

"What's what?"

"What's that instrument?"

"Oh, it's a guitar." Henry stuffed half a slice of bread into his mouth and rubbed his hands shaking a few crumbs onto the floor. Then he picked up the guitar and dragged his thumb across the strings. "Ooh, it's very out of tune," I observed as I put out a hand to take the guitar. I too dragged my thumb across the strings and cringed again. I opened a drawer and took out a recorder. Blowing a top E, I showed Henry what I wanted and passed the recorder to him. He blew the same note without having to be shown where to put his fingers and I began to tune the guitar to the top string.

"What's this called?"

"A recorder." As I was tuning the stringed instrument he began playing a tune on it. "Oh, you know how to play it," I said with a smile.

"Anyone can play a whistle," he replied casually, and I thought, *Well, I can't.*

He was silent for while as I was tuning, then asked, "Is this your music room?"

"Music room? No, it's our dining room. Or our laundry room, as my mum keeps complaining we haven't got a utility room." Having got the guitar vaguely in tune I passed it to Henry, who had watched me tuning it. He immediately began to tune the instrument more accurately. He clearly had a much better ear than me, which was no surprise at all. I am not a musician and I had heard him playing various instruments very well in the music room in his house.

As he plucked and strummed, I put a music stand in front of him and looked for some music books. I found a simple one and put it in front of him on the stand, open at *Blowing in the Wind*. Just a simple three chords, G, C and D. I pointed to the chord pictures and he formed his fingers and practised the three chords – almost perfectly. Having strummed these two or three times he launched into playing and singing the song as if he had been a guitarist for years. I was struck by the anachronism of a man from the 14th century playing a 20th century protest song in the 21st century.

After he had played and sung the song (better than Bob Dylan), he asked, "Is it a religious song?"

"Well, sort of, but probably not in the sense that you mean."

Henry looked around and pointed at a brown bag. "What's in there?"

"Oh that. That's my sister's old violin. She hasn't played it for years."

He leaned down and picked up the bag and began to unzip. "I have seen one of these things before. It was on the trousers you gave me. I worked out what to do. What is it called?"

"A zip."

"Oh yes, very onomatopoeic," he said, pulling the zip up and down to make the zipping noise. The imp told me to tell him there was no such thing as zips, only hook and eye fasteners, but I resisted the temptation.

He took the violin out of the bag and plucked the strings, looking at me. "Don't ask me how to tune it, I have no idea," I told him in complete honesty. "Oh, hang on," and I looked through the music books once more. "Here we are. Violin for beginners."

"Thanks," said Henry. He turned to the first page, which had the tuning sequence. As he was tuning and bowing I remembered he could play violin-type instruments in the music room in Burford House, so this one would just be a little different.

While this was happening the little imp appeared on my shoulder again saying, "Go on, really blow his mind". So I picked the electric keyboard out of the corner, put it on its stand and plugged it in. Henry stopped half way through his noises and once again asked, "What's that?"

"It's a keyboard."

"A what?"

"A keyboard." I struck one note. Henry immediately put down the violin and came over, almost pushing me aside in his eagerness. He began tapping one note at a time, then two or three notes, and then moving from the white keys to the black keys, all with one hand.

"Look," I said and played the C scale. Henry just looked, so I then played the D scale followed by the E scale and Henry said, "Oh yes, all the notes are the same distance apart, just in a higher pitch."

"That's right." I left him to experiment while I looked for some piano music. As I was doing so he asked, "How does it work? It's so small and there's no sound box!"

I could not start explaining about loud speakers and microchips so I said, "Oh, there's a little man inside hitting the strings with a hammer. Like a dulcimer."

Obviously he didn't believe me but he didn't ask more. I found what I was looking for, and to emphasise the scales I put 'Doh a Deer' in front of him.

"What's this?"

"Piano music."

"Piano? This is a piano? A soft?" he said pointing at the keyboard.

"Yes but it can also be a forte. Actually it's a keyboard (running my finger silently along the notes) but it's in piano mode."

Henry looked at the page, pointing to the musical staves, and said, "What's this?".

"Well, er, that's the music. How to play it."

"It doesn't look like music to me," he said, rather dismissively.

"Well, it is, look." I leaned over him to play the song with one hand.

"Oh, I see." He began to do the same. He picked it up really quickly and was soon quite smooth. Then he said, "Oh yes, very clever. This song incorporates those scale things you were teaching me."

Teaching him! I really didn't think I was in any position to teach music to Henry. Then he played again and finished with singing, "Brings me back to doh, doh ,doh, doh."

"It was written by Rodgers and Hammerstein," I threw in quite randomly.

"Are they troubadours?" he asked.

"Well, sort of but a little bit better off."

Then I thought I'd be clever and said, "But what about the bass line?"

"What bass line?"

"Here. This bottom line." I pointed to the bass staves. Henry looked at me and I thought, oh no, he's going to expect me to play it now. I thought quickly and said, "That's a bit difficult. Why don't you start with this?" I started to look for a different piece. "Here it is," I said and put *Für Elise* in front of him. "This requires two hands but only one at a time, if you know what I mean?"

Henry looked at the sheet music and said, "Oh, yes," and began to slowly tap out the notes with both hands.

"It was written by Ludwig Van Beethoven," I told him.

"Oh, was he from Saxony like you?"

"Sort of," I replied. He probably thought I knww him. Still what's three hundred years into the past when you're seven hundred years into the future?

Another little game occurred to me. As he was mastering

Für Elise I pressed the record button and left him to play. When he came to a natural break I pressed the replay and Henry's playing, errors and all, came flooding back. Once more his jaw dropped as he recognised his own playing. He simply said, "How?"

"It has recorded it."

"Re-cord-ed it?"

"Yes." I played it from the beginning again.

"But, how does it know what I've played?"

"It doesn't, it simply plays back what it has recorded."

"Recorded? What you mean written down like a monk copying a document?"

"Well, sort of but it's not *written* down. There is no paper."

"Then how does it know what I have played? Does it just remember what I played?"

"Not really. It just makes a digital copy of it."

I played a few things myself and recorded them to show him. He just looked and said nothing, so I recorded something over what he had played and played the two together in a horrible row. I showed him what buttons to press to record something and he picked that up quickly, but still had no idea what was meant by "recording". I suppose in his world everything is instantly been and gone. There was "evidence" of what happened in terms of sound, photos, films or information. Only the written word, which so few people could understand. The idea that we could relive our past by looking at photos, or listening to something, ws just not in his world concept.

He was getting quicker and smoother at what he played, and seemed to enjoy the playback as it showed his errors, when that little imp appeared on my shoulder again saying, "Go on." With this I pressed one of the buttons and a piano became a trumpet.

Henry stopped and said,

"What's happened?"

I smiled and said, "It's now a trumpet sound."

"A what?"

"A trumpet. A wind instrument."

"Yes, I know what a trumpet is, but...?"

"It can make the sound of *any* instrument. Look, there are 240 possibilities," I said, pressing button after button to produce different sounds. Henry's mouth dropped open once more and I said, "I'll leave you to play with it," and walked out of the room.

NINE

CHURCH

While Henry was making music I was able to get on with other things, like calling friends and, most importantly of all, calling Serene. I had no idea what to say to her and how to convincingly explain why, having been away, I had no time to see her now I was back. I had run various scenarios through my head but had not even settled on how to start. Eventually I plucked up the courage to pick up the phone and dial. The phone rang, and again, and again. *Come on. She must know it's me ringing.* Just when I was about to give up, half relieved, the phone was answered but there was silence the other end.

"Hello, Serene?" I said.

"Yes, Edmund?" What followed was one of the most difficult conversations I have ever had. What could I tell her? Even if I told her the truth she would not believe me, and every white lie I told made me feel worse about the situation and myself. By now I had come to terms with the idea of having to go back to the 14th century at some point, so I had to tell her I would not be around for a few days again. More significantly, I didn't know when I would return. I didn't know whether to be light hearted about it and suggest it's no big deal, I go away for a few days again over the summer holidays, or to make a big deal about really wanting to see her but saying I just couldn't at the moment. During what seemed an interminable conversation I tried both approaches and a few others. At last our conversation came to a silent halt and we left it that I would call her as soon as I could. I pressed the red icon and heaved a sigh of relief, but her most painful words were ringing in my ears: "You seem to have the time to do anything except see me!"

Over the last couple of days I had weighed up all my options and none really appealed to me. I was sitting there in my safe 21st century home, and I didn't want to go back to the 14th century again. Why would I not just stay? Oh, yes; Henry. My conversation with Serene had made me realise I had to do something, and the sooner I got on with it, the sooner I would get back to my normal 21st century life. Or would I? I was fully aware that travelling back again with Henry might not work and he could be stuck there forever. How would I explain him? No birth certificate, no passport, no National Insurance number, no NHS number and no idea of how to survive in the 21st century. Effectively, he did not exist. Convenient if the police did come looking for him after the knife fight, but not much use otherwise.

Supposing we both got back to the 14th century but I couldn't travel back here again to "the present", whatever that was? Worst of all might be the possibility of us both being arrested by The Church, tortured, "tried" and found guilty of whatever medieval crime and burned at the stake. Laughing at thatthe threat when Megan came to tell us to get out didn't seem so clever now. Megan and Henry clearly thought the threat was real, so I could only assume it was.

Having come to terms with the idea of going back to the 14th century, I now needed to do a little bit of research on all sorts of thing. So I picked up my laptop – and immediately put it down again as if it was too hot to handle. *No. Don't take any risks. Only touch it for travelling. Just in case.* So I settled down in the armchair with my phone. Annoyingly small, but at least I could be sure I wouldn't suddenly find myself somewhere else. Or would I?

Henry continued to entertain himself by experimenting musically, and there were a few gaps in the sound, I assumed because he was thinking or pressing buttons. By now he had found the rhythm box controls and was putting together some quite sophisticated sounds. I had already been impressed by his musical abilities, but now I was now wondering how he was so capable, not just with sounds and rhythms he had never heard before but having to deal with the technology as well.

Once more the music stopped and Henry came into the room and went straight into, "When are we going back home?" Fortunately I had about come to the end of what I was researching and my first thought came out of my mouth.

"Well, Henry, you have been very patient, and I have decided what we need to do."

"Oh good, and I need to go to church."

"Eh, church?"

"Yes." Now this really did surprise me, but I suppose it is normal for a medieval mind.

"Well, umm, do you mean the Catholic church?" As I was saying this I realised it was a silly question. Henry looked at me and asked the obvious,

"As opposed to...?"

"Hang on, I'll check on the website when it's open." This produced another strange look from Henry. As I was on the net already I quickly found the website and said, "There's a service starting in 40 minutes."

"Good."

"I'll tell you what, I'll walk round with you and show you where it is, then I can walk on to the pizza shop and meet you back here later." Henry looked at me and asked,

"Aren't you going to Mass?"

"Oh, no," I answered with little thought. Henry took a deep breath and forcefully told me, "You must go to Mass. You're a bad boy if you don't go to Mass". He wagged his finger. I was quite taken aback. Not in the sense that I was hurt, or insulted; just how like a child he seemed. He might rebel against the Church by thinking there must be some other cause for disease than the wrath of God, but he didn't question the idea that the destination of his soul must be through the Lord Jesus Christ and the One True Holy Roman Church. Once more I was reminded that he was a product of his time; a Pre-Enlightenment man. He had no more choice over his religion than did Mohammed the Muslim from Mecca.

I had to decide how to treat this. I immediately rejected the idea of pandering to his prejudices. Yes, I had pandered to them in the 14th century because I'd had to, but I wasn't going to play that game in the 21st century. If I started that in the present, there would be no stopping it. So, I just looked at him and said, "No, Henry, I am not going to Mass."

Henry just looked confused and stood up. Nothing more was said, and we both got ready to leave. I tried to break the ice with small talk, but as we walked I became more conscious of the need to impress upon him that he must be careful what he said to people. Henry listened in silence, then exploded, "You don't have to keep telling me this!"

"Okay," I responded, and silence returned. I could see his point, but I was permanently worried that he might get into a situation where it became clear he did not exist. But then, how could he? People would just think he was another Eastern European with pidgin English. On the other hand, there was the event with the knife, and had the police come along he would not have been able to answer some of the most basic questions, like, where did he live, what was his occupation, where was he born. And that's before any fingerprints or DNA.

I tried to lighten the atmosphere by saying, "Carterton is a newish town. Not a planned one, just an organic growth, but it wasn't here in your time."

"I worked that one out when we came back from Burford to an area I know but with buildings I do not know."

I pushed on and said, "There was a farm here, Rock Farm, and it had a barn which is now the Catholic church. It is the oldest building in Carterton."

Henry scowled and said, "A barn is now the church?"

Oh dear! Anything I said seemed wrong. Just as well I didn't mention that Catholic churches are very rarely in old buildings because the Church of England took all the old churches at the time of the Reformation. Any Catholic churches since then had to be newly built, or be converted from old buildings like the barn in Carterton.

"Here it is," I said as we rounded the corner. "In you go. I'm sure you can find your way back from here."

"Oh, yes. See you there." I watched him walk into the church.

I walked on to the pizza shop, queued up, picked up my

order and walked back to the house with the pizzas. My head was racing with the situation Henry was in and the fact that his presence meant that I *had* to go back to the 14th century. My attitude had changed from regretting the need to go back to wanting to get Henry out of there as soon as possible. The question that occurred to me repeatedly was, how had I got into this situation? Of course, for this I had no answer.

I reached the house, entered and turned on the oven to reheat the now cool pizzas. Having taken them out of their boxes and put them in the oven, I settled down in front of the television for the first bit of "me time" since before I had first travelled. I was hopping from channel to channel in a search for trivia; maybe a panel show or some sort of comedy. Actually, a vacuous soap would do. I was looking at an old *Dad's Army* when I heard the door open and called out, "Henry?"

"Yes."

I jumped up to see his expression was slightly morose. I tried to ignore it as I took the pizzas out of the oven. Henry flinched a little as I opened the oven and a wave of heat came out. He looked into the oven, presumably to try to see if there was a fire, but said nothing. He could not question everything, any more than I could explain everything. I had remembered to put a knife and fork in front of him so he didn't need to "tear the food with his teeth" as he had made it clear to me in the 14th century that this was completely socially unacceptable. As I put the plate in front of him he simply asked. "Did you get these from the bakery?"

"Yes," was my only response, as this was probably the easiest question I had had to deal with. A pizza is only dough with things on top, so it wouldn't be outside his worldly view.

"How did you get them here from the bakery?"

"In these boxes," I said and indicated the pizza boxes on the side. He picked one up and through a mouthful of food asked, "What are they made of?

"Cardboard."

"Cardboard? What's cardboard?"

"A sort of paper."

"Paper?" he said running his fingers over it and probably thinking how expensive paper was.

We finished the meal and Henry didn't seem any happier, so I felt I had to ask him what was wrong. "Henry, you don't seem very happy," I said. His eyes turned towards me, but there was no immediate response. I remained silent as Henry inhaled and exhaled before tentatively saying, "Er, the Mass was strange."

I wasn't really sure what a "Mass" was but knew it was something to do with the church service. "How do you mean, strange?"

"Well, it was correct, but it seemed the priest was talking to the congregation rather than talking to God."

"Well, um, what's wrong with that?"

Henry gave me his confused look again and said, "Eh, ee, ah, obviously the Mass is through the priest." Was it? I wouldn't know. Why through the priest? But I didn't think it would be helpful to say this and simply said, "Go on?"

"Of course, the Pope is God's representative on earth and the priest is the Pope's representative. It is through him God hears us take the Mass."

"Won't God know without the priest?" There was then a period of silence as Henry gathered his thoughts to say, "The Church teaches that we must go to Mass."

Without giving it any real thought I replied, "Have you

never considered doing your own thinking?"

He said nothing, but his face was a combination of confusion and hurt. It had not been my intention to hurt him, but I just could not get my head around the idea that someone else tells us what to think. But then, I haven't got a medieval mind that believes in forest spirits, priests and gods. This was not the Henry I had associated with my time in the 14th century. That Henry didn't seem to be a religious parrot. Perhaps it was just the context of the 14th century, when I expected him, and everyone else, to be deeply religious. As he seemed less obsessed than other people in that time he had seemed quite rational, but now I was judging him by 21st century thinking. I supposed that was more my fault than his. Also, he was clearly very disturbed and frightened to be out of his time, and I supposed the ritual of the Mass gave him a sense of security. But because it was different from what he was expecting, that comfort blanket was denied to him. Of course, it would be different after seven centuries, but if you believe anything is "the word of God" it's difficult to accept the idea of it can change. That would make God look rather silly.

He stood in front of me looking at the floor. I wanted to change the subject, but it was obvious he had more to say.

"Go on, Henry," I said, encouraging him to get it off his chest.

"Well, er, he, the priest seemed to be performing the Mass in English!"

"Well, er, yes. What language would you expect him to do it in, Chinese?"

"No, Latin. The words were the same, but they were in your dialect of English."

"So? Surely that makes it easier to understand."

"Yes, but... oh!" He threw his arms in the air, and no more was said on the subject.

TEN

DECISION TIME

We were both quiet for a while, then Henry said, "So, what's the plan?"

I was taken off guard by his question but had to accept he had been very patient given the situation he found himself in. I had given a lot of thought as to what to do and had almost decided, but was still procrastinating, because what I really wanted to do was to stay there and live a normal life in the 21st century. Now I was put in the position of having to voice my thoughts, which would, more or less, commit me.

Over the rest of the evening I gave him some idea of my plan. I expected to be met by resistance somewhere along the line, as I didn't like what I was planning, so why should he? To my relief, or my surprise, I'm not really sure which, he didn't argue at all and just accepted the plan. He seemed to assume I knew what I was doing. I wished I had his faith! The plan only took a few minutes to explain and Henry quickly moved on to the subject most on his mind: "Where are all the lower orders? Who does the farm work? How can everybody be so well off?"

"Well off? What makes you think they're well off?"

"Because there are so many fat people around."

This confused me at first but then I remembered all those thin, grey, struggling people I had seen in the 14th century. I smiled and said, "These days it's more likely to be the poor who are fat."

"Eh, how can that be?"

"Because they often have a less healthy diet."

It seemed he was not sure if I was telling the truth or just playing mind games with him. He went on to ask about the "social position" of the people in Triumph's. How could I answer that question? I waffled on about things being different from what he was used to, but I could tell he wasn't happy with my reply. What seemed to exercise him most was the position of the "gay girls". Not just the other customers but the staff as well. He also seemed disturbed by what he termed "the lack of respect from people". To this I simply replied, "Yes, Henry."

"What are those things on some people's faces?" was his next question. I looked quizzically at him and he ringed his thumbs and forefingers and put them in front of his eyes.

"Oh, glasses. Spectacles. For people who cannot see very well. It helps them to see." I remembered I had seen a pair of my mum's in the kitchen so I went to fetch them and put them on. As I walked back in Henry said, "Yes, that's it."

"You try them," I said, handing them to him.

He put them on and looked around saying, "It all looks bigger but... distorted, and, uh, it's starting to hurt my eyes."

"Yes, that's because you don't need glasses, but they're very good for people with bad eyesight and in fact for most people over the age of 40."

"Oh," he said, handing them back.

"You remember how when we were in the glass maker I talked about making things to see the stars?" I reminded him.

"Yes, the telescope." He had remembered.

"Well, it's the same principle."

"Oh, interesting!"

"But I don't know if these glasses are mum's real glasses or her £1 glasses." Henry made no reply and I wasn't sure if that was because he didn't care what I meant or because he was beginning to latch on to my silly comments.

There was silence for a while and then Henry moved back to the subject of to how the keyboard remembered what had been played before. As I was trying to explain how this happened, while avoiding talk of binary language, I got my phone out and turned on the speech recording app. After about a minute I started to play back our conversation, saying, "Listen to this". Once more Henry's mouth dropped and his expression turned from one of interest to one of mild fear. He began to gabble about echoes and ghosts, and I showed him how to record us both. He pressed "record" and I made inane comments for half a minute before showing him how to play it back.

I left him to play with it for a while, but then he seemed to get bored with it and suddenly said, "I keep meaning to ask you about these paintings". He pointed to the family photos around the room.

"They're not paintings," I informed him. I took my phone from his hand and took a photo of him, then opened the gallery to show him. This was just too much for Henry and he fell back into the armchair. "That's how those 'paintings' are made," I said. Then I knelt by his side, put my arm around him, took a selfie and showed it to him. This just appeared to reinforce his sense of shock, which made me want to push the game further, so I turned on the video app and recorded us chatting. Switching it to playback, I handed the phone to him once more.

By now it was getting late and I thought about getting on with what was needed to be done. I told Henry it was time, and he stopped playing with his new toy. I gave him the smaller of the two cases I had dug out. We walked out of the house towards the road. I did not want to take the car in case of CCTV around the town, so we walked through the side roads carrying the cases as casually as possible. As we arrived at the back of my father's pharmacy I could hear the hubbub from people getting their kebabs from the mobile food van around the front. This produced a mixture of fear that we might be seen and the pleasure of knowing their noise would cover any noise we made.

Up the fire escape I went with Henry behind me. At the back door I leaned over the railing and banged the fan light window frame a couple of times and the retaining bar jumped up. Wonderful! Perfect! Just what I was hoping for! I knew that this window was a weak point in the pharmacy security and was pleased how easy it was to open. I climbed up on the railing and put my arm through the open window to reach the handle of the larger window and open it. Now it was easy to slip into the building, open the back door and let Henry in. I was filled with a sense of fear of being caught and great guilt about my father's chemist shop.

Henry whispered, "Is this the apothecary you spoke of?"

"Yes. You just follow me around and hold the bag open."

As quickly as possible we went around the store room, picking up anything I thought might be useful but very conscious of the minimal space. Even if we could get all we wanted into the two cases there was still the question of whether we could all travel together. Maybe two of us was the maximum. If that happened I would still have to go back to the 14th century because of Henry. Then a thought occurred to me. If the worst comes to the worst it might be possible for Henry to go back with out me, and without any medicines. Anyway, it was all academic until we tried.

Henry did as he was asked and followed me around holding open the bag as I quickly grabbed whatever I could find that might be useful. I knew what was needed most of all was antibiotics. One of the good things about there having been no antibiotics in the 14th century is that they could not have any drug-resistant bacteria. Soon the bag was full, so Henry closed it and opened the case for me to fill. I was filled with fear of being caught, so I had a mixture of wants: to get as much as possible, but to get out as soon as possible. What surprised me was how calm Henry was. He didn't seem at all concerned about being caught. Perhaps that was because he was from the 14th century gentry and, therefore, effectively above the law.

Having put the larger packs in the case, I stuffed all the corners with smaller objects. Eventually it was not possible to get any more in and Henry forced the lid down and closed the clips.

I picked up the bag and could only just about lift it. Henry didn't seem to have any difficulty lifting the case, which reminded me how much fitter than me he was. I opened the door and ushered him out in front of me, partly because I didn't want to be seen emerging from my father's pharmacy with a bag full of drugs. Of course I had to follow him and we carefully and quietly eased our way down the steps and out the back into the car park. I was breathing fast and felt hot, but Henry still seemed as cool as a cucumber. We worked our way back through the alleyways between the houses to avoid being seen as much as possible. It was quiet, but not so late that no one was around at all.

There was almost a full moon and the sky was clear. I looked up and said, "What a beautiful moon there is tonight."

"Yes, but I am used to the moon and stars being much brighter," he replied with a note of disappointment in his voice. At this the little gremlin appeared on my shoulder again and I said, "I think when men were up there they turned down the brilliance on the moon."

"Eh?"

"Well, I think the men who have been to the moon have done something to it."

"What are you talking about?"

"I'm talking about the men who have walked on the moon."

"Oh, don't be silly, I know you're only playing games," Henry responded dismissively. Yes, I was playing games. It was true about the men on the moon, but Henry wasn't playing. Oh well!

Suddenly we went around a corner to be faced with a couple of old people coming the other way. We nodded and grunted as we passed and my pulse went up about 50 beats per minute. I told myself this was because I felt guilty and not because of any possibility that the other people knew what we had been doing. We kept having to stop, or more honestly, I kept having to stop for a rest, but eventually we made it home without being stopped and I heaved a sigh of relief.

I felt very tired, which was probably the result of the situation I found myself in, so I wanted to get to bed as soon as possible but didn't want to wake up and have to get things ready to travel. So I tried to remember all I would need to take and got everything ready and waiting for the morning. Then I suddenly thought of something else. There were many aloe vera plants in our house and as it scientifically has good healing qualities, it should be useful in the 14th century. The plants were all over the house, so I selected one that was not too big but had plenty of little shoots on it which they could take for cuttings.

As I picked up the pot I knocked over another one, spilling dry compost onto the carpet. Not what I needed when I just wanted to get to bed. Henry was standing behind me and watched as I got the vacuum cleaner out of the cupboard and plugged it in. As I sucked up the compost I looked at Henry's face as the carpet was returned to its clean state. "It's all disappeared," Henry said in amazement.

"No, it's not, it's inside this box."

Henry gently shook his head.

I put the plant pot with the other items and told Henry I was off to bed. "Yes, me too," he said, and we both wandered up the stairs. By now I expected him to know what to do, so I just slipped into my room and closed the door. I was thankful to be alone and able to relax. Soon I was in bed and began to go over everything in my head. This worried me, as the last thing I needed was to lie awake when I needed to get up early and fresh the next morning.

I started to drift off and then woke up again. I felt wide awake. Had I been asleep? Then I realised it was light outside, so I looked at the clock. A little earlier than I had meant to wake, but I obviously wasn't going to get to sleep again.

I lay in bed for a while and then got up to have a shower, conscious that it would be my last for a while and, if things went wrong, maybe my last ever. When I was out of the shower I knocked on Henry's door. He was asleep but got out of bed straight away.

"Do you want a shower?" I asked him.

"Why? I had one yesterday."

A perfectly good answer and he didn't smell, so what was the point? Just 21st century social expectation.

"Okay, but don't forget to dress in the clothes we came here in or we'll look out of place."

"I won't."

Down for breakfast and once more I gave him food rather than asking him what he wanted. Henry had already put the television on, something he was getting quite used to, and a weather forecast came on. Henry looked at the screen avidly and asked, "What's this all about?"

"It's a weather forecast," I answered.

"A what?"

"A weather forecast. It tells us what the weather will do over the next few days."

Henry was silent for a while, then asked, "How can that man predict what will happen?"

"It's not a prediction. Fitzroy was clear about that. It is to forecast what is happening now."

This didn't seem to explain anything for Henry, and he asked, "Is that meant to be England, Scotland and Ireland?"

"Yes, it is."

"But they are all a funny shape."

"Are they?" was all I could say to that.

"And how can anyone know what is God's intention for the weather?"

Oh dear! Here we go again. "Good question," was my only response.

Having finished breakfast, I was clearing up when Henry exclaimed, "What's that?"

"What's what?"

"There's a strange animal in the garden."

I looked out of the window and said, "Oh, that's only Mr Squirrel, he lives here."

"A squirrel? But it's far too big, and it's the wrong colour."

"Oh yes, the red squirrels are extinct around here. That's a grey squirrel and they come from America. They have driven out the red squirrel from most of the country, though I think there are still some left on the Isle of Wight and in Scotland. They were brought here from America along with the mink and American crayfish." They can have them all back if they want them, but we'll keep the rock and roll."

"American?"

"Yes."

Henry watched the squirrel for a while and then asked, "Where is America?"

"Half way to Australia." I answered unhelpfully.

Henry thought and asked, "Where is Australia?"

"Where my parents are on holiday." Poor Henry was getting nowhere.

Having cleared up the kitchen and taken every opportunity to procrastinate, I had to accept it was time to travel and told Henry. Just as I was settling down next to the pile of cases with the laptop on top, the landline rang. Oh no! It would either be someone trying to sell something or my parents. As I wouldn't be back for a few days, I would have to talk to them. I jumped up and answer the phone. "Hello."

"Hello Edmund, it's dad."

"Oh hello, dad."

"I hope I haven't woken you up?"

"No, I've been up for ages."

"The main reason I am calling is because I have just had a call from Petronella, you know, the manager of the pharmacy." My heart jumped into my mouth and all sorts of future scenarios ran through my head. "She tells me there was a break in last night."

"Oh my..!" I cut myself off, not wanting to appear too concerned.

"Yes, they took all sorts of things but nothing of any great value."

"Oh," I replied, and my pulse rate started to drop. "Well, er, eh, what happened?"

"I don't really know, but they seem to have come in through the back door at the top of the fire steps."

I took a deep breath and went straight to the point. "So, what's going to happen?"

"Nothing really. Apparently the alarm went off in the police station and they drove around sometime later but could see nothing, so they went off again."

My mood began to lift more. "Oh dear," I said, trying not to sound too pleased.

"The police aren't going to do anything and there's no point in telling the insurance company, it's not worth it, and they will just complain about our bad security and will probably put up the premium, so there's no point in putting in a claim."

"No, of course not," I agreed wholeheartedly.

"Strange though, what appears to be missing would seem to be the sort of things someone would need to take to a third world country with an epidemic." I laughed nervously, but thought that was exactly what I had wanted them for. "Oh well, son, I'll leave you to get on with your day. We are going out this evening."

"Okay, thanks for letting me know. I'll be away again for a few days so if I don't answer the phone..."

"That's all right, Edmund. See you in a few weeks. Bye."

"Yes. Bye, dad." I put the phone down.

It had not occurred to me that there would be an alarm in the pharmacy. If I had known I would not have done it. Just as well the police were too late and too busy to do anything. And my father didn't think it's worthwhile doing anything about it. It seemed I had had another very lucky escape.

I sat in the middle of the floor rather than on the sofa, so that Henry and I could be on the same level. I motioned to him to sit in front of me and loaded the two cases on my lap with the laptop on top. "Oh no!" I muttered. Just in time, I had remembered the windmill. I unloaded the cases again and groped behind the sofa where I had left my sister's old blue windmill. We would need that as a marker when when we arrived.

My hand went straight on it and I loaded the cases again with the aloe vera plant on top and the windmill next to it. Once more, Henry looked very calm and seemed to think this was just another way of travelling in the 21st century. No different from a car. He gripped the edges of the laptop as I nervously tapped in, "bbc.co.uk/cricke..." I looked at Henry and took a deep breath while pressing "t". Instantly we were both swirling, and I knew something was happening.

ELEVEN

A SUMMER STORM

The mist was clearing but I felt as if a bucket of cold water had been thrown over me. Slowly I realised it was raining. Raining! I have never been in a monsoon, but I imagine they are something like this.

Henry was grumbling as the mist cleared and he came into view. "Henry!" I exclaimed suddenly, remembering the life and death question of whether or not we would both arrive had been answered.

"Eaarhh, this is horrible," he said. He didn't seem to be at all happy to have returned. I supposed that was because he simply assumed that it would work as it had when we went forward in time.

"Yes, more rain than the back of Paperback Writer!" I told him in agreement.

I looked around through the rain to see that the ground was sodden and we were already covered in mud, having arrived sitting down. Henry jumped up and shook himself like a dog, but it didn't seem to make any difference. I closed the laptop, wiping it with my not quite so wet underarm, before bundling it into its case. Now Henry was helping me get the cases off me so I could stand up. Having done so I planted the blue windmill marker in the indentation I had left in the mud, then put the laptop under a thick-leaved bush, hoping this would give it some protection.

I turned towards the cases and said, "Come on, we'd better get going." We both picked up a case and I cuddled the aloe vera plant.

"This is ridiculous. We can't carry these bags in all this rain." Henry was right. We were slipping in the mud as we struggled to get a grip and the weight was just too much in these circumstances.

"Well, we have to," I told him.

"No, we don't, we can leave them here and come back later with a cart." Of course he was right, so we put the cases under the same bush as the laptop with the aloe vera next to it. At least I wouldn't need to water it.

Off we went and I kept thinking the rain would ease off soon, but each step seemed to be taunting me as the rain was not getting any less intense. Maybe it was even getting worse, but that might just have been my imagination as I was now drenched to the skin. I felt as if for every three steps forward I was slipping back at least one. We had five miles to go, which would normally take about two hours on a dry, sunny day, but going uphill on this mud slide would probably take three or even four hours. I remembered how the first time I travelled, and walked to Burford, a couple of horsemen had come out to meet me. I was wishing the same would happen now, but I knew it would be a long time until we were over the brow of the hill, so we could be seen from the road across the top of the hill.

We both kept on slipping and sometimes went flat on our

faces. Both of us were long since past laughing at the other for going down and being covered in mud. By now Henry was ahead of me and kept stopping for me to catch up. It was another reminder that he was fitter than me. I was beginning to think that Henry kept going ahead, and then waiting, to make a point, when he said to me, "There's no point in me hanging back for you, I can go on ahead and get help."

I reluctantly said, "Okay, you go on."

At this Henry picked up more speed and went off ahead. I felt an illogical sense of abandonment as I saw the gap between us slowly get wider and wider. It also gave me a spur to get on myself. It told me he was now back in his time and naturally 'took over' as he would normally do.

By now we had both picked up the old mud track now called Shilton Road, and as I came to the top of the hill I could see down into the valley with the small village of Shilton to my left. I looked ahead through the wall of water and could just about see that Henry had reached the top of the hill on the other side of the valley.

I hastened down the hill and was starting up the other side when through the noise of the wind and rain I thought I heard, "Sir, sir. Sir, sir!" I looked around to see a man slowly coming towards me from my left out of Shilton. I stopped and took two steps towards him, then stopped realising where, and when, I was. He came towards me saying, "Sir, sir, I do not have the disease. Sir, sir, I do not have the disease."

"Stop there!" I shouted through the rough weather. He stopped with his arms outstretched towards me and then dropped to his knees and began to plead. "Please, my family and I do not have the sickness but we are all starving. Do you have anything we could eat? Please, please, please!"

I pulled myself up from my stooped stance and replied, "No, I do not have anything to eat but I will try to send some food." With this I continued up the hill, thankful for the short break. Behind me I could hear, "Please, sir. Please sir. Please sir!" He was obviously in no fit state to listen to what I had said and I became aware of how quickly I had become insensitive to his plight. Yes, I would do what I could, but I felt little pity for him or his family. I did not like this observation about myself.

Lady Burford was sitting at her desk writing when she heard horses cantering towards the house. The arrival of horses was not unexpected, but they usually approached the house slowly so their speed seemed to portend some ill news. She rose from her desk and went into the hall to see Megan opening the door. "Megan!" came a shouted greeting through the half-open door. Before she could see who the newcomer was, Lady Burford recognised her son's voice.

"Sir Henry!" shouted Megan joyously, confirming the Lady's hopes that her son had returned.

"Henry, Henry, Henry!" She ran towards him with open arms. Megan graciously stepped aside, repressing her own joy and her desire to ask about Henry's friend.

"Mother, I am soaking wet," said Henry.

Lady Burford threw her arms around her son's body saying, "You're back. You're home. Where have you been?"

By now the hall was filled with Henry's siblings, Stephen, Ann, Marion and John, together with Peter, Cook and the rest of the household staff.

"Peter, set a fire."

"Right you are, my lady.

"No, two fires. One upstairs and one downstairs."

Henry pulled himself up the stairs and into his room, where he began to peel off his very wet clothes. Soon there was a knock at the door and in came Peter with wood and kindling, leaving the door open as his arms were full. Henry took little notice and carried on taking his clothes off until he heard Megan say, "Ooh, beg pardon, sir!" He turned to see Megan standing with her back to him in the doorway with a lighted taper in her hand.

"Never mind, Megan. The fire is more important." Peter stood up and took the taper from Megan and she disappeared, stifling once more her desire to ask about Sir Edmund. Once the fire was going Peter gave a slight bow and took his leave. By now Henry was dry and had put on some more clothes. He had no desire to go downstairs, as he was still not sure what to say about his disappearance, so he settled down in front of the increasing fire. He might be dry now but he was far from warm.

By now I knew I was more than halfway to Burford and I simply could not get any wetter, so my spirits began to lift. I thought Henry would be at the top of Burford Hill by now and rather envied him. The rain was not getting any lighter, so I kept my head down as I pushed on. Through the wind and rain I thought I heard horse's hooves so I raised my head to look, but could not see much at all. The large drops of rain were actually hurting me, so I lowered my head as the wind changed again and I could hear hooves once more. Once more I looked up. Now I could see two horses coming towards me. As they got closer, I could see that only one horse had a rider.

The thought of the Bishop's men flashed through my mind, but then I heard the single rider shout, "Sir Edmund! Sir Edmund!" My heart jumped and I shouted back, "Yes, I am." A silly thing to say, as who else would he be looking for in this weather?

I didn't recognise the rider but assumed Henry was back and he had sent out a man with a spare horse to get me. He helped me to get on the horse and off we went. It was a few days since I had last been on a horse and immediately felt my little-used muscles complaining again. Even so I was very grateful for the ride, and we were soon at the barrier at the top of Burford Hill.

As we approached the barrier I recognised Edgar and he shouted, "Good day, Sir Edmund." Good? Was he having a laugh?

"Good day, Edgar," I replied.

"Sir Henry has gone on down to Burford House. Shall I escort you there, sir?"

"Escort?" Oh well, play the game.

"Thank you, Edgar," I replied, and we went off down the hill and through the virtually empty town. Who in their right mind would be out in this weather?

At the door to the big house Edgar touched the brim of his hat as I climbed off the horse. "Thank you, Edgar," I said again and passed him my reins, thinking at least he had a hat, which was more than I had. Edgar nodded and wandered off with my horse trailing behind him.

I turned to the door, which suddenly flew open to reveal Megan with a beaming smile. "Welcome back, Sir Edmund," she said. I returned the smile as I entered the house and Lady Burford appeared,

"Good day, Edmund."

"Good day, my lady."

"Henry said you wouldn't be far away. He is upstairs getting changed and warm."

"Edmund!" Henry called from the top of the stairs.

"Henry!"

"Come on up, Edmund, there is a fire waiting for you."

I skipped up the stairs, anxious to get out of my wet clothes and filled with relief that once more, we had travelled without any problem and I was now out of the horrendous weather.

I followed Henry to the room and as we went in he waved an arm and said, "Peter has brought you some dry clothes."

"Oh, thanks." I started to peel off my clothes, which seemed to be just one thick, sodden layer of material. I started to dry myself and felt the warm glow of the fire, which had now properly got going. On with my new set of 14th century clothes, which no longer seemed strange or worth much thought, other than they were dry and warm.

Henry seemed his usual laid-back, calm self. "I have decided on our story," he said.

"Oh yes, go on."

"We simply say we hid when the Bishop's men were around and they didn't find us, nor did Knut and his men. When they had gone we sneaked off to get the two cases and then started to come back when we hoped the Bishop's men had gone. Then it started raining and here we are."

I silently looked at Henry and said, "Well, it's simple and the rain will make it look as if we have been outside for a couple of days."

"That's what I thought. It will all fit together for others."

"Okay, Henry, I agree."

We sat chatting for a while and then when we were properly warm we went down to explain to Henry's mother what had happened. Lady Burford seemed perfectly happy with our explanation (I left Henry to do most of the talking) and sympathised with our plight, having had to spend two nights in the open air – even before it had started raining. Henry had been right; the state we were in from the summer downpour well covered up the fact that we had spent the last two days in the comfort of the 21st century.

Then I remembered the two cases we had left under the bush. "We must go back to get our cases," I murmured. As the words left my lips Henry's foot came down heavily on mine. I winced and bit my tongue and Lady Burford looked at me questioningly. "Oh, er, nothing. I was just thinking of something else," I said.

After a while our interrogation was over and it was our turn to ask questions about what had been happening in our absence. Apparently the Bishop's men had been sent away with a flea in their ear, but Lady Burford was sure it was not going to be the last we heard from them. Alfred had been sent to get Lord Burford back from London and had met Scabbard returning alone. Alfred had gone on to find Lord Burford in Windsor, but Scabbard had returned late last night.

"Where is Scabbard now?" Henry asked.

"I believe he didn't get back until the sun was up, so he's probably still asleep" she informed us, "but I'm very pleased to have him back". She was silent for a couple of seconds. Then she put on a serious face and asked, "What are we going to do when the Bishop's men do return?"

I looked at Henry and he looked at me. We then both looked at Henry's mother, who sat in silence before saying, "I just hope your father returns before the Bishop's men do".

There was more silence and I remembered Matilda, the young girl in Northleach with the disease, so I asked, "any news of Matilda?"

"Who?" replied Lady Burford. Henry jumped in with,

"The little peasant girl in Northleach, mother."

"Oh yes, I'm not sure about her but I think Megan knows." As she was saying this she picked up her little bell and rang it. A few moments later there was a gentle knock at the door and Lady Burford called, "Come in, Megan." Megan demurely entered and her Lady asked, "Megan, do you know anything of the young girl in Northleach?"

"Ooh yes, my lady, I went there yesterday. Matilda is still alive... or she was yesterday, but she is in much distress being away from her mum, who only speaks to her through the food hole. She has to do this so she doesn't infect anyone else."

At this news my heart was filled with sadness as I remembered Matilda's plaintive cries as we had left her a few days ago. I was pleased to hear she had still been alive yesterday, but I wanted to get to her as soon as possible to see if we could do anything for her.

I looked at Henry, whose eyes told me he understood what I was thinking but I was not to voice my thoughts.

"Thank you, Megan. Anything else to tell us?"

"Well sir, I have been doing my duties around the town and throughout the countryside but there is no more sickness in the town."

"Oh, that is good!" I exclaimed, and Henry added, "I am pleased."

"I 'spose you knows about the nuns, sir?"

At that point Lady Burford jumped in with, "Er, I haven't yet told them, Megan."

"Ooooh, I am sorry, my lady. I didn't mean to speak out of turn."

"That is all right, Megan. You may leave now."

Megan walked towards the door. I was longing to ask about the nuns but knew I should wait until Lady Burford chose to tell us.

As Megan was opening the door, Henry said, "Ah, Megan, I meant to thank you for telling us about the Bishop's men." Megan's face changed from one of contrition for speaking out of turn to one of great joy and pride.

I added, "Yes, thank you, Megan. You probably saved our lives". Megan's smile got even broader and Lady Burford said, "That will be all, Megan." The door closed and we both looked at Lady Burford.

"Yes, I have not yet told you the bad news about Sister Cecelia. Unfortunately, she has died."

I was shocked to hear her say this, but my shock seemed illogical to me. After all, I knew she was ill with the plague, so death was hardly unexpected. Perhaps it was because I live in a world where people who get ill usually get better. Death is something I associate with very old people.

As I was taking in this news and thinking what to say I looked at Henry to see that his face showed real upset. Henry and his mother looked at each other and there was silence. I knew it would be inappropriate to break that silence.

After a few seconds Henry said, "I have known Sister Cecelia all my life."

"Yes, I know you have, Henry, and she must be a great loss to you. She used to look after you sometimes when you were a child."

Henry said nothing and then Lady Burford added, "But it is pleasing to know that Sister Florence is still alive, thanks be to God."

This was what I was waiting to hear. I had assumed Sister

Florence was still alive, as Lady Burford had only mentioned Sister Cecelia, but I was much relieved to hear her say it. I knew that Henry had known Sister Cecelia. He knew everybody in the town, but I didn't know she had looked after him sometimes when he had been a child.

There was another silence, and I nervously said, "I am very pleased that Sister Florence is still surviving." As soon as I had said this I wished I had kept my mouth shut, but Lady Burford looked at me and a slight smile crossed her face.

"Yes, Edmund, it is very pleasing that Sister Florence is still surviving." She paused for a while before saying "And it is even better that there have been no new incidents of the sickness. But it was Father MacKenzie who came to tell me of the passing of Sister Cecelia, and he did little to disguise his pleasure that your attempts to save her life had failed."

Very defensively I reminded Lady Burford, "But I did always say the important thing was to avoid further cases of the disease, and that seems to be working."

"Yes, Edmund, you are right but as you know, Father MacKenzie is already intent on pursuing you and Henry, for unspeakable crimes, and he will use anything he can to make you look bad."

"But why? Why is he after me?"

Lady Burford just looked at me, and Henry started to mumble about his father returning soon. Obviously he was trying to change the subject. It had been silly of me to ask why I had upset Father MacKenzie and the whole Church. It seemed the Church taught that it was all God's will and anyone who said otherwise must be a heretic. I was not really sure what a heretic was, but it appeared they liked to burn those who disagree with the Church.

"Yes, Henry, Scabbard told me your father will return within a couple of days and then he will know what is to be done," said Lady Burford. Henry looked reassured and Lady Burford told us she had "matters to attend to", which obviously meant we were dismissed.

Outside the room Henry said to me, "Right, we must send someone to get the cases we left behind, then we can decide what to do."

"Send someone? But we'll need to show them where we left them."

"Why? They'll hardly have difficulty in finding them," Henry told me with a confused tone in his voice.

"But how? There are miles of fields out there for them to look."

"In this weather the tracks we left could be followed by a deaf, dumb and blind man!"

Of course. Not being used to living so close to nature, it didn't occur to me that our tracks could simply be followed. Even Tommy could follow our trail. It reminded me that we were now back in the Middle Ages and I was now the one who was an anachronism.

Just then Megan appeared to see if we wanted anything; a good excuse to be with us, I thought. I reminded myself that she had probably saved our lives and how much we both owed her.

"Yes, Megan, where is Scabbard?"

"I believe he is in the stables, sir."

"Good. Come on, Edmund." I followed Henry out to the courtyard and ran to the stables through the now much lighter rainfall. As I moved off I turned to look at Megan to see her rather forlorn expression. I thought I would try to have a chat with her privately later to express my gratitude. The only problem with that was that I had no idea what had happened on the night she had put me to bed when I was drunk.

TWELVE

MEDICAL TRAINING

Henry entered the stables with me close behind him and said, "Hello Scabbard." Scabbard wheeled around and replied, "Sir, I am so pleased to see you back, and you Sir Edmund. I'd heard you had returned."

"Yes, Scabbard, good to see you too. I need you to do something for me."

"Yes, sir, what is it?"

"We left a couple of cases in the field under a bush. Would you bring them both back here and put them into Edmund's room please, Scabbard."

"Certainly, Sir Henry. I will get them as soon as I have finished this little job, if that's all right with you?"

"Yes, Scabbard." Henry turned to leave, so I followed him. I suddenly stopped and called back, "Scabbard, if you find anything else there don't bring it. Er, in fact, don't touch it."

"No, sir, I won't."

We continued into the house and Henry said, "Good thinking. I hadn't thought about that."

"No, we don't want him bringing the laptop or removing the windmill."

"No, but why is our position so important?"

"Because it will ensure we arrive back exactly where we left and not in the fireplace or halfway through a wall."

"Oh, of course."

As we were entering the house we were greeted by Cook. "Ooh sirs, your food is still waiting for you."

"Food!" replied Henry.

"Yes, sir, food. You haven't eaten properly for days."

"Oh yes, Cook. Thank you," Henry said as he looked at me. We both realised we were not playing the part of people who had been wandering around the countryside for a couple of days.

We went into the breakfast room and got stuck into the feast that had been laid on for us. It had only been a few hours since we had had breakfast in the 21st century, and while I felt I could do with some elevenses, there really was too much there, but we had to eat as much as possible to keep up appearances.

Breakfast also gave us the opportunity to talk things over. My priority was to get to little Matilda in Northleach, but Henry's priority was Sister Florence, who, like Sister Cecelia, Henry had known all his life. Also, it would be politic to go to the Abbey first, and although the rain had almost stopped, waiting a little longer would make the journey to Northleach more pleasant. Whatever we did we could do nothing until Scabbard returned with our cases with all the items from my father's pharmacy. This thought made me feel guilty once more.

I now felt a little callous towards Sister Florence, because I was more concerned with Matilda. Her plight had tugged my heartstrings and she reminded me a little of my little sister when she was younger. I also rationalised it to myself because Matilda was younger than the sister and therefore had more life ahead of her. It was obvious that even with Medieval principles of medicine, those in the Abbey were being better looked after than the child of a serf in Northleach. This made me feel Matilda had more right to be helped. Anyway, Sister Florence had God on her side. Who had Matilda? Oh yes, me, Henry and Megan, who had done her very best for her over the last few days and was, literally, putting her life at risk.

We sat chatting for quite a while and I was pleased to be able to relax in the warmth. We were chatting about all sorts of things then I realised we had not really discussed what to do when Lord Burford returned, so I asked, "What do you think your father will want to do when he gets back?"

"I don't know, but until he does - I'm in charge!"

"You, Henry? But I thought your mother would be in charge?"

"Why? In the absence of the Lord of the Manor, obviously his first born is in charge if he is of age, and I am."

Of course he would be in charge. His mother was a woman. Even so, I'm sure she would "guide" Henry, even if he didn't notice.

There was a knock at the door and Henry said, "Come in, Scabbard." Scabbard entered and reported that he had put the cases in Sir Edmund's room.

"Thank you, Scabbard," I said and Scabbard left the room.

"So, what now?" Henry asked.

"Let's go up and see what we have brought?" a

We went to my room to find the two cases on the floor. I opened the first one and told Henry what each item was for. He could understand what the face masks were for, but seemed very wary about the pills and potions. This made me wonder if they really would do any good at all.

Having been through both cases, we went downstairs and Henry summoned Scabbard and Megan. They both arrived together, and Henry said, "Thank you for collecting the cases, Scabbard." I nodded in agreement and Megan said nothing but I caught her looking at me. Then a thought crossed my mind and I blurted out, "The Aloe Vera plant."

"Er, what?" asked Henry.

"We didn't ask Scabbard to bring the plant."

"Oh no. Scabbard, did you see a plant with the cases?"

"Yes, sir, but you told me not to touch anything else."

"That is right, Scabbard, but please go back and get it."

"Certainly, sir."

Henry then went on to tell them that we were going to see Sister Florence first and that only he and I would be going, which was probably a little pointless as Megan had been in a few times before. After that we, with Megan, were going to Northleach to see Matilda. I left the talking to Henry as it was his time, his home and his servants. Or should I say his serfs?

"If you would go to get the plant while we are in the Abbey, Scabbard, then get the horses ready for us all to go to Northleach," said Henry. "We will need you as well to carry some things for us."

At this point I remembered the man who had begged for food. "Oh, Henry, I forgot to tell you, a man begged for food in Shilton," I said. I rather left the comment hanging, hoping that Henry would arrange something – which he did.

"Scabbard, can you organise some help?"

"Yes, sir, I can send Ned with some food."

I now thought we had never really had a look at Shilton when we were checking for the disease. It hadn't really occurred to me, it being such a small place, so I added, "If he could have a general check around the village while he's there, Scabbard."

"Yes, sir, I will instruct him." Henry looked at me questioningly and then said, "Right, let's go up and look at what we have got."

In my room we went through the cases so that we could brief Scabbard, and more importantly Megan, as she would be the person acting as 'District Nurse'. We told her what each item was and what it was for. Neither Megan nor Scabbard showed any particular shock, or questioned what I was showing and telling them. Was this just because they knew their place and would not ask where it all came from, or was it because they just had faith in me and what I did and said? Maybe some other reason. Maybe lots of reasons.

Then I had to introduce them to the concept of a prophylactic treatment. I was not too sure how to go about this, so I said, "Do you remember what I said about the very tiny animals that get into our bodies?"

"Oh yes, sir, I remember that", Scabbard assured me. Megan just smiled and nodded.

"Well, it only needs one to get in and then they multiply very fast. It is only then that our bodies start to make little things to fight the little animals." I avoided using any technical terms, not just because it was unnecessary and would confuse things, but because I couldn't remember the terms. Both Megan and Scabbard made agreeing noises, so I went on, "In these boxes are little pills called antibiotics that will help our bodies develop the things that fight off the little animals. If we all take them before we get any little nasties in our bodies, then the little fighters will be ready if we do get any of the little nasties into us."

I felt so patronising talking to them like children, but how else could I explain things? Anyway, they seemed perfectly happy and smiled and nodded. Henry said nothing and maintained an air of authority and knowledge – even if he didn't really know what I was talking about either – so I said, "Scabbard, would you get some water please?"

"Water, sir? Would some ale not be better if we are to drink it, sir?"

"Oh yes, you're right, Scabbard." He went off to get some as I explained a little more to Megan.

Henry listened silently, and I became aware that he was doing what I had been doing: taking a back seat when the other had more authority. Megan was clearly very eager to know about all the medicines, bandages, ointments, plasters, antiseptics and face masks, which she could see had a much finer mesh than the probably pointless things I had asked to be made up before, and most strange to her, the sterile gloves. "There are not many of these," I told her, "so try not to rip them and wash them very gently in very hot water each time they are used."

"Oh, yes sir, I will do that, for sure, I will do that", Megan said with growing enthusiasm. I thought, they won't be sterile, but they'll be better than nothing.

Then Scabbard reappeared with a tray, saying, "I have brought four bowls for us all, sir." It was only then that I noticed that the "cups" we had been drinking from in the 14th century were not so much cups as bowls. Not that that made any difference. They still worked.

I had no idea what dose of antibiotic was correct, but I seemed to remember two tablets three times a day, so that is what I told them we should take. To show it was all safe, I was the first to pop a couple into my mouth and wash them down with some ale. Once more, it felt strange drinking beer at that time of day, even if it was very weak. The other three followed my example and I told Megan it would be the same for Sister Florence and little Matilda, if she was still alive when we got there.

I then went on to talk what else I had brought, and when I talked about things for cleaning wounds Scabbard said, "Excuse me, sirs. The barber surgeon is treating a man with a badly-wounded leg that has become infected. I believe he is intending to cut off the man's leg."

"Oh no, he mustn't do that!" I said as forcefully as I could. "We might be able to save his leg." There was a moment of silence then Henry said, "Scabbard, before you go to get the plant you must go and make sure the man's leg is not amputated."

"I will do it as soon as you have finished with me, sir."

"What is the man's name?" Henry asked?

"It is Joseph the Stonemason, sir."

"Oh yes, of course. Not only will he lose his leg but we will lose a good mason. He can't go up a ladder with one leg!"

Megan sniggered and then controlled herself. I felt the need to encourage Scabbard and said, "It is very good that you should have told us this, Scabbard. Perhaps we can do something for him."

"Thank you, sir."

Having given Megan and Scabbard a short medical training session, and told Megan what items to bring with us now, it was time to get on with what we needed to do. So, off to the Abbey.

THIRTEEN

THE ABBEY

Scabbard went off to find the barber surgeon before he could chop off Joseph's leg, and I went with Henry and Megan to the Abbey.

As we approached the Abbey I toyed with the idea of telling Henry and Megan that I would be the only one to enter the sick room, but I remembered what had happened last time I suggested that. Anyway, Megan had been in and out while we were in the 21st century, so what would be the point? As before, people looked at us as we approached the Abbey and I wondered what they were thinking. Not just about us going into the sick house, but it must by now be known throughout the town that the Bishop's men were after Henry and me. Where did their loyalties lie? With their Lord and his family or with the Church, which had ultimate say over what happened to their soul? I wasn't really sure what a soul was, but I remembered my uncle once saying that he didn't believe in the soul until someone pointed out that Margaret Thatcher hadn't got one!

Outside the Abbey we stopped and Megan opened the bag containing the items I had told her to bring. Out came the sterile masks and we tied them around each other's heads. Then the sterile gloves, which they both seemed to have great difficulty in pulling on. Clearly not used to the stretchy rubber – or whatever they are made of. The door was opened by the Mother Superior with a big smile and I wondered if this was for all of us or just Henry.

"Come along in, sirs. You are most well come," she said.

"Thank you, Reverend Mother," replied Henry as we walked in. He added, "We are all greatly saddened by the loss of Sister Cecelia and our prayers are with her soul and all of you."

I mumbled in agreement and wondered if Henry actually believed all of that stuff about prayer and souls. He probably did, as I had seen in the 21st century that it was all real to him. It seemed Megan did not exist – again.

Inside we were immediately hit by the smell of vinegar as we were ushered into the sick room. Then the smell changed to one of putrid, rotting flesh. Of course, I had smelt this before a few days earlier, but then I could hide some of my disgust behind finding the dead pigeons at the bottom of the bed. There were none there this time, so I had to repress my revulsion at the smell. The nuns gave us the usual funny looks as we entered, but they had obviously followed my previous instructions and the nun was still alive. I stood by the bed and said, "Good day, Sister Florence."

Much to my surprise there was a grunt of acknowledgement from the body in front of me. This told me she was succeeding in fighting the bacteria, even without any 21st century help. I looked down and could see that the sheets had recently been changed, and the nun's bedclothes had been changed also, so I could see no reason to examine her. I would only find what I already knew.

I turned to the Mother Superior and said, "We have brought some medicine for Sister Florence." I used the first person plural to attach my words to the authority of Henry, who was, in the absence of his father, the Lord of the Manor.

"Oh, may I know what they are, sir?"

I nodded to Megan, who opened the bag and produced a bottle of antibiotics. She looked at me in silence and I said, "Go on, Megan." She swallowed and looked at the Mother Superior saying, "You should give Sister Florence two of these little things twice a day. She should swallow them with some ale."

Megan held her hand out with the bottle in it and the Mother Superior took it saying, "Yes, Megan." No word of thanks, I noticed, and I wondered if she actually disliked Megan or just didn't like a Welsh serf (Wales not being the most Christian part of the country in the 14th century) telling her what to do. That was the main reason I had wanted Megan to give the instructions: to give her authority and confidence.

The Mother Superior turned to one of the nuns at the doorway and said, "Bring some ale." At this point I had an idea and asked, "Do you have any apple juice?"

The Mother Superior looked perplexed. "No, sir, it's the wrong time of year," she said. "We have used our last apples and won't have any more for another few weeks." Of course, no 24/365 products from all over the world in the 14th century.

"Any plum juice?"

"Well, sir, we can make some of that."

"Good. Get her to drink that and any other juice you can make from fruit."

She nodded, but she made little attempt to hide her disapproval of this idea. The fruit juices would provide plenty of vitamins, which Sister Florence must be lacking, living as people did in this time. It may give her the runs as she probably had eaten little, but it couldn't be any worse than weak beer.

Now was the opportunity to put into practice the brief medical lesson I had given Megan back at Burford House. I looked at her and said, "Get out the antiseptic and swabs." She picked out the items with her gloved hands and unscrewed the lid of the disinfectant bottle. I then turned to one of the Magdalene Sisters I recognised from our previous visit and said, "Please watch what Megan is doing, as you will have to do it later."

"Ooh yes, sir, I will do that," replied the sister. I could not bring myself to address her as "Sister Magdalene" because I knew that was not her real name, just one given to her as an insult to carry for the rest of her life because she had been too flirtatious, or whatever, as a child. I wanted to ask her what her real name was, but I knew that would not help.

Megan took the cotton wool swab in one hand and gently poured some antiseptic onto it. Then she lifted the sick nun's arm on her side of the bed, and carefully began to dab the buboes on her body. Sister Florence winced, which pleased me as it showed she was sensitive, so she was not close to death. By now the smell of the antiseptic was beginning to overwhelm the smell of putrid flesh. Then Megan moved around to do the other side of her body.

While she was doing this I noticed the window was open, so I knew they had taken note of what I had said about fresh air and were not worrying about what they called the "miasma". There were no dead pigeons either as I had found on our first visit. Nor did it seem there had been any further bloodletting, so Sister Florence did not have to fight the *Yersinia pestis* and the lack of blood.

At this point Sister Florence had a bit of a coughing fit, which reminded me that *Yersinia pestis* is the bacteria that causes bubonic plague, which is the most virulent form of the disease, causing the patient to cough up blood.

Now Sister Magdalene caught my eye and said, "Excuse me sir, but Sister Florence has been coughing much less in the last couple of days."

"That is very pleasing to know," I told her.

"Ooh, and there is less blood in her phlegm, sir."

"That is even better to know." Now I took a bit of a gamble and said, "I think I told you, last time I came, that if she could survive a few days she would probably get through. Well, she has survived and is clearly less ill. So, I think with this new medicine she will recover."

There was a very restrained show of joy from the sister and the Mother Superior said, "We had all said extra prayers for our dearly beloved sister and Father MacKenzie has said special Masses for her."

I summoned up my most patronising tone of voice and replied, "I'm sure God was impressed by the prayers and special Masses and has decided to reward your devotion."

The Mother Superior gave a benign smile and I thought, but he didn't reward your prayers for Sister Cecelia, and Florence is not so "dearly beloved" that you won't make her carry that devastating epithet Magdalene.

There was no point in our staying any longer, so we began to leave. I pointedly said, "Megan will be back later to see all is well."

Outside a small crowd had gathered again and I was beginning to wonder why they still took an interest in the odd stranger and tried to express my thought to Henry. Ineloquently

I asked, "Why are people still interested in me?"

Henry was quiet for a while and then said, "I don't think it's just because of your ideas about the sickness. Everybody knows the Bishop's men are after us and that makes them want to come and look."

"You mean I'm some sort of celebrity?"

Henry said nothing as we walked towards Burford House and then said, "I'm not really sure what you mean by a "celebrity", but I think people do like the idea of seeing people who have upset Father MacKenzie and the Bishop so much."

I realised that the concept of "celebrity" did not really exist in the 14th century but viewing public hangings, burnings, or whatever, was a form of entertainment. I tried to come to terms with this and asked, "You mean, like seeing an outlaw before he is hanged?"

"Well, sort of, yes."

We walked on in silence and went round the side of the house to the courtyard to pick up some horses to go to Northleach to see how little Matilda was getting on. As we entered the courtyard Henry said, "Good day, Knut." Knut, who was bowed cleaning out a horse's hoof, raised his head and said, "Good day, Sir Henry and Sir Edmund." Once more it seemed that Megan, who was following a respectful few steps behind, did not seem to exist. "Your horses with their saddle bags are all ready for you, sirs."

"That is good, Knut," replied Henry. Just at this point there was a clatter of horses' hoofs and we all turned towards the sound to see Scabbard riding around the corner.

"Ah, Scabbard!" hailed Henry. "Have you got the plant pot?"

"Yes, I have, sir. Here it is." Scabbard reached down between his legs and picked up the plant pot from the horse's back, then dismounted one handed and passed the pot to Henry, who passed it to me.

"Look, Scabbard, here's what you do," I told him. "You give this plant to someone who knows about plants. Tell them to take cuttings. They do grow quite easily so you should have quite a few soon."

Scabbard looked quizzically at me and said, "Yes sir, I can do that, but, er, what is it for?"

"Ah yes, a very good question, Scabbard," I said, realising I had not mentioned the most important thing about the plant. "The sap is very good for healing wounds, athlete's foot and many other things."

"Oh, I see, sir. Oh yes, I know what to do with that, sir. Er, what is it called?"

"Aloe Vera. Aloe Vera," I repeated for emphasis. As they don't use the word "hello" we wouldn't get any lame jokes about "Hello Vera".

"That is good, sir, but what is, the athlete's foot?"

"Oh, it's when you get very itchy cuts between your toes."

"Ah, I get that sometimes", Henry informed me.

"Well, you'll have to wait till a few more shoots grow."

Scabbard half-opened his mouth and I assumed he wanted to say something, so I asked, "Yes, Scabbard, what is it?"

"I saw Maria. You know, the wife of John who had the voice problem."

"Voice problem?" I asked. I had no idea what he meant.

"You know, the man who couldn't speak because of..."

"Oh, John! The man with laryngitis because of his sore throat."

"That's right, sir, him. His wife, Maria, says he is much better and the family have had some visitors since I told people he had not got the disease."

"That is good, Scabbard. Thank you for that." Of course I praised him and was pleased John was getting better but I was not too sure about the visitors, as tonsillitis may not be the Black Death but it can still be infectious.

"And what about Shilton?" Henry asked.

"Oh, Ned is not back from there yet, sir."

"Well, when he does get back let us know what he found."

"Oh yes, I will certainly do that, sir."

I looked at Henry and asked, "What was the name of the stonemason with the injured leg?"

"Joseph", replied Henry.

"Oh yes, Joseph. Have you been to see him, Scabbard?" I asked.

"Yes, sir. The barber surgeon was just laying out his knives and saws when I got there, but I stopped him from sawing off Joseph's leg." Just Scabbard's words were enough to make me shiver at the thought of sawing off a leg while a man is conscious. Especially if it is not necessary.

"Oh, that is good, Scabbard", I said which seemed inadequate for the situation. Scabbard continued, "The barber surgeon was not pleased to be stopped, but Joseph seemed very happy when I told him you would be around later to make his leg better."

They all thought I could definitely make his leg better. They thought I was some sort of miracle worker, but I didn't even know what the damage was to his leg. It might need to be sawn off anyway.

As it seemed we had covered all the issues, I asked, "Are you busy at the moment, Scabbard?"

"Well, er, yes sir. I am always busy, but what do you want

me to do?"

"We are just off to see little Matilda in Northleach, but I don't think we really need you to come, do you Henry?"

"No, I don't think so. Megan will be enough to help us," Henry said. "You can get on with what you need to do here and we will see you later."

"Yes sir, I will do, sir."

With that Henry, Megan and I mounted the horses and I noticed Megan had already loaded the saddle bags with all we needed in them. I felt a little bad that she was left to carry everything, but reminded myself that that was her job. "Job" is really the wrong word, but what word does one use for the tasks of someone who is effectively a slave?

FOURTEEN

NORTHLEACH

As we trotted up the hill I realised it is far more difficult for the horses on cobble stones than it is on grass or even tarmac. What little riding I had done in the 21st century had been mainly on bridle paths. It felt different from how things felt when I had come to this century the first time, and I think part of the reason for that is that there is now a lot less horse shit around than there was. As a consequence, there are fewer flies too. Even so, there are still plenty of them.

As we came to the top of the hill Henry was in front, and as we approached, the guarded barrier was opened for us. They must be used to Megan coming and going each day and that made me think that she must have been in a very privileged position, as virtually no one else could come and go as they pleased. In her medieval mind Northleach must have been the other side of the world. Serfs were not allowed to leave their Lord's land without permission and Megan clearly had permission. And another thought – Henry had literally been to another world.

As we passed through the barriers there were many

exchanges of "Good day" and "Good day, sir". So much so that it made me think I was in a caricature of an Australian soap. No point in telling them that though. Just more blank faces, and I couldn't be bothered to play games at the moment.

It had to be afternoon by now and the hot, midsummer sun was warming us, but after all the morning rain, what used to be a mud track was now a quagmire with some puddles the horses refused to step into, as they did not know how deep they were. So we had to ride on what used to be the grass verge but now looked more like a river bank. This did slow us down quite a lot, but we were in no great hurry and I was enjoying the gentle summer canter through the Cotswolds. I have driven along the A40 a few times, and have been into a lot of the villages along the way, but this was very different. It was quite slow and I did not need to concentrate on where we were going as my horse just followed the horse in front, so I was able to look around. To my right was the Windrush valley and the varying sights as we travelled the road were very beautiful, and probably unique. The heavy and sustained rain was more than the parched land could deal with and apart from the big puddles up here on the ridge, the little river Windrush in the valley below had burst its banks. Virtually all the broad flood plain had water in it and it was difficult to tell where the river stopped and the land started.

Even though we were travelling quite slowly, I was hot and sweaty. The sun was now beating down and the mid-afternoon heat was fast drying the countryside and all the puddles had steam rising from them. In the valley the effect was even greater and in places the steam rising from the water created so much mist that the river and the flood plain could not be seen. At one point the mist was so thick it looked as though I could step off the road and onto solid cloud that filled the valley. At another point, there was virtually no mist and the sun reflected off the sheet of water so perfectly that it was like having a giant mirror shining in my face. It was so bright that it made every item, such as trees, leaves, flowers and everything else, look sparking and unreal. So much so that I wondered if the meal had had any shrooms in it.

Even though I was enjoying the ride it seemed like hours before we arrived at the turning off the main road into Northleach. There is a gentle slope down into the town which, of course, did not start so far from the centre as it does in the 21st century. I had been here only a few days earlier, but it still seemed smaller in comparison to the small town I am used to.

We arrived at the town barrier and were recognised from a distance; unlike our first visit, and the barrier was raised for us. Perhaps it was Megan they saw from a distance and they were expecting her. Once more there were nods and exchanges of "Good day" and "Good day, sir"

As we entered the old town I began to look for the Mechanical Museum and the Dolls' House I knew of in the 21st century, but of course, they were not there. Henry was still up front, followed by me and then, respectfully, Megan. I could not really remember where we had left Matilda so I was pleased to follow Henry. When we arrived I did remember things and there were a couple of men standing near the door. I did not know if they were just passing, there to help us or if they were guards to make sure Matilda did not "escape".

One of the men recognised Henry, so maybe he had been around last time we were here. He hurried to open the door to Matilda's quarantine prison. We dismounted and handed the reins to the other man. As the door opened a rancid smell hit us and immediately Henry turned to the one of the men and said,

"The windows must be left open all the time when it's not too wet or too cold."

"Yes, sir, certainly, sir", he replied with a nod and a slight genuflection.

Henry virtually ignored his reply as we donned our masks and gloves. This, of course, drew strange looks. Then another couple of men appeared, presumably to see what was going on. Then Henry simply said, "Megan," and she stepped forward and into the darkened building. As she passed Henry she whispered, "Sir, I did tell them about the windows but they said the miasma must be kept in."

Henry said nothing as we followed Megan in, and as my eyes adjusted to the darkness, I could see something on the bed was moving.

Megan stepped forward and said, "Good day, Matilda. I have brought Sir Henry and Sir Edmund with me." There was more moving and grunting from the bed. Then the "object" struggled to sit up and Megan gave her a helping hand. Matilda opened her mouth to speak but no words came out. It now became clear how Megan had taken command of the situation in Northleach, for she said in a loud voice, "Bring me fresh water from the stream as I told you." I looked towards the door and could see one man going away from the crowd.

"Don't try to talk, Matilda, until we have something for you to drink," Megan told her as I stepped forward to see Megan lifting Matilda's arm so I could see the buboes. I remembered the sight of her pus-oozing buboes from the first time we were here and was expecting the same, but what I saw was only a mild version as the boils were a lot dryer than they had been before. There was still some pus coming out, but not nearly as much. It seemed to me, from what little I knew of the disease, that the worst was over in terms of the bacteria. But she was obviously very weak, so it was not clear she would be able to recover.

"This is very good, Megan. She is fighting the disease very well. I want you to clean the boils with what I showed you before and..." There was a kerfuffle outside and a voice saying "Let me through. Let me through." I turned to see the crowd outside hurrying to part and let through the woman.

"Oh, good day, Matilda," Megan said as the woman entered. I assumed this was Matilda's mum, whom I had met before, but I didn't really recognise her. That would explain why the crowd parted so easily. They would have known that she had been in and out of the sick house and would want to avoid her.

"Oh, good day, sirs and Megan. I have been doing what you told me and have been feeding her lots of mouldy bread. I was just about to scream "**Mouldy bread!**" but I managed to stifle it. Of course. Mouldy bread. Alexander Fleming. He who discovered penicillin through eating mouldy bread. Except he didn't discover it, he only showed scientifically what the medieval people knew anyway.

"Oh, er, we, er, I think..." I stumbled for words and eventually pulled myself together enough to say, "That is good, Matilda. But, er, I have something to give her that will mean you don't need to feed her mouldy bread anymore."

"Ooh, ah, sir. That would be good as she don't like to eat mouldy bread. But I made her eat it by not giving her much else to eat." Oh my god! She was restricting proper food to make her eat mouldy bread. No wonder little Matilda was so weak.

"Well, from now on, Megan will give you some little things to give to Matilda," I said. Megan got the antiseptic out of her bag to clean the boils and then went straight back in to get out the antibiotics. She passed them to me and I held them up, saying, "Give her two of these three times a day." As I was saying this I felt just like my father when he is serving people in his chemist's shop. "And you, Matilda, take one three times a day as a prophylactic." I expect she had no idea what a prophylactic was, but she nodded and said, "Ooh yes, sir, anything you say."

At this point a voice behind us said, "There you are, Miss Megan. Straight from the upper reaches of the River Leach where the water is nice and clean." I turned to see a man placing a vessel, presumably full of water, in the doorway. Megan was busy, so I walked a couple of paces and picked up the vessel saying, "Thank you, my man". I really was getting quite into this Lord of the Manor thing. I passed the water to Megan and she began to help Matilda drink as she asked the mother, "When did Matilda last have a drink?"

"Ah, just before I gave her the last lot of mouldy bread."

"So, she hasn't had anything to drink since she ate the mouldy bread?" Megan asked in a cool voice.

"Oh no, missy, she ain't." I shivered at the thought of how a very sick little girl was supposed to get better if she couldn't even have something to drink after being made to eat mouldy bread. I was just about to voice my displeasure when Megan said in an equally cool voice, "Well, you must give her as much water as she can drink, as often as possible." At this I added, while trying to keep my voice as cool as Megan's,

"Yes, you must give her as much water as possible, Matilda." There was a pause, then the mother said tentatively, "But when I gives 'er wa'er she'm do wet 'erself."

So that was the logic! Don't give her water so she doesn't wet the bed. That's almost as good as putting a witch in a ducking stool, and if she drowns, she's innocent.

There was a shorter silence and Megan said, "Well, as I said, you must give her as much water as possible." I just bit my tongue.

I couldn't remember telling Megan that sick people should have as much water as possible, but she clearly knew and I was beginning to see she was a natural nurse. Caring for people came so naturally to her, as it did when she put her life at risk to warn Henry and me about the Bishop's men. All she needed was a bit of knowledge and encouragement. I was sure she could contribute more to medieval society than working as a housemaid, but she would probably never get the chance, being a serf. A slave.

Henry and I watched as Megan showed little Matilda's mum how to clean the wounds, and as she did so I gently said to the mother, "Now you don't need to feed Matilda mouldy bread, you must try to get her to eat as much as possible along with drinking the water. But it was very good that you did give her the mouldy bread. That may well have saved her life." I wasn't exaggerating either, nor trying to boost her ego.

"Oh, thank you, sir. Thank you. I does do me best, sir."

"Yes you do, and you have done very well. Just keep on following Megan's instructions."

"Oh, I will do that. Yes, I will do that. Sir."

Once Megan had finished showing the mother what to do she said, "I will help you help Matilda to use the piss pot before we leave."

"Oooh, thank you missy. Thank you," replied the mother and she went into a corner and came back with a pot which I couldn't help but notice was full of some sort of liquid and I asked, "What's in there?" The mother looked at me and said as a matter of fact, "Piss, sir."

"Well, why haven't you thrown it away?"

Her facial expression changed and she replied, "Because wem's going to sell that later." Of course, people used to sell their urine for all sorts of processes – like washing clothes. The thought made me quiver and I said, as calmly as possible, "You must pour it into some sort of receptacle and keep it outside the house."

"Yes, sir, I will do that", she replied, but she didn't seem too convinced. It seemed we had finished apart from the potty so I said to Henry, "Let's wait outside for Megan to finish." I felt Matilda had suffered enough indignity for a lifetime.

Outside we remounted our horses and waited while Henry gave the gathered population a lecture about windows, water and always carrying out Megan's instructions. I couldn't help but think of the pisspot in the corner all the time. That would explain some of the smell and the flies. It reminded me of something I had heard once about the origin of the term, "He's so poor he hasn't got a pot to piss in". It must mean he can't even sell his own piss because he hasn't got a pot to collect it in.

Soon Megan emerged from the house (I use the word 'house' very loosely) and we were on our way out of Northleach and back to Burford. It was early evening now and the sun was going down behind us, which was warming my back in contrast to the wind to the front as we galloped along. The hot sun had done its work and the roadway was much dryer than it had been coming the other way. Even so, there were large puddles and we spent most of our time off the road, riding along the verge as we had done coming down. Most of the mist in the Windrush valley had burnt off, but it still looked very beautiful. The journey back to Burford was quicker than it had been the other way, but it felt longer and I was now hungry and a little tired.

We arrive at the Burford barrier and were soon in the town

and at Burford House. Food, and the obligatory bath, were waiting for us and we were soon eating. It now occurred to me that we had spent the day with Megan, but now we are back she had to get on with her duties while Henry and I talk over the day. It seemed unfair somehow.

Although I was a little tired I did not want to go to bed, and the evening dragged a little just chatting with Henry. So, when the sun started to go down I was happy to accept nature's call to bed.

FIFTEEN

PENICILLIN

I wanted to continue the same conversation with Henry and then realised the voices I could hear were not part of the conversation I was having but were those of Henry and others downstairs. I had just woken to the sound of Henry's voice and assumed I was still in last night's conversation. Where was I? Oh yes, in bed in Burford House in the 14th century. What time was it? No idea, in this clockless society. Anyway, it was light outside so it must be morning. But then at this time of year it gets light half way through the night. Time to get up, though.

I was used to Scabbard bringing me a bowl of water in the morning and he had not appeared, so it couldn't be very late. But Henry was clearly up, so perhaps Scabbard had not brought the bowl of water to wake me because there was nothing particularly planned today.

As I was getting dressed the voices downstairs continued, but I could not really make out what they were saying. Soon I was opening my bedroom door and I stepped out and straight into Henry, who seemed to be heading downstairs. "Oh, hello Henry. I thought you were..."

"I'm going down to see my father. He has returned."

"Has he? But, I thought..." Then I realised the voice I had assumed was Henry's was actually his father's: Lord Henry Burford. Similar in timbre, perhaps deeper, but through closed doors from a distance, it sounded like Henry; and I hadn't been expecting to hear Lord Burford's voice as I believed he was still in Windsor with the King.

I followed Henry down with him as he shouted, "Father! Father!"

"Henry, my son! So good to see you." Henry flung himself into his father's open arms. No teenage embarrassment about hugging your father then, it seemed. But then, the 14th century didn't really have the concept of being a teenager. It seemed half the house was there, or arriving as Henry and I were, except for Henry's sister, Marion, and Megan.

"Good to see you back, Father."

"It's good to be back, son, and I am sorry to you all for waking you so early."

Lady Burford, who had been standing silently with a big smile on her face said, "Not at all, husband, we are so happy to have you back any time. Did you meet Arthur on the river?"

"Arthur? No, I came across country on horses."

"Oh, so you didn't see Arthur? I sent him to Windsor to ask you to come home as soon as possible because..." Lady Burford stopped in mid-sentence and silence fell before she mumbled, "Oh, we er..."

Lord Burford looked at his wife and said, "You had better come and tell me all about it."

"But, husband, you are just returned, you must rest."

"I will rest after you have told me what has been happening. Come along." He ushered Lady Burford, Henry and me into a room and closed the door. As soon as we were inside the room Henry asked, "But father, what about Arthur?"

"I am sure when he gets to Windsor he will be told where I am and he will return. I decided to come across country because I don't really need any of my belongings, except what I could get in my saddlebags, and I have ordered the stopping of virtually all items coming into the town, so I cannot bring something in that may be infected. I will not put my family at risk."

At this, Lady Burford's smile broadened. She put her head on one side and said, "You are such an honourable and caring husband, father and lord."

Lord Burford went on, "I was also told of the transport horse dealers on the route who would still be trading, so I was pretty sure I could get back and it would be quicker, and less trouble, than by river. So, tell me what has been going on?"

As when we returned to Burford from the 21st century, and we had to tell our adventure – well, half of it – to Lady Burford, I let Henry do most of the talking. He explained how we had returned from Windsor to be immediately warned by Megan that the Bishop's men were coming to get us and we had just made our escape in time as the Bishop's men pursued us across the fields past Shilton and nearly as far as Black Bourton on the plain. There we had jumped off our horses, slapped their backsides and hid under a bush. I realised that Henry was embellishing the story he had told his mother, so he must have given it some more thought.

Lord Burford asked, "And how did Megan know this?"

"It seems she has a friend, David, who is one of Father MacKenzie's assistants and hears most of what goes on", Henry told his father.

"Ah yes, David. I know him."

Henry went on, "And then we talked things over. About what we should do. Should we stay away until the Bishop's men are gone? Should we go back immediately and hope that Knut and his men protect us? Should we try to signal for help? Should we pray to God for his help?"

Steady on, Henry, I thought. Not too much invention.

Henry went on to say how we had wandered around for a couple of days, getting hungrier and thirstier, but too afraid to go back for the Bishop's men. But as we were thinking we could not stay out there much longer, even if it was midsummer, the heavens opened. At first it was warm and quite pleasant, but soon became cold.

"Well, that decided it for us," concluded Henry. "So here we are!"

I had avoided any eye contact with Henry whilst he was spinning this yarn, but I admired his creativity.

There was silence for a while and then Lord Burford let out a long, "Mmmmm! So, the Bishop thinks trying to save lives is a heresy, does he?"

"Yes, Father. I am sorry." I wondered why Henry was apologising.

"It is not your fault, son. I am sure God will judge you well."

"Thank you, Father."

"So now we must call the Council." He picked up a little bell and gently shook it. Immediately there was a gentle knock on the door. "Come, Megan."

"Sir," she said on entering with a little curtsy. She looked as if she had just got out of bed, which she probably had, as she hadn't been downstairs a few minutes ago. Her sleeves were hanging loose and her hair was all over the place.

"Will you call Scabbard, Megan?"

"Yes, sir", she said with another little curtsy and she turned.

"Oh, Megan, I believe you warned Sir Henry and Sir Edmund of the danger from the Bishop's men."

"Er, yes, sir," she replied rather tentatively, turning back again.

Lord Burford looked at her for a few seconds and said, "You have done very well, Megan."

Megan's anxious expression turned to one of relief and joy. There was another few seconds silence and Lord Burford went on, "I believe you got this information from your friend, David, in the church."

"Yes, sir, that is right, sir. And he is in much..."

"Yes, Megan, I understand his fears and I will do all I can to protect him, but we would be much appreciative if he could let us know anything else he hears."

"Well, sir, I really don't know. Can I please tell him you will protect him?"

Lord Burford gently reminded her, "I said I would do all I can to protect him."

"Yes, sir, well, I can tell him and ask him."

"This is good, Megan."

"Well, if it be pleasing you, sir I think he can get out at about midday if I can go to meet him, sir?"

"Yes, Megan, you may go to meet him at midday."

"Oh, thank you, sir. I will do what I can."

"Yes, I know you will, Megan. You have already proved yourself a loyal servant. Now you may go."

"Thank you, sir", and Megan left with another little curtsy. The door closed and Lord Burford looked at us. "I need to get some sleep before the council meets after the noon."

Henry and I mumbled in agreement and Lady Burford said nothing. Then there was a knock at the door and Lord Burford called, "Come Scabbard".

Scabbard walked in and bowed slightly. "Good day to you sirs and my lady." There was a round of "Good days" and Lord Burford said, "You were quick, Scabbard".

"Yes, sir, I was only in the yard sorting out your horse with the groom."

"Good. I want to call a council meeting, but it would be better if, er, Father MacKenzie were not present."

"I understand, sir."

"You know the town, Scabbard. You know how people think. So, could you go and visit whoever you trust on the council and invite them to come to Burford House after lunch?"

"Yes, sir. I think I can do that, sir."

"Thank you, Scabbard."

Scabbard left, and I was again aware of how much trust Lord Burford put in him. Not only was he useful for what he did, he was also his Lord's eyes and ears.

So we were having the council meeting 'after lunch'. I supposed that was more precise than "after the noon" but what time was lunch? This world with no clocks was difficult. Well, if Megan was to meet David at lunchtime then I supposed "after lunch" would be when she got back.

The Lord of the Manor then told us, "The meeting would usually be held in the church and, of course, Father Mackenzie would be there as he is part of the council. I am aware of the dangers this poses, so it must be avoided. The Father will probably hear what has been discussed, but that is much better than him being there and hearing first hand." He then added, in an act of humility, "I may be Lord of the Manor, but this town is ruled largely by the council of the Ramping Cat and I must get their agreement for whatever action we take."

Of course! The Ramping Cat town symbol. I had always wondered what that was about, so I tentatively asked, "May I ask, sir, why the town symbol is the Ramping Cat?"

Lord Burford paused for a while as if asking himself why I didn't know and then he told me, "I would be pleased and proud to tell you of our town's history. During the reign of William Rufus, the town was granted a charter in 1090, by Robert Fitzhamon, giving the town a market, the right to rent out our properties, sell or bequeath our leases, and a town council with an Alderman. Essentially, no residents of Burford are under the feudal system and are all free men. The Ramping Cat is a lion on its hind legs and that was the coat of arms for the Fitzhamon family, so it is the seal for the town council."

"Oh, thank you, sir, that is very interesting to know." And it *was* very interesting to know. So now I realised that Burford really was a very advanced town socially. In 1090 the people of the town already had rights and freedoms that the rest of the country would not have until the 16th century. So it was not a matter of 'serfs you are and serfs you shall remain'. Eat your heart out Dickie the Eleventh! He wouldn't say that for another 33 years, but he was already wrong as far as the people of Burford were concerned.

Sir Henry looked pleased and genuinely proud to tell me of his town's history and asked, "Are you interested in the history of our family?"

"Oh yes, sir." Well, what else could I say? I really was interested.

Lord Burford went on, "I, and of course young Henry here, are direct descendants of Sir Robert Fitzhamon." I wasn't quite sure what to say to that, so I said, "Are you? That is interesting, and impressive." Lord Burford smiled, and I could see that Henry and his mother were grinning from ear to ear.

So, the kind way Lord Burford runs the town isn't just because he's a nice bloke, but because there is a town council and all the residents are part of the town and have some rights. Even so, it was obvious at the last council meeting, when I was there last time, that Lord Burford had the loudest voice and the most influence. Now he closed the meeting by saying, "I'm off to my bed. I will see you after the noon." At this he left the room, and we all filed out behind him.

Henry said, "I'm just going to finish my lavatory, so I'll see you later." He turned left and I went to go up to my room. Just then Megan appeared in front of me, looking a bit better presented than before, and I thought now was a good time.

"Oh, Megan, would you come up to my room a moment?" I asked her. "I have something to show you." As these words came out I thought how this must sound, but Megan simply replied, "Certainly, sir." We entered my room and I opened one of the cases I had brought with me full of medical supplies and one other item that could be called an unnecessary waste of space.

"I have brought something for you, Megan," I said. I pulled out the massive bottle of shampoo I had pick up in my father's pharmacy, and a little shiver of guilt went up my spine again. As I handed her the bottle I realised it was made of plastic and shouldn't be there. But then I had brought so many things that shouldn't be there – what was one more?

Megan just looked at the bottle and then at me. "It's shampoo, Megan," I said. This didn't seem to make her any the wiser, so I said, "Shampoo is a French word. It's for washing your hair."

She was silent for a while and then told me, "But I don't speak no French, sir."

"That doesn't matter, Megan. Wet your hair first and then put a small amount on your hair and rinse it. Then repeat the process with a bit less shampoo." She just looked at me and then at the bottle, so I added, "It will make your hair look even more beautiful, but don't waste it and don't share it with anyone else, as I can't get any more."

"Ooh no, sir. I will do as you say. Thank you very much, sir."

We both sat in silence for a few seconds, and then I realised she was waiting to be dismissed. "Thank you, Megan. You may go now," I said. She left the room, clutching her giant bottle of shampoo, and I flopped onto the bed to have a little rest after my very early start.

SIXTEEN

THE COUNCIL

Sometime later I found myself awake, but I was not too sure if I had been sleeping or just dozing, so I went downstairs to find food and Henry waiting for me. I wasn't sure what time it was as the sky was overcast, so no sun. I felt a little uncomfortable not knowing whether it was early morn, mid-morning or lunchtime, but it didn't seem to worry anyone else, so I assumed it was my 21st century obsession with time.

"We can go and see Rupie before the Council meeting after the noon," Henry said as I snacked on food I assume had been left for me for breakfast.

"Rupie? Who is Rupie?" I asked.

"Rupie, the man whose leg the barber surgeon wants to cut off."

"Oh him, yes, we must go and sort that out before gangrene sets in." As I listened to myself saying this, I became aware of how confident I must sound that we could sort it out. Confident or arrogant? I'm not too sure. Me, a 17-year-old school kid offering medical advice to a whole town. Then I thought of my meeting with the king last time I was here and corrected myself;

medical advice to a whole country.

I then said, "Rupie, that's an unusual name."

"Is it? Why? It's quite a common name. I was at school with a couple of Rupies."

"Oh well, I just hadn't come across it before and I thought his name was Joseph." I did not want to appear argumentative.

"It's the colloquial form of Rupert. It's his middle name and he prefers it to Joseph."

"Oh yes, Rupert! I know that name all right. I have just never heard it called Rupie." There was a Rupert on one of the market stalls that visited Carterton each Thursday. I hoped it was not the same one.

"How about Megan coming with us? I asked.

"Yes, I expect so, but she needs to be free to meet her friend David at lunchtime."

"Of course," I replied and thought, it must be about a couple of hours before noon. Between 10 and 11 am. Illogically, it made me feel more secure simply knowing what time it was.

Henry picked up the little bell and shook it, and I began to stuff my face faster so we could get on with things.

The door was gently knocked and Henry called out, "Ah, Megan, come in." She entered and stood in front of Henry, facing me across the table. "Megan, we are going to Rupie's house today, can you come with us, providing we are finished in time for you to meet David?"

"Ooh, yes, I thinks so, sir, but I shall have to tell Cook."

"Yes, Megan, meet us by the door in a few minutes." With this, Megan, left the room with another little curtsy.

This reminded me that Megan and Henry were about the same age as I was. All three of us were contemporaries, yet we lived in completely different worlds. Me in the 21st century; not rich but very privileged in comparison to how people lived in the 14th century. Henry lived a privileged life in the 14th century but quite poverty-stricken in comparison to the way I lived. I don't know of anyone in the 21st century who lacks running water, has to walk or ride everywhere, has to live with the constant, and realistic, fear of dying of some terrible disease, and, ultimately, has a much shorter life expectancy, even if he is rich and privileged. Though, that does help. Edward III would rule for about 50 years.

Megan lived at the same time as Henry but in a completely different world. She was poor, effectively a slave at Henry's command. Her time was not her own and, worst of all, she had no chance of ever bettering herself. She would probably die in the same world she was born into, in terms of her wealth, social position and expectations. On the other hand, she was alive and would probably not be had she not been brought from Wales after some battle, as a prisoner slave. After all, both her parents were killed so what chance would she have had? Anyway, she seemed pretty happy there and maybe that was because she didn't know anything else. She had no idea what her life could be like had she been born into the 21st century. Unlike Henry.

A few minutes later the three of us were leaving Burford House. We walked to somewhere near the church that I did not recognise, so I supposed it was long since gone by the 21st century. We arrived at the house and Henry knocked on the door. From the outside it looked like a substantial building, not like the hovel Edward and his epileptic son lived in. Or where John and Maria lived. I wondered how he was getting on. I would have to ask Scabbard.

The door was opened by a woman and Henry said, "Good day to you, Catherine."

"Oh, hello, Sir Henry, oh, er, and Sir...."

"Edmund", I informed her, as she clearly either didn't know my name, and why should she, or she had forgotten.

"Ooh yes, come along in sirs, and Megan." I was pleased that Megan had been acknowledged. Inside there was a small hallway with a couple of doors leading off it. Catherine opened the first door and we walked in to see a man sitting in a chair with his foot on a stool. This I assumed was Rupie. He smiled broadly as we entered. He had clearly been expecting a visit and had heard our conversation at the door.

"You are most well come, sirs," he said.

Catherine then echoed her husband's sentiments. "Yes, we have been waiting for you since Scabbard came to see us when the barber surgeon was here."

"He wanted to cut off my leg, you know, sir."

At this I thought it was time for me to take command. "Yes, Rupie, I know that. That's why we're here, but I cannot promise anything." I now approached the leg resting on the stool. It was bare except for some rough bandaging around it, which I started to unwrap. As I did so there was a strong fetid smell of something unpleasant and I looked down to see a horrible mess of flesh, bits of which seemed to be detached from the leg. I reached into the bag that Megan was carrying and got out a spatula stick to poke about at the flesh. As I was doing so I realised we should have put on our masks before entering. This might not be the Black Death, but it was still an infectious wound, and they would have covered up some of this smell.

Yes, there were bits of loose flesh in and around the wound. It seemed his flesh was falling to bits. The more I poked about, the less it seemed to be part of his leg, yet Rupie showed no sign of pain as I poked it. I asked, "What's all this?"

Henry leaned forward and said, "That must be meat the barber surgeon has put on the wound."

"Meat! What on earth for?"

"Well, to help heal the wound." I was almost as astounded by this as I had been by the dead pigeons at the bottom of the nun's bed. I took a deep breath to calm down and asked, "Why would rotting meat help heal a wound?"

"Well, because the flesh will help the flesh. It is the same material."

I could see there was some sort of logic to this. Rather like the principle of homoeopathy where you give something similar to the problem to fight the problem. It is equal nonsense and a lot more dangerous. Homoeopathy may not do any good, but it doesn't make the situation worse. What surprised me most was that Henry seemed to give credence to the idea.

I heard a loud knock at the door, and Catherine jumped up to answer it. It was the barber surgeon. He entered and loudly proclaimed, "That wound's never going to heal. The leg will have to come off."

Once more I took a deep breath. "No, meat will not help a wound heal. It will make the situation much worse as it rots."

The barber surgeon looked affronted at this. Henry's face was passive.

"Well, I always puts meat on a wound. It is known to help heal wounds."

"No, it is not known to heal wounds. You may think it does, but it doesn't." I then had a change of tack as there was no point in telling him he didn't know what he was doing. This man just needed a bit of medical training. So I added, "Megan and I will show you what to do with a wound". I looked at Megan, who, without being told, opened the bag and brought out antiseptic and cotton wool balls. I told her to remove the bits of dead animal and clean the wound. This she did as I watched and, more to the point, the barber surgeon watched, though, he was hopping from foot to foot, clearly uncomfortable. Now we could see how damaged the leg actually was. The wound was deep but it seemed not that bad as it gently oozed. But had the dead animal bits caused an infection? Only time would tell.

I then addressed the barber surgeon directly, "Do you know how to sew up a wound?"

There was a pause, then, "Sew up a wound, sir?"

"Yes. Get a strong, but small and very sharp, needle and some fine thread. Then put it all into boiling water for a couple of minutes and wash your hands rigorously."

The barber surgeon pulled himself up to his full height and said, "I always washes my hands before I start work!"

I replied, "Good", and then I had a thought. "Megan, you can sew, can't you?"

"Yes sir, of course, I can sew."

"Well, can you do this and show, er, the barber surgeon (I realised I didn't know his name) what to do?"

"Yes sir, I can do that."

"Good. The antiseptic will be an anaesthetic as well, so Rupie will hardly feel it." Megan looked at me quizzically, so I added, "Anaesthetic. It means he will not feel much as you are sewing his leg."

"Ah, like wine." I didn't know if Megan meant putting wine on the wound or drinking wine, so he felt less pain. Only spirit would really work for cleaning a wound, but I didn't know if they had spirit stills in this period. It was too complicated to get into anyway.

Megan then turned to Catherine and said, "I can get back

here later today if you could have some boiling water ready."

"Yes, Megan, I can do that", she said. I realised the two knew each other. Well, I suppose they would.

I then turned back to Rupie and told him, "Megan will give you some little things to take that will help kill any infection there is."

Rupie looked a little confused and said, "Take, sir? Take where?" I was now a little confused as to what he meant, then it clicked.

"I mean put in your mouth and swallow."

"Oh yes, sir, I understand what you mean."

I then had another idea and turned back to the barber surgeon. "Sir, you know lots of people get the pox?"

"Yes, sir."

"And you know cows get the pox?"

"Yes, sir."

"And you know milkmaids don't get the pox?"

"Err, yes, sir."

He didn't seem too sure, but I pressed on. "Well, I'd like you to help lots of people not to get the pox."

"Oh, yes, sir. I can do that."

He didn't even know what I was going to say, so I went on, "If you find a cow with the pox, bring someone close to the cow, and get a little bit of the pus on a sharp knife, and put it on a very small cut in the person."

"Ah! You want me to do that, sir?"

"Yes, sir, I do. You are a skilled surgeon and I need someone I can trust to do this properly."

Once more he pulled himself up to his full height and said, "Oh, yes, sir. I am sure I can do this for you."

To my surprise Henry then offered his help by saying, "I can get Scabbard to find a cow that is suitable." This meant that my suggestion had now been sanctioned by the son of the Lord of the Manor, so it had a lot more authority. I was pretty sure Henry was as sceptical as the barber surgeon, but he probably accepted I knew what I was doing and was being supportive.

I felt we had done all we could do there and began to pack the things to leave, saying to Rupie, "Well, that's about it. I cannot be sure it will heal and only time will tell."

"Oh, thank you, sir. Thank you, thank you." With this Catherine joined in with, "Yes, thank you, sir. Thank you so much. Oh and you too, Sir Henry, oh and you too Megan."

I wasn't sure we could save the man's leg and felt a bit of a charlatan, a quack, taking all this praise. What did please me was the thought that if the cow pox thing worked it would save a lot more lives long term than anything I could do about the Black Death.

We left with their thanks ringing in our ears, and I was thinking that now I had seen how the not-so-poor people lived in the Middle Ages. Rupie's house was substantial, with good furniture in it, so he was quite well off. This must have been how the skilled workers lived. Artisans, I think they called them. I suppose he would be a free man, not a serf, even outside the socially-enlightened world of Burford.

On our way back Megan left us to go to meet her friend David. Back at Burford House, we had something to eat and chatted about nothing in particular. I raised the subject of Megan's status by asking Henry, "If the people of Burford have rights, how come Megan is a serf?"

There was a long pause, and I got the feeling Henry was uncomfortable, but he eventually replied, "Megan was brought back here as a prisoner from Wales. Both her parents are dead, so my father took her in. She is free to go, but where would she go to? She has nothing."

This brought home to me that it was not just a law that kept people in one place, it was also the lack of any alternative.

"I see that, but does she have rights and privileges like the other people of Burford?"

Henry thought again. "Not really. All she has is owned by my father and she cannot sell anything, even herself, so in that sense she is not free. Not like the stonemason or the barber surgeon. She was captured by those in my father's service, so she belongs to him. Why do you ask?"

"Oh, I just wondered, nothing really."

The door opened and Lord Burford appeared, telling us the council meeting was about to begin, so we followed him out. As we were emerging from the room a soft voice whispered, "Your lordship! Your lordship!" It was Megan.

"Yes, Megan, what is it?"

"May I speak to you, sir?"

"What is it? he repeated.

"I... er... I" He realised the problem and said, "Yes, come in here where we can talk privately." They both disappeared into the room we had just left.

Henry and I stood around waiting and I was tempted to listen at the door, but did not. After all, I thought I knew what was being talked about, and I would be told later.

After a while the door opened and Megan came out, followed by Lord Burford. She gave me a little smile and went towards the kitchen. Henry's father just said, "Come along" and we followed him to another room where Scabbard and five other men were waiting. I did not know if Scabbard was a member of the council or if he was there because he was Lord

Burford's right-hand man.

We went in and his lordship looked at me and asked, "You know Alderman Smith and the other council members?"

I vaguely remembered them from the meeting in the church a few days ago but I didn't know any of their names. I just replied, "Yes, sir." Knowing Alderman Smith's name was enough. It occurred to me that it was a great achievement for a smith, a person who works with metal, to become an Alderman. Not only a great achievement for the Alderman but for the town of Burford, which had a culture in which such a man could rise to the top. But then, I suppose a blacksmith is a lot further up the social scale than a serf, who works in a field that he doesn't own.

Lord Burford then began by telling the meeting about the Bishop's men coming for Henry and me. I was sure they already knew, the whole town must know, so he was just summarising the situation. There was nothing he said that was news to me. He went on, "The Bishop and Father MacKenzie will not let matters lie there. I happen to know the Bishop now knows that Sir Henry and Sir Edmund have returned, and he is determined to see the two young gentlemen arrested and, er, examined."

I realised that this must have been what Megan had learnt from her friend David and had wanted to tell Lord Burford in private. And I knew from my study of Chaucer's time that the term "examined" meant to be tortured until the victim said what the examiners wanted to hear.

Lord Burford went on, "They will be coming back to the town at some point soon". There were mumblings of agreement and worry expressed around the table as their Lord paused before asking, "So, what are we going to do?"

The council members looked at each other and at Lord

Burford before the Alderman spoke. "Sir, the town is already closed to outsiders and all the entrances are blocked and guarded so, how will any of the Bishop's men get in? It's not like last time when the guards on the gate did not know what they had come for."

"Yes, Alderman, you are right, but the Bishop will know that and he'll send a large force."

There was more mumbling around the table and Alderman Smith said, "The people of Burford are very loyal to you, sir, and will do all they can to defend our lord, the town and all the privileges we hold dear." I assumed this last reference to 'privileges' was to Burford's non-feudal status. "I am sure every able-bodied man in the town will want to serve you, sir."

There was a period of silence as Lord Burford's eyes went from man to man around the table, including Henry and me. He then said, "Scabbard, I think you know what is necessary and will make sure all is put in hand." Scabbard had been silent until now, presumably because he was simply there to know what was going on and what was required and to ensure it happened.

The meeting appeared to be coming to an end, and what was to be done had been decided, and then Lord Burford looked at me and said, "And I am sure that Sir Edmund will have something to contribute to the town's defences."

At this, all eyes fell on me, including Henry's. Then silence, and I swallowed hard, stumbling. "Er, I, ah, don't know anything about military matters, sir." There was another silence and Lord Burford allowed himself a faint smile, saying, "Your knowledge has saved lives and I know His Majesty is impressed with your capabilities, so I am sure you can think of something to contribute." He then turned to the council and told them, "Gentlemen, you all know your roles. I think this meeting is closed."

The council members stood and bowed to Lord Burford. I just sat there frozen in my seat as Lord Burford's words echoed in my head: 'I am sure you can do something to contribute!' What on earth could I do? I might know things they didn't, but I couldn't do anything to stop the Bishop's men. I was not a miracle worker! Yet it was becoming very clear that a miracle worker was what they thought I was. How was I to tell them I could do nothing to contribute? This made me feel useless and very guilty and for the first time I wished I had not come here in the first place.

The room was almost empty, but I continued to sit motionless. Then I felt a nudge on my shoulder and Henry said, "Come on".

I pulled myself up and followed him out of the door to find his father waiting for me. I shook myself and put on a silly smile as Lord Burford said, "Edmund, would you come in here please?"

We went into another, smaller room, perhaps his "office", and the lord motioned us to sit. He looked at me silently for a second, though it felt like a lifetime, and said, "Now, Edmund, tell me about these little things you have told Megan to give to the sick?"

I held my breath and wondered what he was referring to. "It. was... I'm not really sure what you mean, sir."

He leaned forward on both forearms, screwed up his eyes and pursed his lips slightly. "The little round things Megan has been giving to those who are sick in any way." I then realised he was asking about the antibiotics. But what did the question mean? Was he asking because I had done something wrong? In which case I had better answer defensively. Or was he asking simply out of interest?

I looked him in the eye and tried to work out what he was thinking. After a second I decided to risk it. "Do you remember I told you about the very small animals that get into people and make us sick?"

"Yes, I do and I have given it much thought." I held my breath once more. "We do know that the cold of winter kills many animals, and humans, so, if you say it is little animals that make us ill, the cold of winter would kill off many of them. That would be why what you called "epidemics" become much less in winter time. This much I understand, but, what I don't know, is, how can we encourage the little animals to die off?"

I slowly let out my breath in relief, thinking I had made the right decision; he was asking about how to kill the "little animals". I summoned up all my Biology GCSE knowledge, plus what I had researched on the net before we returned to the 14th century, and began. "The little animals eat us from the inside, so we need to find a little animal that will eat the little animals without eating us." I paused for him to absorb that, or to ask me something, and he slowly moved his head down looked at me. I imagined what he would look like looking over the top of a pair of glasses, a wise old owl. Perhaps the glass maker I had tried to tell about making magnifying glass could do something for him. He seemed quite old, and my dad had told me that most people over the age of about 45 cannot focus close enough to read a book. So he could be no more than that.

So, I went on, "Let's call these little animals "micro-organisms". I paused to ensure understanding and acceptance, and went on, "Well, when one micro-organism comes up against another they fight for territory they can grow on. When this happens it is known as "antibiosis". Like the antonym of "symbiosis". So those little round things are called "antibiotics".

They contain little animals that eat the nasty little animals, but don't eat us."

I threw these words around with no idea if they were of Greek or Latin origin but hoped he would understand them. To be honest, I was playing a little game too, just seeing if he would understand what I was talking about. Judging by his body language, he did. Even if the words were not used in the literal Greek sense, which he would have understood, he still seemed to get the sense.

"And where did you get these little round things?"

"From a passing apothecary, sir."

"Ah, I see."

"He told me how to make them, but I have never made any."

"Oh, I see. Can you remember how to make them?"

"I think so, sir. But I can't be sure, so it might not work. We need lots of mouldy bread."

"Mouldy bread? Aha! Well, I shall speak to Cook and you can tell her what to do."

I had given this a lot of thought since I had heard Henry embellish our terrible time in the wilderness. I had practised in my head what I was going to say, so when it came to the obvious question being asked I was ready with an answer. I had wondered if the idea of a wandering apothecary, who just happened to have this wonder potion, would just be too implausible, but apparently not. He seemed perfectly happy with the explanation. "Certainly, sir. It will be an honour." With this, Henry and I were dismissed.

The next day Captain Scarlett marched through the cloisters to the Bishop's office with the setting sun streaming between the pillars. Over the last few days he had felt a distinct sense of humiliation over his failure to capture those two young men. Now he was determined to reverse this humiliation. His heart was beating a little fast as he knocked on the Bishop's office door.

"Come!"

Captain Scarlett pushed on the door and it opened fully to reveal to the Bishop his large silhouette in the door frame. "Ah, Scarlett. Come along in. Sit down."

"Your Grace," Captain Scarlett replied with a little bow and sat opposite the Bishop.

"So, I assume you have guessed why I wish to speak to you today?" the Bishop asked.

"I presume the heretics have returned to Burford, your Grace."

"God has seen fit to allow a message to reach us from Father MacKenzie." The Bishop now leaned forward to ask, "Are your men all ready?"

"Yes, your Grace. We have been preparing since we returned and we are ready with equipment and victuals."

"Good. You are ready to march then."

"Yes, your Grace, but we need to arrive after nightfall and if we leave now we will probably arrive at Burford tomorrow morning."

"Yes. Then you have time to make final arrangements and for your men to have a good night's sleep before you march tomorrow."

"That would be good, your Grace, and we can have the element of surprise."

The Bishop sat up straight and took a deep breath. "We do not know quite what you will find in Burford. It seems the Devil has infiltrated the minds and hearts of many in that town and some may be...er... misguided enough to try to protect the heretics. Lord Burford is a powerful man and the council of Burford is very defensive of the town's rights."

"Yes, your Grace, but I can assure you they will not escape this time, even if sorcery is involved as it was before."

"Good. Then go about your duties, Captain Scarlett, and do not restrain your efforts. Remember, you are doing God's work and those who would stand in your way cannot be godly people."

"Yes, your Grace." Captain Scarlett marched out with great enthusiasm for his task ahead. After all, what is a soldier for if not for fighting?

SEVENTEEN

DAY OF REST?

Early the next morning, Lord Burford summoned Scabbard.

"Good day, Scabbard. First of all, tell me about what was found in Shilton."

"Good day sir. Ah, that was not good news, sir. The village was much blighted by the pestilence and seven houses were boarded with the families inside. It seems all are now dead."

Lord Burford sucked in a large gulp of air. "This is grave news indeed."

"Yes, my lord, and those who are still alive are starving. I have arranged for supplies to be sent to the survivors."

"This is good, Scabbard. Let's hope God spares those who are still alive."

"Yes, sir."

"On to the main reason I have called you, Scabbard."

"Yes sir."

"I need a very urgent message to be delivered to the King. Who do you think we could send?"

Scabbard paused for a moment. "Well sir, Alfred is a strong rider."

"Then give him this letter to take to Windsor. We are facing the unknown and need all the support we can get. If we can get the king's help we... well, we may yet survive."

By the slight faltering in his voice, Lord Burford was clearly afraid, for his son, his family and all those in the town who were supportive of this "heretical" medical intervention.

"Thank you, Scabbard. The sooner he can go the sooner we will know whether the king will support us against the Bishop and the Church – or not."

"Yes, my lord."

"Now please tell Henry the situation in Shilton, and explain Alfred's task."

Henry and I were at the back of Burford House chatting and soaking up the sun. This was our first opportunity to do nothing since our return and, although that time had not been particularly physically demanding, I was pleased to sit and think of nothing except enjoying the sun. Then Scabbard approached us.

"Gentlemen, I have instructions from Lord Burford."

"Yes, Scabbard, what is it?" Henry asked in a rather weary voice, not welcoming the interruption to our leisure.

"Sir, I have been asked by his lordship to inform you of some matters." He went on to tell us about the deaths and starvation in Shilton and the fact that Alfred was to be sent to Windsor with a letter for the king. The knowledge of what had happened in Shilton was saddening, and I was filled with a great feeling of guilt that we had not been there before to try to do something to save lives.

Henry sensed my thoughts and said, "You know, we can't be everywhere all the time. And we cannot save everyone. We have done much to help people, preventing the spread of the disease, and your ideas seem to be effective as there are no new infections within the town. You cannot do the impossible."

I knew Henry was right, but I still felt very guilty and began to wonder if the Burford of the 14th century would have been better off had I never come. Henry seemed to understand what I was thinking and listed some benefits that we had brought to the town. I wanted to believe him, and knew in my own mind that if the barber surgeon did things properly, then more people would be saved from mutilation and death from smallpox than were now being saved from the Black Death.

Then Henry changed the subject. "Have you given any thought to what my father asked?"

Suddenly my leisurely sunny afternoon was brought down to earth with a bang. I had given little thought to Lord Burford's request and had not taken it particularly seriously. After all, what did he expect me to do? Pass arrows to an archer? I was a soft 17-year-old from a comfortable 21st century home. What did I know about warfare? When Henry had disarmed that knife-wielding man he had demonstrated medieval fighting skills. I could never come anywhere near what was needed. I would be more a hindrance than a help.

I looked at Henry, then looked away. Then I looked back again, almost hoping he would not be there. But he was.

"Er, I have been thinking about this. And, um, I'll tell you soon." I could see by Henry's face he was disappointed that I had not immediately come up with a plan to save the world. Even so he did not push the point and we got on with our day. But of course, for me the bubble had been burst. We continued our somewhat stilted conversation, but my mind was racing. What could I do? I felt inadequate, a failure and a fraud.

Later on, in the early afternoon, we were outside having something to eat when I heard footsteps behind us. We turned to see Megan approaching us.

"Oh, begging your pardon, sirs. I didn't know you were still eating."

Henry replied through a mouthful of food, "It's all right, Megan, what do you want?"

"Well, sirs, I have just been to Northleach to see Matilda." My ears pricked up, and I looked at Megan. She put her hand around her neck and tossed her hair.

"Go on, Megan."

"She has not been taken, sir. Her fever is less and she is eating better. Especially now her mother does not make her eat the mouldy bread because I give her those little things." She put both hands behind her neck and tossed her hair again. What was she doing?

"She seems a little stronger and needed a lot less help when I got her onto the potty." With this she shook her head vigorously and brushed her hair from her eyes.

"Megan, this is wonderful news," I said. "I am so pleased."

She smiled broadly and flicked her hair once more. Then I clicked. She was playing with her hair because it had been washed in the new shampoo I had given her. And indeed, it did look lovely. I let out a little laugh when I realised what was going on, then quickly composed myself, saying, "If little Matilda is getting stronger, then perhaps she is past the worst."

"Yes sir, I think she may be." I looked at Henry, who was also looking well pleased. He asked, "What about Sister Florence?"

"Oh yes, she seems to be getting better too," Megan answered. Her perfunctory tone gave away her thoughts of priority. Clearly Megan thought the life of a little girl was more important than that of a middle-aged nun. I had to admit to myself that I agreed with the sentiment.

"Anything else to tell us, Megan?" Henry asked.

"Ah, the townsfolk of Northleach have done all I asked of them. Food, clean water, clothes washing."

"That's good. And have you yet told the people of Northleach that Matilda is getting better?"

"No sir, I thought I'd talk to you first, sirs." Megan looked at me.

"How about we wait to see tomorrow if she is the same, better, or she has relapsed?" I said. There was silence and she looked at me quizzically. I went on, "I mean, is she the same as she was, is she still getter better or has she gone back to being more ill?"

"Oh, I see, sir. Oh, well yes. I will tell you tomorrow how she is, sir."

At this point another thought occurred to me. "If we are not around tomorrow, and you are sure little Matilda is recovering well, then you may tell the townsfolk that she is getting better."

"Oh, yes sir, I will do that."

"But she and her family are still to be kept in quarantine until I say so." She looked at me. "Quarantine, Megan, away from everybody else."

"Oh, yes sir, I will do that." It then occurred to me that I was giving instructions above my station and I turned to Henry. "Is that all right with you, Henry?"

"Yes, that sounds fine to me. Is there anything else you have to tell us, Megan?"

"Not really, sir. Everyone else in the town seems to be

healthy still, but everybody is still very frightened. They don't come near me when I am there," she said with a smile. "Oh, and of course, when I got back I had another bath and," she flicked her hair again, "I washed my hair in the new..."

I cut in quickly with, "Yes, I can see that, Megan. Very lovely."

Henry seemed to have no idea what was going on with Megan and her hair, and I felt it was easier if it stayed that way.

Henry looked at me and said, "Well, Megan, I think that is all for now. You have done very well, and I'm sure you will continue to do so. You may go now." Megan gave a little curtsy and turned to leave with a backward glance at me. I felt this was a little dismissive of Henry, but then, that's the way things were in the 14th century.

When Megan had left, Henry was quiet, and I was not minded to break the peace. The sun was beating down and there was a light breeze. A perfect English summer's day. I wondered about some sun block but, of course, I had none. Anyway, the people here didn't seem to worry about skin cancer, so why should I? But then, the average life expectancy there was only about 35. Not a lot of time for skin cancer to develop.

Suddenly Henry asked, "Do you have something planned for tomorrow?" I had given a great deal of thought to the request from Lord Burford about what I could do to help, but the suddenness of Henry's question put me on the spot..

"Yes, Henry, I have. You have been to the place where I live and you know I cannot bring back any armies or weapons. You also know I have had no military training."

"Yes," replied Henry. His tone indicated that he was confused by this and did not really approve. So I went on to explain what I was thinking. This brought a few questions from

Henry, but no real discussion. He just seemed to think my new ideas had the same value as my statement that little animals inside us make us sick. He thinks I know what I'm talking about, so he just goes along with what I say.

Later that evening we were in the yard preparing to mount our horses. Henry had spoken to Scabbard and all was prepared for us to leave. I quietly asked Henry, "What about the horses coming back? Won't it raise any questions?"

"No, I have just told Scabbard we will meeting some people with new horses, so we will send ours back. Don't worry about it." With this we mounted our horses and slipped out of the back of Burford house towards Swinbrook.

It was now virtually dark and we were soon sitting on the ground holding the laptop between us, having dismounted and slapped the horses' backsides to send them home. Once more, I was extremely nervous about what would happen, though Henry was as cool as a cucumber. He seemed to be less stressed than when we were zipping along at 60 miles an hour through the Cotswold countryside. I pressed the keys and eventually reached the final "t". The mist swirled and I closed my eyes. There was a bump and I opened them again to see Henry getting to his feet in my sitting room. We had arrived back safely – again.

This was very different from when I had arrived there with Henry a few days ago. No shocked look on Henry's face and no need to explain things. He was far more blasé than I was and it all seemed perfectly normal to him. I really was not in the mood for clubs, pubs or parties, so I said, "I'm off to bed."

"Me too," he agreed.

EIGHTEEN

MALTING

The next morning I woke before the alarm went off, Probably because I had got used to keeping time in a society that didn't have any artificial lighting, except for candles, so they start the day as soon as it gets light. At this time of year that was pretty early.

Immediately I was out of bed, eager to get on with the day. I banged on Henry's door and shouted, "Don't forget to wear some of my clothes". There was no reply, so, hoping he had heard, I jumped into the shower.

Downstairs I was eating breakfast in the kitchen when Henry came in and went straight to the cereals cupboard. He had obviously decided what he wanted to eat, which did make my life easier. We both ate and prepared to leave as quickly as possible, and soon I was approaching my father's car. I wanted to take it because it was smoother and had more go-faster goodies.

We went down the drive and stopped at the end for a cyclist.

"What's that?" Henry asked, watching as the cyclist rode past.

"It's a bicycle."

There was a pause and then Henry said, "Oh yes. Two circles. Two wheels." He watched it as we drove past and asked, "How does it work?"

This was something I had never thought about before, but it didn't take much to work out. "The things under his feet, the pedals, are attached by a chain to the back wheel and that turns the wheel."

"Mmm, very clever, but is it any easier than walking?"

"Oh yes, I think so, by a ratio of about seven to one I think." Henry glanced at me, puzzled, so I added, "It takes about seven times less energy to get the same distance, and it's a lot quicker."

"Yes, I can see they are quick, but not as fast as one of these."

I just grunted.

It was still quite early and there was little traffic around, which was just what I wanted as I was trying to avoid the morning rush hour. As we were leaving the town, Henry pointed into a field and almost shouted, "What's that?"

"It's a combine harvester. It…"

"Stop. Stop. Stop. I want to look at it. It's a gigantic engine. Almost as big as a trebuchet."

"A what?" Now it was my turn to ask questions as I pulled off the road close to the fence where the combine harvester was about to pass.

"You know. A siege engine."

"Oh yes. One of those giant catapults used for chucking big rocks at castles," I said, remembering what the word meant.

"Not just big rocks but burning oil, rotting dead animals and prisoners," Henry kindly informed me.

As we got out of the car, the combine harvester was slowly coming towards us and quite near to the fence. "There is another big car behind it," said Henry.

"Yes, that's a tractor pulling a trailer to collect the ears of wheat when they have been stripped off the stalk."

Henry looked at the vehicles as they slowly passed and asked, "But how does it do the threshing?"

I paused while I thought of some clever, technical answer, but none came to mind, so I just admitted, "I don't know."

Henry bent down and put his arm through the fence to pluck a stem of the crop and looked at it.

"As I thought, it's not wheat, it's barley."

"Sorry Henry," I said with mock sincerity. "I don't really know the difference."

"How can you not know the difference? They look completely different. Wheat is used for making flour and barley is mainly malted for beer."

"Malted? I don't even know what malted means."

Henry huffed and puffed as the vehicles moved ahead of us. "Barley is encouraged to germinate and is then stopped by roasting it. How can you not know that?"

I thought for a moment whether or not to ignore this question, but decided to explain. "This is not an agricultural society any more. Very few people work in farming, so we don't know about these things."

Henry continued to watch and then said, "But your town is surrounded by fields full of crops, some of which are being harvested early. How can you not know the difference between wheat and barley? And, anyway, why is it being harvested so early? It's not harvest time yet." He paused and added, "But it does look ready to be harvested, even if it is a couple of months early".

Having been made to feel so ignorant about cereal crops, I

felt the need to get my own back by sounding knowledgeable. "Ah, that's probably because of global warming and selective breeding of the different sorts of barley. It might even be genetically modified."

Henry didn't seem to hear this as he continued to study the stem of barley in his hand and slowly said, "The ears are so large and there are so many of them."

"Are there?"

"Yes, there's a yield of three of four times what I would expect."

Now this really was my opportunity to sound knowledgeable and important. "Well, you see, Henry, the population has grown so much we need more and more food to feed everybody and we no longer have harvest failures, or famines in this country." Saying this not only made me feel knowledgeable but superior in our modern times. It seemed to have no effect on Henry as he watched the vehicles move down the field. Then suddenly, the harvester coughed out a bale of hay wrapped in black plastic.

"What's that?"

"A bale of hay. What's it look like?"

"A bale of hay? But it's black."

"That's because it's wrapped in black polythene. Look, there are some more all over the field." I pointed to all the round bales.

Henry picked another stem at its base and held it up. "This straw is too short," he said. "The thatcher would not want this."

"Ah well, there's not a lot of work for thatchers these days, not even as prime ministers," I told him enigmatically and added, "And anyway, I think the lower the stem the less damage is done by wind and rain."

As the two vehicles moved towards the end of the field,

Henry asked, "Why has the harvester not got anyone in it, like your carriage car?"

Another opportunity for me to feel knowledgeable and superior with our technology. "Well, that's because it is controlled by GPS." I waited for the next question, but it never came, so I added. "GPS means it knows exactly where to move to." And then, just to prove my point, the two vehicles reached the end of the field and began to slowly turn. "There you go. It knows it's reached the end of the field so it's turning the corner." Henry just seemed to accept this as a part of my world. Which it was.

"So why has the other smaller one got someone in it?"

I thought for a moment for something clever, then just told him, "Because that one has to carry away the grain onto the roads, which is a lot faster and more complicated, so it needs to have someone in it."

Just to prove my point, another lorry sped into the field and lined up behind the lorry collecting the grain. Then they both moved forward at the same speed, so that the second lorry neatly slipped into the space of the first and the first one zipped out of the field the same way the new one had come in.

"So, where are the people who work the fields? The peasants and serfs? Where have they gone? How do they live if they don't work on the land?"

I was not sure what to say to this. How does one explain seven centuries of development? I simply said, "People do other work. Other jobs." This clearly did not fully answer Henry's questions. He continued to lean on the fence and silently watch the barley being harvested.

It was a beautiful summer's morning and, although it was still only just after 6 am the sun was still warm on my back. The main reason for starting off early was to try to avoid much of the morning traffic, so, enjoyable as the lesson in modern farming methods was, I did want to get on.

"Come on, Henry. We need to get going to avoid the traffic."

Henry turned towards the car and asked, "Traffic? What do you mean, traffic?"

"You know, lots of vehicles all on the road at the same time as people go to work."

"Hmm."

We continued our journey up to the A40. We had been on this road before, and Henry looked at the countryside on each side of the road as we sped along the dual carriageway. As we approached the end of the Witney bypass I could see the slow-moving traffic ahead and we joined on to the end. Fortunately, it was not moving too slowly.

Henry mumbled, "So many of them, and so many different types." He wasn't really talking to me, so I made no response, but was aware that he was still having some difficulty coming to terms with the 21st century. Then he was quiet again and I broke the silence with, "This is what I meant by traffic. Lots of cars on the road at the same time, all going to roughly the same place."

"Mmmm, well, it's not how I'd use the word." I assumed the meaning of the word had changed and said nothing.

Further down the road Henry asked, "What town is this?"

"Oxford."

"Oxford? It doesn't look much like Oxford."

"These are just the outskirts. It's a lot bigger than it used to be."

"Is it?"

The traffic was not too heavy and before long we were

approaching the motorway. I put my foot down and merged with traffic which was moving normally. I could see Henry looking around once again as he saw yet another even broader road and even more vehicles. Suddenly, we rounded a slight bend in the road and the cars in front slowed down significantly. I wondered why, but then I was blinded by the sun and I realised why all the cars had slowed down.

Henry asked, "Is there something wrong?"

"Not really, Henry, it's just the sun in people's eyes. They cannot see."

Henry peered forwards and said, "I have never seen the sun so bright."

"Ah, that's just because we are behind glass."

We eased forward and began to speed up as the angle of the road moved away from the rising sun, but I could see its brilliant rays flooding the Watlington cut, and the birds circling above.

"They look like red kites", Henry observed.

"They are."

"Herrumff!" Henry exclaimed. "They are bad birds."

"Bad birds? Why bad birds?" Once more Henry's tone of voice went into the 'how can you be so ignorant' mode.

"Because they take lots of lambs and even babies if they get the chance."

"What a load of nonsense. They only eat carrion. That's why they like the motorway. Lots of roadkill to eat. It's attitudes like that which led to their extinction in England. This is the Getty estate we are passing through. They gave their land for a reintroduction programme nearly a century ago."

Henry just looked rather bemused and asked, "What is the Getty estate?"

"Oh, just some oily family who live around here. They have

a lovely cricket ground." As soon as I said this I was regretting it, as I now expected the question, "What's cricket?" but it did not come.

We carried on up the cutting and Henry wanted to know, "Why don't we slow down as we go up this steep hill? Horses always do." There was nothing I could say to this that would not be far too long and too technical. Anyway, it seemed it was only a rhetorical question. Soon we were looking down on the town of High Wycombe, and Henry commented, "So many houses." Once more there was no need for me to comment.

We were soon at the M25 junction, and the traffic was slowing as we were coming into London.

"Ah, this is it I think," I said as I signalled left. "My dad brought me here once before. It's possible to park and get the tube in." I drove down the road slowly looking out for a tube station then saw the station. "Good. Now to find a place to park."

"Park?"

"Yes. Somewhere to leave the car."

Henry looked around the road and asked, "Why not here?"

"Yellow lines. Yes, I think this was the residential road he parked in. This is Ruislip station."

"Station?"

"Yes."

"What, like the stations of the cross?"

"Sort of, yes, but without the crucifixion and not a lot of Romans. Oh look, there's a place!"

We parked, walked a couple of hundred yards back to the station, bought the tickets and walked down to the platform. Henry looked either side of the platform at the tracks as a train came around the bend. He looked up and said nothing. The train pulled in and I said, "Not that one. It's going the wrong way." Henry remained silent. Then another train came the other way and stopped in the station. "Come on Henry, this one's ours," I said.

NINETEEN

DIPPY NO MORE

We got on the train and sat down but Henry was looking around so much he was attracting attention. People would think he had never seen a train before let alone travelled on one! We were lucky to have got a seat as by the time the train moved off there were a lot of people standing. Henry was looking out of the window on both sides as we travelled through the suburbs then he asked, "Where is this place?"

"Outskirts of London."

"Outskirts?"

"Yes, the edge of London."

"But I have been to London. It's nothing like this. I don't recognise anywhere."

"Ah, you may do when we get into the centre."

At this point the train entered a tunnel. Henry looked up and said, "Candles! Dark outside." A couple of people looked at him and I quietly explained to him that we were in a tunnel and that this system was called the Underground. He did look a bit perplexed, but with all the other new things he had experienced this was just one more, and then the train pulled into another station and more people squeezed on board.

As we moved from station to station Henry didn't say much, and I wondered if this was because he had little to say or he was gobsmacked by the whole experience. Then he broke his silence and asked, "What's that?" pointing to the tube map above the seats.

"It's a map of this rail system."

"Rail?"

"Yes, this thing we are on is called a train and whole system that trains run on is called a rail system. Look, that map there shows the line we are on and all the stations on it. Near the beginning is South Ruislip, where we got on. It goes all the way to Epping in Essex. We are going to get off at St. Paul's."

Henry stared at the map, taking in all I had said. Then he came out with, "I have been to St. Paul's a few years ago when I was at school in London."

I thought to myself, this should be fun. There will have been a few changes. I also felt a little guilty about wanting to play time-travel games again.

Having given him time to absorb the idea of the Central line I moved on to say, "And that map next to it is a map of the whole system under London. Look, that red line is the Central Line we're on and all the other lines fit around it." At this point I thought I'd sound knowledgeable again and added, "This is not an analogue map. The stations are not where they seem to be on the map because that would be far too complicated and confusing. It was invented by a man call Henry Beck in nineteen..." I stopped before I had finished saying 1931, as we had yet to touch on how far into the future we were, and then was not the best time to start. I quickly moved on to say, "He was known as Harry Beck."

A smile came across Henry's face and he said, "Yes, my school friends call me Harry."

At this point my eye fell on Gloucester Road Station, and an idea popped into my head. Did we have time? Of course we did. We had all day. I quickly checked where we were and told Henry, or Harry, "I've changed my mind, we'll get off at Notting Hill Gate." I jumped up as the train entered the station and Henry followed me onto the platform.

Once we were off the train Henry stopped and looked back along it. "Yes, I can see why it's called a train. Lots of carriages linked together."

"That's exactly right. Lots of carriages linked together." No linguistic problems with 'carriages'.

As we headed towards the exit, following everybody else, Henry asked, "Where are we?"

"Notting Hill Gate." There was a pause then, "No, I meant this building."

"Oh, it's not a building, it's a system of tunnels between platforms." At this point most of the crowd walked on and we turned onto the Circle Line platform.

"What now?" Henry asked.

"We will go from here to Gloucester Road station, there's something I want to show you. It's only a couple of stops." As I was saying this the train came into the station. We could not get a seat, so it was just as well we were only going two stops. I thought about how some people do this every day – both ways. Soon we were at Gloucester Road and we alighted onto the platform. Round the corner and onto the escalator. Another new toy for Henry.

"Why is this here?"

"What do you mean, "why is it here?""

"Well, what is it for?"

"It's to take people upstairs so they don't have to walk. Which reminds me, could you stand the same side as me so people who want to get up quickly can get past?" Henry looked around and moved over, just as a man came up behind us to prove my point. Henry was clearly not satisfied with my answer and asked, "But why don't they just walk? That man did!" Fortunately, we were now at the top, so I didn't need to give any answer.

Now there was an unforeseen problem, as Henry did not know you have to start walking at the top of the escalator and he nearly fell over. Then he asked, "And where are all these people going?"

"To work."

"Work? What, in the fields?"

"No, in shops, offices and restaurants. I have told you, Henry, very few people work in fields any longer; that's why we have the combine harvesters."

Henry thought for a couple of seconds and then asked, "So, are all these people of the lower orders?"

How was I to answer that? "Oh, Henry, I have told you. Things have changed. I doubt if there are any aristocrats in this station, although there might be."

As we came to the barriers I showed him what to do with his card. It was quite difficult to get his attention, because he was looking around all the time. His face looked a mixture of excitement and fear. Despite my game playing, and occasional boredom and exasperation, I was trying to be aware of what he must be going through in this strange world. When I travelled back to the 14th century I had a pretty good idea of what to expect. We all know something about the past, and I knew more than most as I had studied the period in history at school. I had also taken the Chaucer unit in my English exam. But when Henry came here he had no concept at all of what to expect. The world he was born into in the 14th century was virtually the same as the 13th century. Nothing really had changed. Just a few more wars, famines and plagues and a couple more kings. The technology, lifestyle and culture when Henry was born, nineteen years previously, were exactly the same nineteen years later. Mine had changed so much. When I was born people still used paper maps. But, against all that, he was young and should be adventurous, inquisitive and reckless. That's what life is for. He was still a teenager, just, though he had no concept of the word. Even in my world, the 21st century, I found it difficult to appreciate that there was no concept of being a teenager in the first half of the 20th century. Boys left school at thirteen, went straight into full-time employment, or unemployment, and were expected to behave as men in terms of earning and responsibility. A girl would leave school at 13, spend a few years skivvying at home or for someone else, then get married and carry on skivvying for the rest of her life. These days it seems schooling goes on until middle age. Oh well, not everything's better, then!

Outside the station the vehicles were crawling past and Henry observed, "Traffic!" He was learning. I also liked his sense of humour. Then he went into his looking-around thing, walking backwards to have good look at something, so much so that I envisaged people looking at him and thinking he had got some sort of tic, but people just walked past without a second look. I suppose they get all sorts here. Not like where I live. We're all "Ooh aargh", with a bit of straw in our mouths, we are.

"These houses are so big," Henry said as we walked along the street.

I looked up at the three-storey terrace. "They're not all for one family, you know. There may be twenty families living along this terrace of houses. They're probably flats so there could be a hundred households along here."

By now we were at the crossing and we joined the people waiting to cross.

"Why are we all standing here?"

"We're waiting for the traffic to stop." Henry thought about this for while and asked, "Why would the traffic stop... Ah! Like when you stop your carriage car for no reason."

For no reason? Just as well we are not in Germany.

Now the lights were changing. Across the road and up the steps to the Natural History Museum. At the top of the first flight, Henry stopped, looked up at the building and said, "A great man lives here!"

I took a deep breath. "Henry, no one lives here. This is a public building. A museum. Anyway, this is just a fascia. It's red brick around the sides and back."

"A Museum?"

"Yes, a building full of things to look at."

"Ah, things to muse on."

"I suppose so. This one's full of dead animals."

Henry screwed his face up and I walked forward. He followed. Into the entrance hall and Henry exclaimed in a loud voice, "Chinese!"

"Shhh! Yes, Henry, there are a lot of them in the world. About one in five people is Chinese."

"But why are they here?"

"They are probably all here on a coach tour."

"Why?"

"For the same reason as we are, I expect. To see the dead animals!" We stopped to join the queue to have our bags searched and Henry said, "Black men."

"Yes, Henry. Shut up, please."

We went in and Henry walked more and more slowly, looking up. Finally he came to a halt and asked, "What's that?"

"It's a blue whale. The biggest creature ever to live on earth."

"A whale! I have heard of whales but never seen one."

"I have. I saw lots off the coast of Nova Scotia when my parents took us on holiday."

"Nova Scotia? Somewhere off Scotland, I assume."

"If you like, Henry." Nova Scotia is nowhere near Scotland, but I wasn't going to discuss it.

"It is enormous. So much oil, flesh and bones."

"Yes, Henry," I said and changed the subject. "There used to be a different skeleton here. He was call Dippy."

"Dippy?"

"Yes, Dippy the diPLODocus. Or is it Dippy the diploDOcus? I'm not too sure."

"But what was that one? Another whale?"

"No, he was a dinosaur. This skeleton is real bone, but the other was just a plaster cast." I left this to sink in, expecting the question, "what's a dinosaur?" but it did not come, so I asked, "What do you call a dinosaur with no eyes?" Henry looked at me and shrugged his shoulders. "A Douthinkhesaurus."

He looked at me blankly, so I asked, "What do you get after a vindaloo curry?" He shrugged again. "A Megasorearse." The blank look continued, so I just said, "Come on." We walked off slowly, and Henry continued to look back at the blue whale until it was out of sight.

We spent the next couple of hours going around the museum with me answering many questions from Henry but no fundamental questions about evolution, thankfully, and then as we were looking at one display he said, "This is just a circus show!"

"Circus show? What are you talking about?"

"This thing here – it says it is from 232 million years ago. Well, that's just silly."

I had no idea how to respond to this and I really did not want to go down the road of evolution, or how old the earth was, so I simply responded with, "It's a good show, though, isn't it Henry?"

Before lunch we popped into the loo, which was no real problem in itself as he had used them in my house, but he did have some difficulty with waving his hand under the tap to make it produce water. It was the same problem with the hand dryer, as he had never seen one before. After this we went to a restaurant to have some lunch. Getting the food was easy, but Henry did have a little difficulty with the idea of having to get his food rather than someone coming to serve him.

We spent an hour over lunch talking about all the exhibits and Henry was clearly enjoying the 'circus show'. We did talk about many of the exhibits being of extinct creatures, but that didn't seem to cause a problem as he was quite happy to believe that they had all gone extinct within the last 6,000 years, or whatever the bible reckons is the age of the earth. As for the size of the creatures, the blue whale being the largest, and their weird shape, he thought a strange, far-off land was enough explanation of why he had never seen or heard of them. After all, he did come from a time when they believed in unicorns and dragons and thought swallows hibernated in holes during the winter.

Did they not watch thousands of swallows flying in and out of the country each spring and autumn? Where did they think they were coming from or going to?

Having finished lunch, we had a quick zip around the museum again and left as some more Chinese people were entering. I pre-empted Henry by telling him, "I think they might be Japanese". Henry shrugged and said, "What's the difference?" I had no answer for that.

Outside, Henry stopped to look back at the building's front. He clearly liked it, so I used my phone to take a picture and showed it to Henry. Even though I had shown him how to take photos before, he was taken aback that there could be an instant 'painting' of something.

Back into the tube station and onto the first train. The journey was far less traumatic for Henry than the first one, and we soon emerged from St. Paul's station into the centre of London. Outside Henry stopped and looked around. I did the same, as I wasn't too sure where we were or where to go, so I got my phone out and put the postcode into the GPS. Once it had planned the route I said, "Come on, Henry."

As we walked off Henry looked up at St. Paul's and said, "That's not St. Paul's."

"Yes, it is. The last one burned down in sixteen... During the Great Fire of London." I nearly talked about dates again. "This is a new one. Apparently criticised for being too Roman Catholic." Henry just said, "Eh?"

We walked about half a mile, then looked for a sign saying 'Fabulous Fireworks'. To my surprise, having only found this place online, there was a sign on the wall with an arrow pointing down a flight of stairs. Down we went to find ourselves in a large underground warehouse. "You all right there, guys?" came a cheery voice, and a young woman had appeared.

"Oh, er, I'm looking for some fireworks." I answered.

"Well, you've come to the right place. In fact, we have Fabulous Fireworks. My name's Victoria."

"Well, Victoria, I'm Edmund and this is Henry. I want some of the loudest and most dramatic fireworks you've got."

"Loud as well as dramatic? That's a little more difficult these days."

"Is it? Why?"

"Because these days manufacturers are leaned on to make them quieter."

"I thought half the point of fireworks was the fact they are loud."

"Yeah, well, health and safety and all that, I suppose. But we do have some things we do for special events. They can be pretty noisy."

She then showed us a range of her wares and I explained I wanted the shock and awe effect. Victoria was then joined by Francesca and the three of us selected as many of the loudest and brightest products they had and that I could afford. My parents had left me £1,000 and I had spent none of it during my time in the 14th century, but this would blow a big hole in the money. Henry hardly said a word during all this and I didn't know if this was because he didn't know what was going on, because it was all getting too much for him, or some other reason.

Then came the best bit of news. "We can get that packed and dispatched to you to arrive by tomorrow morning," Francesca told me.

"Oh great! I was wondering how long it would take. Thank you."

"That's all right, my darling. No problem." I had been wondering how long delivery would take as I wanted to get back to the 14th century as soon as possible. I was not sure why. What I really wanted to do was to stay here and live a boring teenager's life. But I did feel some sort of responsibility for Henry, his whole family and household, and of course, Megan. I tried telling myself I had delusions of my own importance and it would make no difference if I never went back, but I wasn't really winning the argument with myself. Even if I did convince myself I didn't need to go back, Henry was here, so I had to. End of story.

Outside I said, "Come on, Henry, let's get a bus."

"A bus?"

"Yes, an omnibus."

"An all-bus."

"That's right. A bus for all. A bus for everyone. Look, that one over there will do us."

We ran across the road, dodging the slow-moving traffic, jumped onto the bus and ran up the stairs. This gave us both, but especially Henry, a good view of modern London. When I say 'modern London', some of the buildings were hundreds of years old, but I didn't think any dated back to Henry's time. We went past the Gherkin and the Shard and Henry was clearly impressed, rather than looking frightened and stressed as he seemed to be sometimes on his adventure.

The bus stopped at traffic lights near to the river and Henry exclaimed in a loud voice, "I know that castle!" The Tower of London was coming into view. "Yes, Henry, that is the Tower of London."

I looked around, expecting people to be looking at us after Henry's outburst, but no one seemed to take any notice. I supposed they were used to tourists. He was so full of excitement at recognising something he knew, something connected to his world that made him feel less alien, that I said, "Come on then Henry, let's get off and have a look." We ran downstairs, just as the bus was stopping, and jumped off.

As we stood looking at the Tower, Henry proudly told me how his Norman ancestors, along with King William, had come over to defeat King Harold and build this magnificent building from stone brought from his home town of Caen. I knew all this, but Henry clearly wanted to tell me, so why not? Then I noticed an ice cream van with virtually no queue, so I pulled Henry's arm and he followed me.

"Two double ninety-nines, please," I asked the vendor and he produced two, creamy, brilliant white, soft ice creams with two flakes of chocolate in each.

"What's this?" Henry asked.

"Ice cream. What's it look like? Eat it quickly before it melts." Henry licked the ice cream and said, "Mmmm, I see, ice-cream."

"Yes, Henry, cream frozen nearly to ice."

"Very nice, but what's this?"

"Chocolate. Made from cocoa beans and milk."

"Cocoa?"

"It doesn't matter." I walked off a few feet to end the conversation.

"What's that?" Henry now asked, pointing to Tower Bridge.

"It's a bridge, Henry."

"Yes, but it's moving." Now I could see what he meant, as the bridge was beginning to open and the road was opening from the middle.

"You see that ship coming towards the bridge?" I said,

pointing. "It is too big to get under the bridge, so the bridge lifts up to let it through."

Henry ran towards Tower Bridge for a closer look and I followed. We watched as the bridge became fully open just as the ship reached it. It sailed through quite quickly and as soon as it had passed, the roadway began to be lowered. Soon the traffic was flowing across it again and I said, "Come on, Henry, let's go."

We walked along the Embankment up stream and Henry commented on how much narrower the river was than when he had been at school in London. I told him that was probably because it had been channelled and while the river was narrower, it was much deeper for the ships. We talked about the many changes there had been and how different things were from when he was at school. Once more I avoided precise dates. I got the impression that he thought things had changed this much just in the short time since he had been at school here a few years before.

After a while we turned right and worked our way through the streets until we found ourselves in Regent Street. Henry surveyed the sweeping terrace of tall buildings. He was clearly into architecture and impressed by what he saw. At one point he stopped and tapped a wall. Then he scratched it, as if to see if it would bleed and asked, "What sort of stone is this?"

"I really have no idea," I replied and thought about something I had read when my parents took me to Portland Bill. "I know Portland Place, not far from here, is built of Portland stone, so maybe this is as well."

"It is high quality stone, but I don't think it's as good as Caen stone."

I didn't argue as I didn't know, and I really didn't care.

Now I felt it was time for another little game, so I led him into a busy department store. As we pushed through the crowds Henry fell back a bit and I stopped and looked at him. He looked stressed again, and I wondered if it was the crowds that were causing him a problem. He couldn't be used to it; in his town crowds opened to let him, or any member of his family, pass.

He caught up and we waited outside a lift. Soon the doors opened and we pushed our way in, along with about 20 other people. The doors closed and everybody was silent. Henry turned to me and asked, "Why are we in here?" There was a slight movement as the lift began to rise, but Henry didn't seem to notice it.

"Because we're going upstairs," I told him as quietly as possible. Fortunately, people had started chatting so I didn't feel so embarrassed by Henry's question.

After a while the lift stopped and people got out. "Not here, Henry," I said and put my hand on his arm to hold him back. There were a couple more stops and at each one Henry peered out as the doors opened briefly. When we got to the top floor I gave him a slight push and out we went, but as soon as we were through the doors he stopped and stood still. People were moving around him as he twisted and turned to look at his new environment.

"It's... different. It's not where we came in."

"No, Henry, this is the top floor." I pointed towards the window. Henry almost ran to the window and looked out, up and down Regent Street.

"But...how?" I smiled and told him, "We came up in that lift thing."

"You mean that little room we were all in?"

"Yes, Henry.

"Is it magic?"

"No, Henry, it's not magic."

"Then how? How did we get up here? Is it like your carriage car?"

"No, not really. The room, as you call it, is pulled up and down by strong steel ropes."

"Steel?"

"Yes, a kind of iron."

This seemed to confuse, frighten, impress and excite him all at the same time, and I was not sure which emotion was the strongest. He clearly liked looking up and down Regent Street, but eventually I got him back into the lift to descend. However, it wasn't that simple, as at every stop he insisted on getting out to have a look at the new world that suddenly appeared as if by magic.

Eventually, we were back outside the store and we walked on towards Trafalgar Square. We entered the square and Henry asked, "What's this?"

"Trafalgar Square. Named after a battle."

"A battle? A battle where?"

"Trafalgar."

"Who's he?" Henry asked, pointing to Nelson on his column.

"Nelson, the bloke who commanded the naval fleet."

Henry stood looking up at Nelson, then all around the square and I suggested we go to have a closer look. We stood under Nelson's column and Henry asked, "Why are these lions here?"

"Oh, I think they're something to do with his other battles."

"I see. Who was he fighting?"

"The French and Spanish I believe."

"Really? Christian countries." He continued to look up and observed, "Very Romanesque." I looked up at the column and nodded in agreement, but it was clear he knew a lot more about it than I did.

I edged Henry towards Whitehall and we slowly walked down the road as he admired the buildings on either side. I didn't mention to him that this was where the machinery of government was based, as it would have raised a thousand more questions than it answered. We looked at various statues and mostly I had no idea who they were or why they were here. One was of General Montgomery, but I really didn't know who he was or what he had done. At the Cenotaph I could tell him it was a war memorial and he commented, "It's just a lump of stone."

"Yes, Henry, I think that's the idea."

Eventually we entered Parliament Square and Henry exclaimed, "That's Westminster Abbey."

"Yes, Henry, it is." I had not thought about Westminster Abbey, as I had brought him here to look at Parliament.

"Let's go inside."

"Oh well, I'm not sure, time and all that."

"Oh, come on." He was now taking the lead.

At the massive doors Henry crossed himself and then looked at me. I think this was to ask why I wasn't crossing myself also, but I really couldn't bring myself to play the game, though many around us were. I wanted to ask him why he did that. What did crossing himself do? What would happen if he didn't do it? I felt this wasn't the time to discuss the logic of theology, so I kept quiet. Even if I had asked, I wonder if I would have got a sensible reply. Did he know why he did it, or was it just something he had been taught to do from a very young age and he had never questioned it? Dogs bark, cats meow and Christians cross themselves. There's no point in asking why, they just do.

Then we came to one of the reasons I was reluctant to go in. We had to PAY! An exorbitant amount, as well. I did hope it would be worth it.

In we went, and Henry obviously knew the building well, though some things were not as he expected. Poets' Corner, for example, left him a little confused. Then we got to Charles Darwin's grave and of course Henry had no idea who he was. I touched briefly on how he had done a lot of the research that was now represented in The Natural History Museum, which we had just been to, but once more I avoided the subject of evolution. I did tell him Darwin had had a break with the church and had wanted a simple, non-religious funeral, but the had church ignored his wishes and buried him here.

It was quite a while before I could get him out of the Abbey, but finally we were walking across Parliament Square and I said, "This is where Parliament sits, Henry."

"Here? It is a beautiful building but why here? Surely Parliament sits wherever it is?" This confused me for a while. I thought about it and then I said, "No, they always sit here. They are in there now passing laws."

"But where is the king? Is he in here?

"We have a queen and she is not in there. She's about a mile away I think. They don't need the king or queen to actually be there any more."

"Oh!" Henry responded. This was just one more thing that Henry didn't really understand. He didn't comment on my mention of the queen, not the king, but was that because he hadn't really hear it?

"You know I told you about the man who fought the king for Parliament, Oliver Cromwell?"

"I think so, but you have told me so many things."

"Well, that's his statue there." I pointed to Cromwell's statue on horseback. "As I said, he was no democrat."

Henry said nothing, then asked, "But why would he be?"

"Er, be what?

"Be a democrat?"

"Good question, Henry," was all I could think to say in answer to his question. He must have known what a democrat is because he spoke Greek.

I felt a mixture of pleasure and concern at Henry's pleasure and the fact that time was passing. I was also very hot now, even though the sun was past its zenith. I slowly walked out of the square and Henry followed. We had not eaten, except the ice cream, since we were in the museum, so I suggested we stop in a pavement café. Henry didn't know what to order, so we both had burgers and chips. Once we had finished this I thought it was time for another little treat for Henry. He had liked the soft ice cream, so I ordered him the biggest knickerbocker glory the café sold. As the waitress approached with it, his eyes bulged like a little boy. He started to eat and observed, "This ice cream is hard."

"Yes, Henry, it is a different sort of ice cream. Do you like it?"

"Oh yes, so many different flavours." I just had a fruit salad and ice cream.

After we had eaten, we walked through many more streets and Henry was looking at everything, and everyone, around him. I was embarrassed about how he stared, but no one else seemed to take any notice of him. Eventually we found ourselves on the edge of Hyde Park and I remembered I had been shown a tree there with little models in it, and I wanted to go and look for it. Childhood memories and all that. But by now it was early evening and people were pouring out of London, so I knew we had better join them. We were near to Marble Arch tube station and I said to Henry, "I think this one is on the Central Line", and we entered the station.

"This isn't where we came out," Henry told me, as if I didn't know.

"No, Henry, but it doesn't matter. We can still get back to where we left the car. There is nearly 500 miles of this rail network. More than any other underground system in the world."

He said nothing and we went through the barriers. Down the escalator, this time with many people hurrying past us, but Henry seemed to be enjoying the experience too much to want to run like them. We got down to our level just as a train was arriving alongside the platform, so we squeezed on, along with hundreds of others.

"Nowhere to sit," Henry moaned.

"No, we'll just have to stand."

As we moved along the line from station to station, people were getting on and off, and after a few stops we were able to sit down. The journey seemed to be causing him less trauma than the one into town and he was quite quiet until he said, "Those young women where we bought the fireworks."

"Yes, Henry."

"They were writing things down."

"Yes, Henry, our order."

"Can they read and write?"

"Of course they can." He was silent for a while and then

asked, "Are they members of an aristocratic family?"

I smiled and as gently as possible told him, "No, Henry, everybody can read here."

Henry put his head on one side and raised his eyebrows.

"I am serious, Henry, everybody, everybody in this train, everybody in this town, almost everybody in the country can read." His eyebrows dropped back and he looked more perplexed than anything else. I supposed that if he had grown up in a world where few people could read and write he assumed there was something genetic, something of the gentry, that enabled them to read.

The train became emptier and emptier as we moved out of town and when we arrived at Ruislip Henry said, "Here already!" We were soon in the car and queuing to get onto the A40. I was going to say to Henry that this was the road that went past Burford, but I couldn't see the point. It was evening now and we were driving towards the setting sun rather than the rising sun we had seen on our journey in. At this time the commuter traffic was beginning to thin out and we were quickly on the M40. Miles on and the sun was streaming into the Watlington cut and the circling red kites looked even more impressive. This time Henry said nothing.

Before long we were signalling to leave the A40 into Carterton. As we approached the town we passed a cyclist and Henry gasped, "What's that?"

"That's a bicycle. I told you that yesterday."

"No, not the wheel thing. What's on it?"

"Oh, him! He, or she, is our local transvestite."

"A transvestite?"

"Yes, Henry, a man who likes to dress as a woman." He looked behind us at the vanishing cyclist and asked, "But, but the hair, the dress?"

"Oh yes, not very convincing is it? It's a wig of course. He has various different colours and she has a few different dresses." Henry was silent for a while then asked, "But why?"

"Well, why not? Some women wear trousers, so why shouldn't he wear dresses?"

Whether or not this satisfied him I don't know, but he didn't mention it again.

A few minutes later we had to stop at the traffic lights in the town centre.

"Look!" Henry shouted.

What now? "Yes, Henry, what is it?"

"That woman. With the strange birds."

"Yes, they're beautiful, aren't they? They are cockatoos. I think she has got three."

"But are they tethered like falcons? Are they hunting birds?"

"I don't know if they're tethered but they are definitely not hunting birds."

"But, but why?"

I paused for a while then told him, "Well, I suppose because she likes them. She's known as a girl who likes a cockatoo."

Soon we were turning into my drive, just as someone was walking out of the neighbour's drive. I pressed a button to open the window and shouted, "Hello Nicole!"

"Hello, Edmund," she called back.

"Who was that?" Henry asked.

"My next-door neighbour."

Inside the house I said, "I'm absolutely knackered, Henry, so I'm off to bed".

"Me too," he answered.

TWENTY

THE BISHOP'S MEN

Captain Scarlett entered the courtyard where his men were lined up waiting for their orders. They were not a standing army, and most of them were not part of the Bishop of Gloucester's guard, although the commanding officers were. Most of the men were locals from the town of Gloucester and surrounding villages. All were expected to practise their archery and other military skills in their own time. Most were serfs and had no choice in where their landlord sent them. They were as much his property as were the cows and pigs on his land, and if he told them to join the Bishop's militia at short notice, then that was what they had to do. Some were battle-hardened as they had fought at the Battle of Crécy a couple of years earlier. Even so, most had never been in battle and they could not be described as a well-trained, disciplined army. They were fired up and ready for combat but had no idea where they would be sent, or why. That was Captain Scarlett's task.

"Men!" Scarlett shouted, "Today is a day for God's work. There are two heretics and sorcerers hiding in the town of Burford who have evaded capture before. They ran away to escape the Lord's justice, but it seems they have now returned." He took a long pause before going on: "One of these heretics is the son of Lord Burford and is under his protection. The town is barricaded and well defended on the orders of the lord. Of course he pretends this is just to protect the town from the pestilence, but we know it is to protect his heretic son and his sorcerous accomplice. This accomplice of the Devil seems to have the lord, and most of the town, in his thrall. He claims to perform miracles and takes God's own gift of recovery for himself. That is why we must have such a large force to arrest them. Our force will be so large that once they know we are at the town gates they will surrender without a fight and we can arrest these heretics!" This last word was spat out with great venom.

The captain waited a few seconds for this to be absorbed and then went on, "We shall march today and spend the night in Charlton Kings, a village the other side of Cheltenham. There we will be joined by some more men from Bishop's Cleeve and we will feast and provision for our long march the next day. We expect to arrive outside the town before nightfall and then surround it from all entrances from its west, before we attack under the cover of night. Remember men, this is God's work we do and should it be necessary for you to spill blood in his name, your souls will be washed clean by the grace of our Lord Jesus Christ."

There were mumblings among the men. Captain Scarlett finished by saying, "You may have a short time to pray, men, and then we march."

Captain Scarlett marched out of the courtyard and the men broke up into small groups; some praying, some just chatting among themselves about the task ahead of them. Many felt disappointed that they were not off to a foreign war, to repeat, or gain, the glory of Crécy. Others felt relieved that they would soon be returning to their families, alive and safe. The people of Burford were not expected to put up much of a fight, so they did not feel they faced much danger. Some of the men had heard of Burford but none of them, except for the Bishop's men, had ever been to Burford, and even they had not been into the town, only nearby, when they had tried to capture Henry and Edmund, the two heretics, before they had disappeared before their eyes.

These Bishop's men were the only ones who had any real idea of what was going on, but their story soon spread among the force. They related how they knew of the heretics because they had been sent, along with Captain Scarlett, to arrest the men, but that they had disappeared into thin air just as they were dismounting their horses to arrest them. These men could attest to the fact that sorcery had occurred. How else would the two young men have vanished? Therefore, they must be in league with the Devil.

These men, who had pursued the heretics before, had no doubt they were on a mission to do God's work. Their conviction of their just cause spread among the other men and all of the assembled force were sure they were entering into a small, holy war. Some did not like the idea of having to fight their own countrymen, rather than the French, but all were secure in the knowledge that this was God's will and they would receive God's grace on their day of judgement.

Before long Captain Scarlett re-entered the courtyard and shouted, "Form up, men. It is time to march".

Cheltenham was only eight or nine miles from Gloucester,

so by mid-afternoon they were marching through Cheltenham and attracting much attention from the locals. Why were the Bishop's men here? Where were they going? And how much trade could be done provisioning the force for its journey? Normally, travellers would be greatly discouraged from entering the town because of fear of the disease they might bring. But it was different for the army of God. It was impossible to prevent their entry and they were safe in the belief that if they were doing God's work, they must be clean, and God would approve of any who assisted them.

Cheltenham being the only major town between Gloucester and Burford, having stocked up with all their needs they continued on to Charlton Kings, where the local church, its grounds and the surrounding houses were used to billet the small army. Although the force was not expected – how could it be? – it was usual for those on the Bishop's business to be welcomed by the parish priest and his parishioners. The men were fed in the church and then bedded down wherever they could for a good night's sleep. Some were sleeping outside, but fortunately it was a warm midsummer's night. Captain Scarlett was to sleep in a comfortable bed in the priest's house.

Early the next morning breakfast was provided before the men collected their equipment for the long march on to Burford. Off they marched and after a few miles they stopped in Andoversford, where they were allowed to rest and get food and water from the local hostelries and houses. This would be paid for, unlike in a foreign war when they would be expected to live off the land and steal anything they wanted. It was still mid-morning, but Captain Scarlett knew that if he wanted to be outside Burford by nightfall, they had better get moving.

By midday they were passing Northleach. Normally, this would be a place where they could rest and eat, but the captain knew the town was sealed off from the world because of the plague. This was where Matilda and her family lived – if indeed they were still living. He was also aware that this was Lord Burford's land and if it were known in the town where the force was headed, someone might get to Burford before them to warn of their arrival. Marching on foot is limited to two or three miles per hour, but a man on horseback could do it in less than an hour. The only man on horseback in the army was the captain.

Along the ridge overlooking the village of Sherborne, the men could look down on the River Windrush and wish they could bathe in its cool waters. It was now mid-afternoon and the heat of the day was tiring the men more than the marching. This was where a few days earlier, Edmund and Henry had looked at the mist rising off the river after the great storm the morning before. There was no mist this time as it was a rather overcast, humid and hot day.

On they went and by early evening they had reach Upton, where they waited for nightfall. This also enabled the men to rest before the night's task. Even though a real fight was not expected, Captain Scarlett wanted his men to be rested, fed and watered before they surrounded the town. It was not long before he gave the command to split the force, some going down the hillside towards the town on the road that entered through Sheep Street and the rest of the force along the main Oxford road. The Sheep Street force was to split again, with some men going down to the river to prevent any escape from the town to the north. The west side of the town could not be blocked as that would require going past the barrier at the top of Burford

High Street where they would definitely be seen by the Burford town guides.

Around midnight, the attacking army was in place.

TWENTY ONE

READING AND WRITING

I could hear music and thought I was in a dream. After a few seconds I decided the music was in the real world and stretched out my hand to switch off the radio. It was already off and I realised the music was coming from downstairs, so it must be Henry, up already and playing with the keyboard. It was not late, but I supposed Henry was awake because it was light, and in a medieval world each moment of daylight must be made the most of. Oh well, I was awake, so I may as well get up.

"Good morning, Henry."

"Oh, good day, Edmund."

"Have you had breakfast?"

"No, I was waiting for you." Oh no, he couldn't get it himself. I was beginning to think like my mum. We were not in a hurry, so, for a change, I made us a couple of omelettes with cheese and baked beans in them. While I was cooking, the noises from Henry's playing became more like a tune than a collection of noises. He was learning fast with his new toy, and I could hear the same basic tune being played separately on three different instruments. Then I heard all three played together, and realised he had mastered putting different instruments together for a playback. He was obviously better at it than I was.

"It's ready! Come on Henry."

He came through to the kitchen and looked at the plates on the table and asked, "Can we eat it with the television?" This was not something my parents let us kids do when we were young, but he was probably making the most of the 21st century technology that he would never see again. As we ate he was channel hopping. He seemed to be most attracted to wildlife programmes and the children's programmes.

"What are these things?"

I looked up to see him holding up his fork with a few baked beans on it. "Baked beans."

"Baked beans?"

"Yes, haricot beans in a tomato sauce. Actually, I think they are steamed rather than baked. In the tin." He continued eating and now seemed to be settled on a programme about New Zealand wildlife. I just hoped he wouldn't ask me where New Zealand was. There were certain subjects I wanted to avoid, as they would just be too difficult to deal with. As we ate and watched, the programme began to explain continental drift, but Henry just continued to watch in silence as he ate. I don't think he understood the difference between a fictional programme and a factual one. It just seemed all made up to him.

"Toast?" I asked.

"Yes please," He answered eagerly. He obviously liked toast, so I made him two pieces, one with peanut butter and one with apricot jam. We sat munching as he continued to watch the same programme. Then I had an idea and rushed upstairs. I came back down again and said to him,

"I found this book I had at school for biology. It's called

Human Anatomy and I thought I'd take it with us to give to Megan. It could be useful to her."

I handed it to Henry who began looking through the book. After a few seconds he said, "Yes, I have looked through your books in the music room. Interesting, but the calligraphy is not very good." This confused me for a while. Then I clicked and said, "Books are no longer written as works of art. They are merely factual."

"Hmm", was his dismissive reply and he continued to look through the book and then gave his opinion. "Yes, very nice, but you do know Megan cannot read our language, let alone this."

"Well, yes, I do know, but it is full of pictures she could learn from. Anyway, she could learn to read and write your English, then she could start to make sense of this. You can, so why shouldn't she be able to?"

Henry gave a cross between a harrumph and a laugh. Normally I would have let this drop, but we were talking about Megan, whom I knew and had grown to like. Not just that, but she struck me as a clever girl in a terrible situation. But then, she probably thought she was very lucky to be still alive.

"Come on Henry, tell me why you think she can't learn to read and write?"

He giggled and I continued to look at him, expecting a reply. Eventually he said, "Edmund, there are many reasons, but just let me give you three simple reasons. First, she is of the lower orders. Second, she is a gay girl. And thirdly, she is Welsh!"

I was gobsmacked by this but got my thoughts together to respond. "Henry, everyone you have met here is of the "lower orders", as you term people. All the gay girls here (I was getting used to the idea that all boys and girls are girls and the females are gay girls) can read and write, and as for the Welsh, I think all of them can read and write also. What makes you think Megan is incapable?"

"Hmm, maybe." I was getting nowhere, so at this point I gave up, rather disappointed that Henry thought of Megan in this way, especially after she had saved our lives.

There was silence, so to move things on I collected the plates and went to the kitchen. I was loading the dishwasher when the doorbell rang. I opened the door to a delivery man who announced, "Two parcels for Edmund Decovny!"

"Oh yes, thanks." I signed for them, picked up the two large parcels and brought them into the hall. Then I went into Henry and told him, "They're here, so you had better stop watching that."

"Oh, all right. So, we'd better get changed back into our normal clothes," he replied. I thought of picking him up on 'normal', but could not be bothered and thought it was just as well he had remembered about changing our clothes, as I had forgotten. That could have caused a few more problems. We got changed and I had one final look around the house to see if we had forgotten anything. Also, the thought was on my mind once more that I might never be able to return here again.

We sat on the floor, piled the two parcels on our laps and grasped the laptop as before. I typed in bbc.co.uk/cricke and took a deep breath before pressing the "t". I looked at Henry who, as usual, didn't look the slightest bit worried about what might, or might not, happen.

The mist swirled and I felt a bump and fell backwards, letting go of the laptop. Fortunately, we were back in the 14th century. Henry jumped up and said, "Come on, we can leave the boxes here for a man to pick up and bring back for us later." Now in his own century, Henry was taking command again. I was perfectly happy with this.

Unlike our last return it was not raining, so four miles to the Oxford Road did not seem too onerous. As we came in sight of the defended barrier, as expected, a couple of riders came out to meet us.

"Good day, sirs," said one.

"Good day, Knut and Jasper," said Henry. I knew Knut but had never met Jasper before, although he clearly knew me.

Henry jumped up behind Knut and I pulled myself up behind Jasper, with a little help. As we were riding off I heard Henry telling Knut to go back later and pick up the two boxes from the same place as last time. They must be wondering how we had got them to that place but could take them no further, but no one asked; it was not their place to ask questions. Fortunately.

In a couple of minutes we were at the barrier and it was raised as we approached. We went through to a chorus of "Good day, sirs", and "It's good to see you back, sirs". Soon we were dismounting outside Burford House. The door was opened for us by Rachael, the Housekeeper.

"Good day, to you, sirs."

"Good day, Rachael." We both said. Once inside, Megan came bounding down the stairs with a beaming smile, but there was anguish in her voice when she spoke.

"Oh, sirs, thank the Lord you are back. Miss Anne has fallen sick with the fever."

My first thought was, who was Miss Anne? Then I realised it must be Henry's younger sister. I looked at Henry, who had turned very pale.

"Oh Megan, is it the sickness?" I asked.

"I don't think it is the same one, no sir, I think it is swamp fever."

"Swamp fever?" I questioned, screwing my face up in confusion.

"Yes sir, you know, from down by the river, the wetlands, the swamp."

"Oh, malaria," I guessed.

Megan threw her hands up and said, "I don't know what you call it, sir."

"From being bitten by mosquitoes?" I asked for further clarification.

"Mask...?"

"Little flies, Megan."

"Could be, sir, I don't know." There was silence as we looked at each other, then she added, "She is in her bed, sir," with the clear implication that I should go to see her.

I ushered Megan in front to lead the way and she bounded up the stairs and I followed with Henry behind. Outside the door was a chair with Megan's mask on it. She picked it up and I said, "If it is malaria I don't think we need the masks, Megan." To be honest, I couldn't be bothered. We went in to find little Anne in bed, continually moving in discomfort. I felt her brow and she was very hot and was dripping with sweat. She was talking but saying nothing that made sense, so I assumed she was delirious. Then her mumblings turned to shouting, and Megan tried to calm her down.

"Have you given her anything, Megan?"

"Yes sir, I have, I gave her some of those little round things you gave to the sister and to little Matilda. I hope I haven't done anything wrong, sir."

"No, Megan, you haven't done anything wrong, that is good."

"And I gave her some valerian."

"Valerian?"

"Yes sir, you know, valerian." There was a pause, then she went on, "You know, sir, cure all." I didn't know, but I assumed it was some sort of herbal remedy and probably harmless, if ineffectual.

"Ah, that is good, Megan" I said, and a smile of relief came over her face.

In my research on medieval diseases, before Henry and I had returned last time, I had read about malaria being endemic in England up until the 19th century and I had picked some quinine tablets when we were in the pharmacy. I didn't know if antibiotics were useful for malaria but they could not do any harm, so I said, "Please bring me the medicine cases, Megan."

"Yes, sir." She left the room. Henry had been quiet, but when Megan left he asked a stream of questions, mostly wanting to know if Anne would be all right. I answered as honestly as I could.

"Henry, I don't think she has the pestilence. Megan is probably right, this is swamp fever. Whether or not she will be all right I don't know, but I do have some special medicines for this sickness."

Henry approached Anne, who continued to thrash about in her bed. It seemed she did not recognise her brother. Then the door opened and Megan reappeared with both bags of medicines. I quickly rifled through the bags and found the quinine. I had no idea how much to give her so I told Megan, "Give her one of these, four times a day, but two the first time."

"Yes sir, I will do that." Then she added, "The Lady Burford was much distressed about Anne so I gave her some valerian as well, so she is sleeping now, but it doesn't seemed to be working with Anne."

"Lady Burford is sleeping now?" I asked, rather surprised.

"Yes sir. Do you think I should give Anne some more valerian?"

I had no idea how much, or how often, Valerian should be given, but if it had made Lady Burford sleep perhaps it did have some real effect.

"When did you last give her some, Megan?"

"Oh, soon after dawn, sir."

"Yes, Megan, you can give her some more." With this I felt I had contributed all I could and left Megan to nurse her patient.

TWENTY TWO

PUS

That afternoon I was sitting with Henry chatting about not very much when there was a knock at the door. "Come," said Henry, and the door opened to reveal Cook.

"Sorry to disturb you, sirs," she said.

"Oh don't worry, Cook, I've been disturbed for years," I joked. She looked at me, and Henry intervened by asking, "Yes, Cook, what is it?"

"Begging your pardon, sir," she said with a curtsy, "Lord Burford would like to speak to you, sirs."

"Thank you, Cook," I said, and she gave another little curtsy and closed the door behind her.

A few minutes later we were entering Lord Burford's office to find Scabbard, Megan and Lady Burford were already there. "Ah, Lady Burford, I see you are um... feeling better."

"Yes, Edmund, I am rested and pleased to see you are back to cure Anne." I gave a nervous smile. They seemed to think I was some sort of miracle worker. What if she died? Sister Cecilia had died but they still seemed to think I could cure all I touched. I supposed it was desperation. This was how those quacks made money and why the churches were so full.

Lord Burford opened the proceedings by saying, "Now Edmund and Henry are here we can begin. Megan, let's start with you telling us how Miss Anne is."

Megan pulled herself up to her full height, took a deep breath and reported what she had obviously prepared. "Well, as you know, Miss Anne became very ill and I did what I could for her but could not make her sleep or keep still. But since Sir Edmund came back she is calmer and seems cooler. When I left her to come here, she was asleep I think."

There was a collective release of breath, especially from Lady Burford, and Lord Burford said, "Thank you, Megan, that is good news. And you don't think she has the same sickness as the sisters?"

"No sir, I think it is the swamp sickness and, er, Sir Edmund thinks I am right."

All eyes fell on me and I wanted the floor to open up and swallow me. I smiled and gave a gentle nod and thought, Megan knows more about this than I do.

"So, thank you for all you have done, Megan, I'm sure we're all very grateful." There was a mumbling of agreement around the room and Megan's face went a bright puce. She hugged herself and twisted from side to side like a seven-year-old. Lord Burford cut her embarrassment short by asking her, "And what about sister Florence?"

Megan pulled herself together and replied, "Oh, she is very much better, my lord. Sitting up in bed, eating her food, and this morning, do you know what she did? She went to the abbey chapel to pray! Of course, the other sisters helped her but, well, I think she was giving thanks."

"And she should, Megan. That is more good news. And what about Matilda?"

"She is becoming a real handful. She's up all day and running around that barn she's in thinking she's all better."

I was really pleased to hear this and wanted to ask more, but thought I had better not try to usurp Lord Burford's role. I did not want a repetition of what had happened when I had talked about the dirty water in the church.

Lord Burford then asked, "Do you think she is ready to come out, Megan?"

"I don't know, my lord. She seems well and full of life, er, most of the time, but I don't know, sir."

At this point Lord Burford looked at me and I took my opportunity to join in. "Well, I don't know either, sir. All I can suggest is that I go and see her."

Lord Burford nodded and I said, "May I ask Megan a question please, sir?"

"Please do" he replied, waving towards Megan.

"Megan, when did you last see Matilda?"

"Oh, this morning, sir. I haven't long been back."

"And...?"

"Well, sir, as I said, she was running around. I made her have a bath."

"A bath?"

"Well, sir, an all-over wash. I thought it was time she started being like a normal girl."

I smiled and replied, "You are entirely right, Megan. We must go and see her."

"Oh, yes, sir."

Lord Burford regained control and asked, "And John? The man who could not speak?"

"Oh, sir, I think he is fine now. Up and out. I believe Scabbard put it about that John had not got the sickness so, er, all is well now I think."

Lord Burford looked at Scabbard, who nodded in agreement. "And the stonemason?

"Rupie, oh yes, sir. His leg is healing well. I have changed his bandage and put on some of that creamy stuff Sir Edmund brought. I also gave him some valerian. Oh, I hope that's good, sir, I don't..." She was looking at me. "Oh, and Catherine, Rupie's wife, well, she is so happy because she thought Rupie would never work again. They are both happy. Everyone is happy. Oh, maybe not the barber surgeon."

There was a ripple of laugher around the room and Scabbard indicated that he wanted to speak.

"Yes, Scabbard, what is it?" said Lord Burford.

"I would like to talk to you later, and Sir Edmund, about the Barber Surgeon, sir."

"All right, Scabbard." Lord Burford looked around the room and added, "Do you have anything else to tell us, Megan?"

"Er, no, I don't think so, sir."

"Then you may leave. Thank you, Megan."

"Oh, thank you, sir." Megan hurried out.

"Now, gentlemen, we need to decide what we are going to do if or when the Bishop's men return. But first, Scabbard, what did you have to say?"

"Herrumm! I have been talking to the Barber Surgeon and we need some help from Sir Edmund about the cow pox."

"Oh, over to you, Edmund."

"Er, well, I... what did you want to know, Scabbard?"

"Sir, the Barber Surgeon does not know how much pus to use and where to put it?"

This rather caught me off guard and I replied, "Um, well do you have a young child for the purpose, Scabbard?" *My God, what am I saying? I cannot seriously be involved in giving a young child cow pox pus.*

"Yes, sir, we have. It is Edward's son, Jake."

"Edward's son?"

"Yes, you know, Edward and Marie whose son Edward is, is, er, not possessed by devils."

"Oh yes, of course. So he's the brother of the epileptic child."

"Yes sir, they wanted to show their gratitude for what you did for young Edward."

"What I did? I didn't do anything. I told you all, he was born with it and can't change."

"Yes sir, but you also said he was not possessed by devils, so he and his parents are not shunned by the townsfolk, so life is much better and his father has been given all sorts of work he didn't have before. Why, my lord has even had him cleaning up the horse shit." *What a lucky man!*

"Ah, yes, good, but are Edward and Marie aware that there is much risk in this? It may not work and he could be made very sick. Maybe even..."

"Well, I don't really know, sir, but they do want to show how thankful they are."

Their gratitude was very gratifying, but there was no reason to put their child's life at risk. I really did not know what the outcome would be. It might not work. Well, in the 21st century we know it does work. We know for a fact that the smallpox vaccine has saved millions of lives, and this is how it started. But I didn't know how to give it or how much. And it seriously could kill Jake. I really hated the idea of playing about with cow's pus, but I supposed I would have to go through with it. Not to do so would cause so much embarrassment, and I would lose the 'white coat authority' I had. And anyway, it may work and do some good.

"All right, Scabbard, can we go and try soon after we finish here? If that's all right with you, Lord Burford," I said, belatedly remembering my place.

"Yes, that's fine with me."

"Then I will go to find the Barber Surgeon as soon as we are finished here, sir," said Scabbard, and Lord Burford nodded his approval.

"So, we have to address the matter of the defence of the town because we can be fairly sure the Bishop's men will be back. To let it drop would be too much loss of face for the Bishop. Scabbard, you will be in overall charge of defence, of course, and you, Edmund, I believe you have brought a box of tricks?"

I was rather unprepared for this, and wanted to avoid telling him that all I had brought was a load of fireworks, so I replied, "Yes sir, and I need a high point to set things up."

"Well, there is the house at the top of the hill. We will be using that as a lookout point anyway. It is possible to see all over the town and for miles around. Would that be suitable, Edmund?"

"Oh yes, I think that would be perfect, sir. That way we can see who is coming."

"Well, yes Edmund, but not at night." I smiled and thought, we shall see!

"So, if it's all right with you, sir, can Scabbard arrange for my boxes to be taken there?"

"Scabbard?" Lord Burford asked.

"Yes, sir, I can arrange for that to be done."

"Good, then, if we are finished; we all have jobs to get on with." With that we stood and left the room.

Just outside I turned to Henry and asked, "Where is Megan?"

He responded by shouting, "Megan!" A few seconds later a door opened and she emerged. Silly me, all I had to do was shout for her! I supposed that was what servants were for, but I really couldn't get used to it.

"Yes sir, what can I do for you? she asked.

"Edmund wants you, Megan."

"Yes, what can I do for you, sir?"

"If you come with me I will show you," I said, and I started to walk to my room. As I looked back I could see Henry smiling.

In my room I picked up the book. "I have brought this for you," I said, offering it to her. She was silent and looked a little confused, but then her hand slowly rose to take the book.

"A book? For me?"

"Yes, Megan, a book for you." I came to her side and took it from her hand. "It is called Human Anatomy". I pointed to the title. "I know you cannot read, and this is in a strange language, but maybe you could learn to read your language, and then you could learn to read this. Anyway, it is full of pictures of how the human body works." I flicked through the pages. "Look, here is a section on childbirth. It shows all the inner workings of a woman. Why don't you look through it?"

She tentatively took the book back and began to turn the pages. "I know what a human is, but... ana...?"

"Anatomy. It means how the human body is made up and what everything does." I left her to look through the pictures, then asked, "Do you understand what it is all about?"

"I think so, sir."

"Good. You read it, well, look through it, and if you have any questions, just ask."

Her face was now a mixture of confusion and joy, and she almost skipped towards the door. Good, I thought. She seemed to appreciate it, even if she couldn't read it. And she could learn a lot just from the pictures.

Before she closed the door behind her she said, "I've never had a book before."

When she had left I lay on my bed and had started to drift off when there was a knock at the door. The door opened to reveal Scabbard.

"Good day, sir. If it is convenient for you, sir?"

"Yes, sure. Let's go," I said, and I followed him out of the room, out of the house and across town towards the fields. As we came around the corner I could see three people standing by a fence in a field next to a cow. I could see two of them were Edward and Marie. Marie was holding a bundle and as we approached I saw it was a baby and assumed it was Jake. The other man I assumed was the Barber Surgeon, but I couldn't remember what he looked like.

"Good day to you all," Scabbard said as we got close.

"Good day to you, Scabbard. Good day to you, sir," they chorused.

"Good day to you, Edward and Marie." I then realised I did not know the Barber Surgeon's name. Everyone referred to him as the Barber Surgeon. I looked at him and merely said, "Good day to you," then turned to Marie saying, "Ah, is this Jake?"

"Yes sir, and we have brought him for you to make healthy."

"Ah yes. Did Scabbard explain to you it might not work and he may get very ill?"

Marie looked at Edward, who said, "Oh yes, sir, but we have faith in you."

This really was not what I wanted to hear, but what could I do? I couldn't back out. I then looked at the cow and thought, yuk, it's dirty, it's covered in sores and it doesn't look at all happy. I then turned to the Barber Surgeon and asked, "Have you sterilised your knives?"

"Steri...?"

"Yes, boiled them in water before you put them back in your case."

"Oh yes, sir, I have done that."

I wasn't too sure, but said, "Good. I want you to take one knife and get a small amount of pus (the mere word made me feel sick) on it and then hand it to Edward."

The Barber Surgeon approached the cow and began to dig about in one of its sores. The cow twitched its skin and I said, "get down deep, so it's fresh pus."

"Yes, sir." The knife emerged and I could see some horrible slimy stuff on it and felt sicker. He passed it to Edward and then looked at me.

"Now get your sharpest knife and make a small scratch on the baby. Er, on his thigh."

Marie pulled back the blanket around the baby to expose his thigh. The Barber Surgeon moved towards the baby and I watched as he made a small nick in the child's flesh. Jake made a small noise but didn't really cry. A small amount of blood started to flow. I had to admit he had done it skilfully, and the knife was very sharp so that Jake hardly felt it.

"Now get the pus on the knife and put it on the wound." This he did and then wiped the knife on a cloth that didn't look too clean. He went to put it back into his case and I said, "No!

Not until you have boiled it again."

He looked chastened and mumbled, "Yes, sir." I wondered why I was worried about a bit of dirt when we were putting cow pus into a child.

"Now, all we can do is to wait. If it has some effect the cut should get red, and he will probably get ill, but not too ill I hope. I need to be told tomorrow what is, or is not, happening."

"Oh, yes sir, we will do that," Edward promised. Then I looked at the Barber Surgeon and asked, "Are you sure you know what you're doing now?"

"Yes, and now I am going to do it to everybody in the town who wants it."

This filled me with horror. I said, "Ah, no. You had better wait a few days to see what happens with Jake."

"Oh, all right sir." His head dropped. His chance to reassert his reputation and authority had been delayed, now that he had been told he could not cut off Rupie's leg.

With this I motioned to Scabbard to leave, and we all went our separate ways. I had a strange feeling of great guilt that I had done something terrible. But what else could I do? And maybe it would help. As we walked back, Scabbard and I talked about the process and the possibilities, and I was further frightened by the unquestioning faith they had in me.

TWENTY THREE

ESCAPE

When I was back at Burford House I found food and Henry waiting for me. As I entered the room he said, "You've been off with Scabbard, I hear."

"Yes, we went to vaccinate little Jake."

"Oh, Edward and Marie's baby."

"Yes, that's right."

"Vac-cin-ate? Is that what you call the process of making him never get the pox?"

"Yes, I think it comes from the Latin for cow."

"Oh yes, of course, *vacca*."

I was filled with guilt again and felt the need to expunge some of it by saying, "I can't promise he will never get the pox. In fact, I may have given him the pox. It could well kill him, Henry."

"Oh well!" was Henry's response, which didn't make me feel any better at all. He moved the conversation on by talking about our going to Northleach to see Matilda. Apparently the horses were ready and Megan would join us as soon as we finished eating.

In the courtyard three horses were waiting, and we quickly mounted as Megan appeared from the house looking flustered. "Come on, Megan. Your horse is waiting and it looks like the medicines are in your saddle bag," Henry gently chastised her.

"Yes, sir. Sorry, sir. Scabbard helped me get the horse ready a few minutes ago, then I had to..."

"Don't worry, Megan," I reassured her as I wondered if we would actually even need any of the medicines.

Off we went through the town and this time we left via Sheep Street. Very quickly I was feeling the strain on my legs. I had done quite a lot of riding since the first time I had arrived in the 14th century, but I was still not used to it and not much better than I had been then. However, I had done this journey a couple of times now, so it passed much more quickly than before and soon we found ourselves approaching the Northleach town barrier again. As we came near we were recognised and the barrier was opened. We passed through to greetings of, "Good day, Sir Henry. Good day, Sir Edmund." Megan was hardly acknowledged, despite visiting regularly and being responsible for cleaning up the town and probably saving many lives. It reminded me of Henry's comments that she was of the lower orders, a 'gay girl' and worst of all, Welsh. And this is in an area that was less rigidly socially structured than other parts of mediaeval society.

We went quickly on to where Matilda was quarantined. Outside we once more donned our masks, watched by a couple of people. One of them I assumed was guarding Matilda to make sure she didn't "escape".

I gestured to Megan to enter, and she opened the door. The open door cast a beam of light into the gloom as we entered.

"Megan! You are back again," a joyous voice greeted us.

"Ooh, sorry, sirs. I didn't see you there."

"That's quite all right, Matilda," Henry reassured her. "We have just come to see you."

"Good day, Matilda," I said as I approached her. "Would you sit down please?" She sat on the pile of bedding and raised her arm almost automatically. She had on a loose garment that I could easily move aside to look at her armpit, but my first thought was that she was a very different girl from the last time I had seen her. I could see why Megan said she was becoming a bit of a handful. She must be climbing the walls with boredom here.

I looked at Matilda's armpit and noticed there was not the stench there had been last time. I moved her round a little so I could see better in the dark, musty barn that had been her home since she got ill. I could see that her armpit was very scarred and there were scabs in various places. But most importantly, they did not appear to be oozing any pus. This was very pleasing. Not just for her but having just been playing with a cow's pus I was a little fed up with it, and I was not getting used to it at all. I didn't want to!

"A cloth please, Megan," I requested rather like a surgeon in an operating theatre. She dived in to the bag and passed me one. I wiped around Matilda's armpit and it seemed to be clean. "You say you gave her an all-over wash earlier, Megan?"

"Yes sir. Is that all right?"

"Yes, Megan. You have done well. As usual." Megan allowed a little smile to cross her face. Through the cloth I rubbed quite hard on the scabs but got no pus reaction. Nor did Matilda wince, which showed me she was no longer in pain. Having assured myself, I pulled down Matilda's garment and she lowered her arm.

"Well, what do you think?" Henry asked.

"I think she is almost better. Definitely not going to die!"

Megan let out a little repressed whoop. "So does that mean she can go out, sir?"

I thought for a second. "Well, I'm not sure. She might still be contagious." She looked at me blankly and I added, "She might still be able to make other people sick."

Now came my biggest decision since I had come to the 14th century. Should I allow her out and risk many more people getting sick? To be honest I had no idea how long *Yersinia pestis* remained active. Could I take the risk? Could I leave this poor little girl in here any longer?

I pondered this for a while and took a deep breath before saying, "Yes, I think she can." Megan did not restrain her 'whoop' this time and slowly Matilda realised what was being said. Henry smiled benignly. Now my main concern was how to give this news to the world outside Matilda's prison. I told Megan that all we needed were some clean clothes for Matilda.

"Oh, I think I... May I go outside, sir?"

"Er, yes, of course," I replied, wondering what she was talking about. Megan opened the door and left, and I could hear a commotion outside.

I looked at Henry and shrugged. He shrugged back. Soon the door opened and Megan reappeared again with a bundle of clothes. "I washed these this morning, sir, and hung them out to dry. They are all dry now, sir."

"Oh wonderful, Megan. Help her get changed." This Megan did, while Henry and I discreetly looked the other way. When I turned around Matilda had a smile that split her face from ear to ear.

"There we are, sir," Megan proclaimed.

"Come on then, let's take our masks off so everyone can see we don't need them any more," I said, and went towards the door. As I opened it I took Matilda's hand and said to Megan, "Take her other hand".

The door opened and I stepped out, pulling Matilda behind me with Megan on the other hand. Henry followed last, not a position he was used to. As we came out there was a deep gasp from the crowd. "Matilda!" a loud voice exclaimed, and I looked to see a woman, a little separate from the crowd, now rushing towards us. As she threw her arms around the little girl I realised this was Daisy, Matilda's mum.

The crowd perceptively moved back and Henry stepped forward to address the people of Northleach.

"As you can see, Matilda is well now. Sir Edmund has assessed her and has said she is healthy and no danger to anyone else." I didn't remember saying that! "She is as good as anyone else and must be treated the same."

Someone in the crowd shouted, "Praise the Lord!" and the crowd chorused, "Praise the Lord!" Although most of the crowd physically held back, a couple of young children, who, I assumed, were Matilda's friends, ran towards her. This seemed to make her less threatening to the rest of the assembly, and as the celebrations were continuing the three of us began to slip away almost unnoticed.

TWENTY FOUR

RECOVERY?

The next day there was a strange sense of waiting for something to happen, something that might or might not happen. But what? I really had no idea, and had to admit to myself that I didn't want to know. I was somewhat at a loose end, and Henry was not around. Whether he was still in bed, or he was doing something, I didn't know. I decided to visit the library again to see what I could find to fill my time.

As I was running my finger along the books on the shelf, moving a wave of dust as I went, there was a knock at the door. "Come," I said, and the door opened.

"Beg pardon, sir" said Megan, "Cook would like to speak to you, sir".

"Oh, all right, I'll come down then."

"Oh no, sir, she will come up here to you. I was just looking to see where you were."

"Oh, okay!" and Megan exited. I wondered what that was all about. - *did she really come to find me so that Cook could then come to find me?*

I fiddled about with the books for a while until there was another knock at the door. "Yes, come in Cook," I said rather irritably. A head and a shoulder came around the door as if she was afraid to come in properly.

"Sir, I have got some mouldy bread ready, sir, but I, er..."

"You don't know what to do with it?" I interrupted to save time.

"Oh yes, sir, I think I, er..."

"Why don't I come down to see, Cook?"

"Oh well, sir, if you wouldn't mind."

"Let's get on with it, Cook." I ushered her out and then we found ourselves having a little dancing session outside the door as she stopped to let me pass so that she could follow, rather than lead, her better. As we were walking towards the kitchen I was thinking that I had no idea what sort of mould was best and how to "harvest" it.

As we entered the kitchen I was pleased to find Megan was in the room. Whether this was by design or chance I didn't know but I said, "Ah, Megan, you can be useful here," and she came over to join us. I then managed to manufacture a conversation in which I gave the impression that I was kindly involving her in things, when really I was trying to pick her brains.

Cook picked up one of the mouldy loaves and dropped it again. There was a cloud of dust, or spores, that began to fill the kitchen.

"Let's get this mouldy stuff outside so the spores don't go over everything in here," I suggested.

"Oh, right you are, sir." Cook and Megan gathered the mouldy old dough into a cloth to take outside. Even to me this seemed rather silly - if we were gathering the mould as an antibiotic why would we worry about some going on other food? Except, of course, it would plant quick-growing mould on everything else.

Outside I got them to scrape off the excess mould around the sides but to try not to get too much of the bread that had not yet gone mouldy. "As much mould as possible and as little bread as possible," I told them.

"Yes sir, that's how I tried to give it to Matilda, but the more mould there is the less she wants to eat it."

"Yes, Megan, I can understand that, so that is why we must mix it with honey, or maybe some fruit, anything to make it more palatable."

"Oh, I see, sir, but I thought I had to make it into those little round shapes sir?"

I was confused, then I worked it out. "No, Cook, the shape of what we gave Matilda and Anne is not important, it is what is in it."

"Oh, I see, sir. Well, er, should I give some to Anne when we have made it up?"

Oh no, I thought, this is crunch time. Do I feed this foul concoction to the daughter of the Lord of the Manor?

"Er, yes Cook, do so, but Megan, you continue to give her what you call those little round things. And the other stuff; the quinine." I told her that to cover myself as to what would happen, though I was aware that that would confound any effects of the mould concoction. I thought ensuring Anne's recovery was a more important priority than some sort of medical experiment.

"Yes, sir," replied Megan and I dismissed myself from the process, thankful to get away. I returned to the library and was going through the books once more when the door opened without being knocked, so I knew it must be Henry.

"Oh, here you are, Edmund. I have been talking to my father about the swamp sickness and what to do, so you should come and talk to him as well."

"Um, all right then. Now?"

"Yes, now, Edmund." I followed him out, not knowing what sort of nonsense I was going to have to come up with this time to give the impression I knew what I was doing. At his father's "office" door Henry knocked and walked in.

"Ah, Henry, Edmund, come and sit down." We did so and Lord Burford began, "Edmund" (I froze), "you have shown us the importance of prevention of sickness and, from what I hear from the surrounding country, we are much better off here in Burford." I nodded in agreement and appreciation of the veiled compliment. "So, do you think there is anything that can be done to prevent future swamp sicknesses?"

As I had done some research before I left the 21st century, I did know something about this and was quite relieved to be able to pontificate again about something they thought I was an expert on.

I began by saying, "Well, yes sir, but it's a very big and long job." We looked at each other for a couple of seconds and then he told me, "Go on." I launched into an explanation of how the mosquitoes breed in open, stagnant water and the long-term solution was to drain the wetlands down by the river. I had no idea how to go about this, but assumed this would not be the first piece of swamp ever to be drained. This turned out to be right, as Lord Burford said he would get Scabbard on the task as soon as possible.

As Lord Burford was winding the meeting up I told him, "It would also help if any little pools of water left around after rain could also be dried up or brushed away so that they are not breeding grounds either. It only takes a few hours for the eggs to be laid and then to hatch." I didn't know if this was actually true, but neither did Lord Burford, so it didn't matter. We were bid good day and left the room.

Outside Henry turned to me and said, "I think Scabbard wants to talk to us about what you brought back with us."

"Eh?"

"You know, those boxes."

"Oh yes, the fireworks."

"Yes, those things. I believe Scabbard is in the courtyard, so let's go and find him."

As we entered the courtyard Scabbard dropped what he was doing and came towards us. "Good day, Scabbard," hailed Henry and stopped walking to allow him to approach us.

"Good day, sirs."

"I believe you have something to show us," Henry said as Scabbard reached us.

"Yes sir, if you wouldn't mind, I need to take you to the lookout roof up the hill."

"All right, Scabbard, let's go." We walked off towards the High Street. As we progressed up the hill Scabbard, who I thought was leading us, somehow dropped back to follow behind. Henry and I chatted and Scabbard spoke only when spoken to. I still could not get used to this social position thing, but they both seemed happy with it. It reminded me of the hymn *All Things Bright and Beautiful* we used to sing at school: "The rich man in his castle, the poor man at his gate." All happy and content to know our place in God's creation.

When we were half way up the hill I began to feel a little tired and out of breath, but I felt I needed to hide it, as neither Henry nor Scabbard were showing any sign of tiredness. It was a further signal for me that the Middle Ages might not be very healthy in many ways, but in terms of physical exercise, they were better off than we were in 21st century. I did manage to make it to the house without stopping or starting to breathe heavily, and we entered the building. The house was filled with men doing various things, mainly marching noisily up and down the stairs, although there seemed to be no family there and I did not ask why.

As we entered Henry urged Scabbard to lead the way, and we followed him up the stairs and through a window onto a half roof that ran around a sort of chalet upper storey. Then I saw the boxes we had brought from the 21st century. I began to open them and unpack what I had brought. I then turned to Scabbard for advice on how to launch the rockets. What I wanted was some milk bottles, but I knew that would mean nothing to them, so I started to describe something with a little round hole at the top. During a pause in what I was saying Scabbard opened his mouth, so I stopped and said, "Yes?"

"Would empty bottles do, sir?"

"Er, yes Scabbard, that would be perfect." I felt silly for trying to avoid talking about milk bottles.

It did not take long to set things up and soon we were making our way back down the hill of the High Street. After a few steps, Scabbard said behind us. "Sir, may I speak to you about Sister Florence?"

My first thought was, who was Sister Florence? Then I remembered she was the nun suffering from the plague but not yet dead, unlike Sister Cecelia.

As I was thinking Henry replied, "Yes, Scabbard, what is it?"

"Well, sirs, it is known in the town that Matilda has been set free and they are wondering..."

"Why Sister Florence is still in quarantine?" I finished his sentence for him.

"Yes, sir, I think so."

"All right, Scabbard, perhaps we can pop in on our way back." I directed this question more to Henry than Scabbard and he responded, "Yes, we can do that, I think."

As we continued on down the hill, I noticed the street was more active than usual. Some men were in chain mail and clearly armed. I had seen swords at the barriers to the town, but not being carried in the street. It reinforced my realisation that this was real, actually happening, and not just a dream or a computer game.

As we were approaching the door to the Abbey I could see Megan waiting for us, so this appointment was not quite so spontaneous.

"Good day, Megan," said Henry as we got closer.

"Good day, Sir Henry and Sir Edmund," she replied with no acknowledgement of Scabbard. Was this because she had spent half the day with him, or because in comparison to Henry and me, Scabbard was not important? She had with her a bag which she bent to open. Assuming it contained the masks and things I told her, "I don't think we'll bother with all that, Megan." I said this partially because, if we had been exposed to the bacteria a few times already, we might have had some sort immunity. Also, Megan had told me the sister was getting better. But the main reason was because I really couldn't be bothered.

"Oh well, if you're sure, sir."

"Yes, I think so," I reassured her. "Lead the way, Megan."

She opened the door and walked in. Scabbard stayed outside. A couple of the sisters saw us as we walked through and deferentially nodded. Soon we were at Sister Florence's bedside.

"Good day, Sister Florence," I said in my best bedside manner.

"Good day, Sir Edmund and Sir Henry. I would like to thank you both for all you have done for me," she croaked. She obviously had a lot more strength and mental capacity than last time I saw her.

"That's what we're here for, Sister Florence," I responded inanely, as I couldn't think of anything else to say. "And how are you feeling today?"

"I am much better, thank the Lord." She obviously was, as the last time I had seen her she could only wheeze.

The window was wide open, so they had continued to do as I had asked, and there were no dead pigeons around as there had been the first time I had been to see her and Sister Cecelia. I lifted her arm to look at the buboes and there were some horrible scabs there, but none seemed to be oozing pus. In fact, from the little I could see above the bedclothes, her whole body seemed to be covered in scabs that were obviously not going to heal completely. They would leave some horrible scars. This was much worse than I had seen on Matilda. Was this because Matilda had had a milder dose of the disease or was it that Matilda, being so much younger, was able to fight it much better?

"Can you stand, Sister Florence?" I asked.

"Oh yes, sir, I think so."

"Well, have you been out of bed?"

"Oh no, sir, I haven't been out of bed," she said in a tone that gave me the impression she was saying she had been a good girl.

"Then, you should do so. It is time you had some exercise for your muscles, especially your heart. But nothing too strenuous at first. You are not completely well but I don't think you're contagious any more."

At this I became aware that voices behind me were

expressing their pleasure at this news. I turned to see the Mother Superior and a couple of other nuns at the door. I had felt bad that Sister Florence was being "inspected" by me with Henry and Megan in the room, but to have a crowd at the door as well? Then I reminded myself that nuns don't expect any sort of privacy.

I used this opportunity to turn to the door and say, "Mother Superior, you and the sisters have looked after Sister Florence very well indeed. Now she is on the mend thanks to all the good nursing you have given her."

There were simpering noises from the nuns and the Mother Superior said, "We have prayed to God for her recovery. There has been a vigil in the chapel every day for her and Father MacKenzie has said a special mass for her."

A serene expression came across her face. I didn't know what to say except, "Yes, that will be what saved her."

There were mumbles of agreement and the Mother Superior added, "He has also said a special Mass for the soul of Sister Cecelia." I bit my tongue.

I then turned to Megan and the assembled to say, "But especially you, Megan. You have diligently carried out all my instructions, and that has been a big part of Sister Florence's recovery. Please keep bathing her wounds and giving her the little round things. Most of all she needs to eat to recover her strength." Megan had gone bright red at such acclaim, and in public, but I didn't feel bad about her embarrassment. She deserved it and the public accolade was calculated.

As we left the Abbey, a small crowd had gathered again, rather larger than that which had followed us around the town. I had hardly noticed them, so I must have been getting used to it.

Soon we were back at the house with not a lot to do. No television, no computer to play on and no phone to chat on. I whiled away the time until the night was replacing the day, which was the signal for bed.

TWENTY FIVE

THE BATTLE OF BURFORD

"Wake up! Wake up! Come on, Edmund, Wake up!"

I found myself standing up straight, though I cannot remember getting out of bed.

"Henry!"

"Yes, Edmund. It is thought there is an army surrounding the town."

"Eh?" I tried to think what he was talking about, and then remembered we were expecting an attack on the town by the Bishop's men, and Henry and I were their quarry.

"My father is commanding the soldiers along the river and we are to join Scabbard at the lookout." I stood and looked at Henry, hoping I would wake up soon and be safely tucked up in my bed at home.

"What?" I muttered pathetically.

"Come on, man, get dressed. I am going to finish my dressing. I will see you at the door." And he left.

It was only now that I realised it was dark outside. It must be the middle of the night. I pulled myself together and began to dress. I hurried down to find Henry by the door – in chain mail and a sword at his side. I looked him up and down and he declared, "There is not enough armour for all able-bodied men and I thought you were not versed in warfare". Although he tried to say it in a matter-of-fact manner, his voice could not disguise his negative thoughts about my lack of warfare skills.

"Er, no. You are right," I mumbled, pleased to find I was not expected to fight. I had given no thought to the reality of an armed attack on Burford. Now I had to face it.

We rushed out of the house and the main thought in my head was, What about breakfast? At the gates to Burford House were two armed men, and I could see the outlines of others in the dark. Now I realised that the House was actually outside the town and therefore more difficult to defend.

We moved down the road to the bridge, which was more heavily guarded than before. Into the town, and there were all sorts of men running around doing whatever one does to prepare a town for battle. Henry was almost running, and I was finding it hard to keep up. Even more so as we started to ascend the hill to the lookout house where my fireworks were waiting.

I pushed myself to keep up and managed to make it to the door of the lookout without appearing too wimpish. Up the stairs we rushed, avoiding men coming the other way, to the window which led on to the lower roof where we had been the day before. I followed Henry through the window and as I emerged I could hear Scabbard's voice, "Ah, Sir Henry... oh and Sir Edmund."

"Yes Scabbard, what is the situation?" demanded Henry.

"Well, sir, we believe the Bishop's men are down by the river banks, and up the hillside, massing for an attack. We don't think there are any at the top of the town, because that would be too obvious a place to attack, so they will attack at our weak points.

They have chosen a cloudy, moonless night so, of course, we can't see anything sir."

"I think I may be able to help you there, Scabbard," I threw in. I walked across the roof a few steps to where I had left the fireworks and found a row of bottles next to the boxes. "Bring me a light," I commanded, and Scabbard looked at me and said, "A light?"

"Yes, Scabbard, fire." He stood there and loudly requested, "Ember!" There was movement behind Scabbard and I began opening the boxes to find one of the particular fireworks I was looking for.

"Ah, here it is," I said, to myself as much as anyone else, and I popped the rocket into the bottle as a soldier came towards me with a glowing splint. I took it from him and said, "Now watch," then I touched the blue touch paper with the lighted ember. The paper at the base of the rocket began to smoulder and I stood back. A couple of seconds later the rocket whooshed into the air and all eyes around me watched it rise with a chorus of whoops. It was like being at a kiddies' bonfire party.

"No, don't watch the rocket. Look down over the valley." As I said this the rocket burst at its zenith and filled the night with brilliant light. I looked down to the valley to see many, maybe hundreds, of figures all across this side of the river Windrush. Not just men but many other items of equipment which I assumed were for their attack on the town. The whoops behind me changed to sharp intakes of breath as Scabbard and the soldiers looked out to see revealed all the hidden soldiers waiting to attack the town.

This was followed by total silence. I turned and looked at Scabbard, who eventually stuttered, "I...the...what was that?"

"A sky rocket. One designed to make a bright visual display, rather than a lot of noise." Scabbard stood looking at me. "I thought it would help you see what was going on in the valley."

"Er, yes. Now we know where they are, they have lost their advantage of being hidden until they attack. But they will not stay in one place."

"No, but it helps, and I have other bright rockets, but not many. I was thinking of something a little different." Scabbard said nothing and eventually Henry, who had remained silent, said, "What is it you have in mind?"

I began to explain to Scabbard and Henry what I was planning to do. We then had a discussion. We could hear a growing commotion in the valley below and thought that as the attackers' positions had been exposed, they were planning to attack immediately to avoid losing momentum. After a while Henry said, "We must let my father know".

Scabbard shouted,

"Ned," and he stepped forward as Henry began to write a message for his father. "You must go to Lord Burford and give him this message from Sir Henry." At this Henry folded his message and passed it to Scabbard, who passed it to Ned, who disappeared through the window.

We waited to see if Ned would come back with a reply, but before he did the sounds of battle erupted from the bottom of the town. It seemed Scabbard was right and our exposing the enemy's positions had pushed them into attacking. There was no time to wait for a reply from Lord Burford, so I began to line up the bottles as I needed them and picked up the smouldering splint from the floor to light the next volley.

Whoosh, another rocket shot into the sky. We needed to see what was happening now that the attack had begun, so this was another bright sky burst. As it burst high above the town we saw men rushing towards the bridge area and the back of the abbey. The defenders could be seen with bows, pikes and swords. As the battlefield was lit the attackers stalled, probably frightened by the sky burst. Their commanders could now be seen, and heard, urging them on to attack the "enemies of God". Unlike with the first rocket, the defenders did not seem to be traumatised, and whooped in applause, so it became clear that Ned had delivered the message and the defenders knew this was us making the light and not some act of God to frighten the "enemies of God". Their spirits were up, and that was part of my intention.

Now it was time to add a little more shock and awe. The glowing splint touched the blue touch paper of the next rocket and I moved quickly to light others before the first one went off. *Whoosh*, and the first new rocket shot into the air, not straight up like the last two but at more of an angle over the town. When the second rocket took to the air, the first one burst with not nearly as much light as the first one, but an almighty bang the like of which I had never heard. Nor had anyone else, by the reaction of the soldiers on the roof of the lookout. This was exactly what I had wanted, and I was so pleased I had bothered to go to a specialist firework dealer to get some very noisy "under the counter" fireworks, rather than buying some normal ones off the internet.

Although there was not nearly as much light from the banger, it still lit the ground under it and we could see the attackers coming to a halt, probably frightened almost to death. Good!

Down on the field of battle Captain Scarlett was trying to maintain discipline and prevent the stalled attack turning into a rout. "Come on, men! It is only noise. No one has been harmed by it." He ran forward, waving his sword in the air, and the retreat was halted as another rocket burst in the air above them. There was a common cry among the attackers and many men fell to the ground as the last one had been a lot lower when it went off.

Once more Captain Scarlett rallied his troops, saying, "Come on men! This is God's work we do against the heretics. They will all burn in hell, you don't want to burn along with them, do you?"

At this reminder of the fate that would befall them if they failed, the force turned once more to advance towards the town. The soldiers may have been petrified by the brilliant flashes and huge bangs, but their fear of the unknown cause them was as nothing to their fear of what their loving God would do to them if they failed to get the heretics.

At this moment a rocket failed to go off and landed near to Captain Scarlett, who saw it fall out of the sky. The men near to it, who had also seen it land, backed off, but Captain Scarlett took a few quick steps forwards and leaned over it for a closer look. Then he bent down to pick it up – by its tube, not by its stick. "Look, men, look. It is nothing. Just one of the Devil's tricks. There is nothing to fear from it."

Just then the "dud" firework went off in Captain Scarlett's hand. He let out an almighty scream that rose above all the other sounds. With this, those men who had been rallied to God's standard by Captain Scarlett's words of encouragement and threat turned and ran for their lives away from the town of Burford and towards their camp in Upton. More rockets burst above them, adding to their fear and encouraging them to run away, but as they did so the sky bursts seemed to follow them, impelling them to run faster.

I watched the events unfolding down in the valley from the lookout, along with Henry, Scabbard and the other soldiers. Some soldiers had left, as Scabbard thought they were needed more by the bridge where an attack was actually taking place, rather than up here at the top of the town, which was not currently under attack. I felt very pleased with myself that the rockets had been directed so effectively, but most of all with the effect they seemed to be having on the attackers. Volley after volley of rockets went off and sped towards the besiegers and we watched the forward rush being halted, and then advance again, only to be stopped by the next salvo of fear. Their mediaeval minds believed in ghouls, ghosts, gods and things that go bump in the night, so flashes and bangs merely confirmed the fears their society had conditioned into them from birth. At one point I felt a little sorry for them, but that thought was quickly dispelled.

We could see the back and forth movements in the valley but were not sure what was going on. Then we heard a loud scream above all the racket and saw the attackers begin to run away. Some dropped their swords, or whatever weapons they were carrying, perhaps in some vain attempt to not have any incriminating evidence on them. There was a large cheer from those defending on the bridge, quickly followed by those on the lookout. As we watched, the defenders began to pour over the bridge and into the marshlands surrounding the river in its flood plain.

"Oh no!" said Scabbard quietly.

"What is wrong, Scabbard?" Henry asked.

"They must not pursue. They must not break ranks." I know little about military tactics, but I do remember that breaking ranks to pursue the enemy was what probably what did for King

Harold and the Anglo Saxons. Now the pursuit halted and the men hurried back to their points of defence.

"They have been called back", observed Henry. "My father must be commanding them," he added, with an obvious sense of pride in his voice.

Now for a slight change of direction for my missiles. I repositioned the bottles so as to point them in the direction of their rout. Whoosh, whoosh, whoosh they went and exploded neatly over the heads of the laggards to those at the front of the shambles. This may have been a waste of the fireworks, as I didn't know if we would need them again, or it may have been helpful to continue to frighten them so they did not feel emboldened to return.

TWENTY SIX

FREEMAN

The sound of birds singing filled my consciousness and sunlight filled the bedroom. As I opened my eyes I didn't wonder where I was, as I had done previously, but I was questioning my memory of last night. Had that really happened? Had there really been an attack on the town by the church with the intention of capturing Henry and me on charges of heresy? Had that attack been scared off with little more than a few fireworks? What was happening now? Only one way to find out.

I jumped out of bed and quickly dressed. Downstairs I was greeted with warm smiles and Cook told me to sit in the breakfast room and food would be brought.

"What time is it?" I asked.

"About mid-morning, sir." Mid-morning? What does that mean? Mid from when? Dawn? From when the first person got up? I was still not really used to having no clocks around and having to accept vague estimations of the time.

"Where is Sir Henry?" I asked next.

"I don't know, sir, but I believe he is still asleep."

I rushed off to Henry's room and knocked on the door.

"Yes?" came the response and I opened it and walked in to find Henry getting dressed. Soon we were both downstairs at the laden breakfast table. We began chatting and, yes, it had all happened. We really had frightened off an armed force with little more than a few flashes and bangs. And it seemed that once again I was the hero. As we were chatting the door opened (there had been no knock, so I knew it could not be a servant) and Lord Burford's head appeared around the door.

"Oh, hello, Father."

"When you have finished, gentlemen," Lord Burford said with a smile.

"Certainly, father. Won't be long." The door closed again.

"What does he want?" I asked.

"I have no idea, but he looked happy. After last night, I am not surprised. Our forces were all prepared for the fight of their lives with my father pulling one way and Father MacKenzie pulling the other. We know he has been talking around the town and making sermons from the pulpit about loyalty to the Church."

"Has he? I didn't know that," I told Henry in all honesty.

"Oh yes, my father was not really sure which way the town's folk would go. But I think the events of last night show whose side God is on."

Oh, him again. He gets everywhere, I thought to myself, but kept my mouth shut.

Having finished our meal we left the breakfast room and I followed Henry, who knocked on his father's door and walked in. "Ah, Henry and Edmund. Good to see you. Come and sit down." This we did and Lord Burford leaned back in his chair with his hands behind his head and a beaming smile on his face. "Well, what did you think of last night?"

"I, er, I think it all went very well," replied Henry. I just sat and smiled.

"Of course, your thunder and lightning frightened them, Edmund, but they knew the defending force would be too much for them." I smiled once more.

"Yes, father, we could see from the lookout."

There was a silence and then Lord Burford went on, "Alfred is back from Windsor."

"Who is Alfred? I asked quietly.

"The man my father sent to see the King in Windsor a few days ago," Henry replied equally quietly.

"Oh, yes, him", I remembered.

"He has brought with him a letter from the King." Lord Burford picked up a letter on his desk and waved it in the air.

"Oh, what does His Majesty say?" asked Henry eagerly.

"Ho, ho, more of that this afternoon, my boy." With that we were dismissed and told to be in the town that afternoon, along with the rest of the townsfolk, where he would tell us more.

It was a lovely, sunny day after the clear night, so I filled my time wandering around Burford House grounds. At one point I came across Scabbard, who waxed lyrical about the events of the previous night. Then he said, "Oh, and that plant you gave me, sir".

"Yes, the Aloe Vera."

"Yes sir, it has been replanted and is doing well."

"Oh, I am pleased, Scabbard. Well, you know what to do with the sap, don't you?"

"Yes sir, and it is very easy to take cuttings from."

"It is very easy to transplant the shoots," I replied and with that, Scabbard excused himself.

Rachael, the housekeeper, entered the kitchen and said,

"Megan, come to my room, I need to talk to you."

"Yes, Miss," replied Megan and silently followed the housekeeper to another room.

"Now, Megan," Rachael said with a smile. "You know the whole town is to be addressed soon by his lordship and there will be celebrations afterwards?"

"Yes, miss, we are all looking forward to it."

"Well, you must dress extra prettily this afternoon with some lovely clothes." There was a silence and then, "I have only my..."

"Yes, Megan, we will provide you with some new clothes. I don't really know why, but these are the lord's orders."

"Will I have time for a bath and wash my hair please?"

"Yes, Megan, go and get on with it now," and Megan left the room thinking of the lovely shampoo Edmund had brought back for her.

Later on Henry and I walked into the town, where a large crowd had already gathered around a rostrum. We pushed our way to the front, which wasn't difficult as the crowd parted for us. At the front I looked around to see all of the Burford House household and, of course, Megan, who caught my eye and gave her hair a flick. The rostrum was still empty, but it was not long before there was the sound of marching soldiers and an armed force appeared around a corner, at the back of the rostrum, with Lord Burford at its head. There were mumblings and rumblings among the crowd, which calmed down as Lord Burford mounted the stage.

"People of Burford town!" This prompted loud cheering and clapping. "Last night God granted the town of Burford, and its people, a great deliverance. We have shown the world what we are made of and have maintained the special independence of Burford." I gathered by this that he was referring to the fact that Burford seems to be outside the mediaeval system in that people were allowed to own property and bequeath it to whomever they chose. They were all free men, not serfs – except for Megan, of course, who was brought there after a battle in Wales when both her parents were killed. She was officially the property of Lord Burford.

"In the battle of Burford our forces fought very bravely and chased away the attacking forces." He seemed to be putting a lot on HIS forces and little to the frightening effects of the unknown phenomenon of the fireworks, I thought to myself. "The town is still at risk." There were now low mumblings of disapproval and fear. "But I have received this letter from his Majesty the King," he said, waving the letter in the air, "in which he gives us his full support and…" – he paused for dramatic effect – "he has sent us this force you see behind me to help defend the town."

Wild cheering now followed, and this seemed to be genuine relief. Once more I felt that I was not taking this all as seriously as it should have been, or as seriously as the poor people of Burford did.

Eventually, above the dying applause, he said, "God was by our side last night and today he has sent reinforcements to stand by our side. For this deliverance, we must thank Christ, so there will be celebrations for the rest of the day and night." This was greeted by even louder and longer cheering. When it quietened down he went on, "There will be a special Mass said in the church tonight". This was greeted by very muted applause as the church, and Father MacKenzie, were known to have been behind the attack on the town last night.

"Not only has the King sent us soldiers, he has also sent us something else." At this Lord Burford turned to look behind and gave a nod. Then a man dressed all in black, who had been among the soldiers, stepped forward and climbed onto the rostrum. Lord Burford ushered him forward and declared to the almost silent assembly, "This is Father Mafeking. The king has written to the Bishop telling him that Father Mackenzie..." – he paused – "will no longer be the priest of St. John the Baptist and Father Mafeking will be relieving him."

Almost hysterical excitement now ran through the townsfolk. I was not part of this society, and did not really understand the mediaeval mind, but even I could see that Father MacKenzie was a great threat, not just to the Burford family but to the whole town and its way of life. This was the removal of their fifth columnist and the danger he posed.

Lord Burford raised his arms to quieten the crowd and said, "And just one more thing, David!" he shouted, "David from the church?

"Yes, sir", a quiet voice emerged from the crowd.

"David, come up here." David pushed his way forward to the front and a soldier helped him onto the rostrum. He was clearly very nervous and almost shaking as he stood before the lord in front of all the townsfolk.

"David", said Lord Burford, looking at the quivering mass. "I am in need of an extra stable lad and Father Mafeking tells me that he can spare you to come and work for me."

David's tense face broke into a broad smile and a soldier helped him back into the crowd, where his back was slapped so much the poor lad must soon have been black and blue. Henry and I looked at each other and exchanged a knowing smile. David was Megan's friend, the man who had warned us of the arrival of the Bishop's men so that we could escape just in time.

Without him we might both be dead by now. Or even worse, waiting to be burned at the stake. We both knew that Lord Burford did not really need another stable lad, and that this was in thanks to David for all his help, at the risk of his life had Father MacKenzie found out. He would have a better life in the Lord of the Manor's household than in the church.

As David was absorbed back into the crowd Lord Burford began again. "Megan," he said, looking at her in the front row along with rest of the household. I was struck by the thought that the lowest person in the town, the only serf as far as I knew, was in the prime position at the front of the crowd along with the rest of the Burford household. "Please come up here if you will." Megan stepped forward and the soldier helped her onto the rostrum. Unlike David, Megan was used to being talked to by the Lord of the Manor, but not in front of the whole town. Even though she was nervous, she did manage a flick of her lovely flowing newly-washed locks as she walked towards her lord.

Silence return to the crowd as they waited to hear what their lord had to say to Megan. Lord Burford looked again at his people and began, "I am sure you all know that Megan came here because of the wars in Wales, in which both her parents were killed. She was brought here by one of my men in the King's force and is, therefore, my property. She is the only serf in Burford, and since the arrival of the pestilence she has given invaluable service to the town, the surrounding countryside and to the sick in my own family. In gratitude to her," – at this he turned to the subject of his words – "Megan, I declare you to be a free man!"

More raucous applause and cheering. Everyone in the town had known Megan since she was brought here and knew of what she had done for the town and other places. She was genuinely loved and highly regarded. I looked at Henry, who gave me a knowing smile, and said, "You knew your father was going to free Megan, didn't you, Henry?"

"Well, I did speak to him about her," he answered honestly and modestly.

Megan's face was a mixture of confusion, joy and trepidation. Confusion because she could hardly believe what was happening, joy at being freed and trepidation as to what would happen to her now. If she was no longer a serf in the Burford household, what would she do? Where would she live?

Lord Burford raised his voice above the crowd once more, this time to address her directly. "You will continue to live and work in the Burford household, Megan, if that is what you wish. And I have one further task for you. I will appoint a tutor, and you will learn to read and write."

The response of the crowd to this was more bemusement than anything else. How could Megan, a Welsh serf girl, possibly learn to read and write?

He went on, "And you will have books on herbs and medical practice". Megan was now reduced to complete silence. Tears began to run down her cheeks and Lord Burford told her, "You may return now". A soldier took her hand to help her down, and she managed to say, "Oh, thank you sir. Thank you. Thank you. Thank you, sir!"

I wondered if the medical books would be of any use at all, but the herb potions might well be. And, of course, she would eventually be able to read the book I had given her on human anatomy. I looked at Henry, who gave me another knowing smile. Despite what he had said to me about Megan never being able to read and write because she was a gay girl, a serf and

Welsh, he must have thought better of her capabilities and persuaded his father to give her the chance to learn to read and write. Both of us knew that what Henry's father had said about Megan's help with the pestilence was true, but the main reason for his gratitude was that she had saved his son from the Bishop's men.

TWENTY SEVEN

GOOGLE

That evening I took myself for a walk to relax and gather my thoughts. I could not walk through the town, as I would be continually acknowledged as some sort of celebrity. I realised that this was what it must be like for those who really were celebrities, and I was not sure I liked it. Like most of my friends at school I would like to be famous, but it does have its downside. Therefore, I went the other way, out the back of Burford House and up the hill towards Chipping Norton.

The hill seemed to be one big field full of sheep. Hundreds of them, thousands maybe. They were the origin of the great wealth of the area and the reason why there were so many big churches for such small communities. With there being no consumer goods or foreign holidays, what else could they spend their money on other than praising the Lord and securing their place in heaven? I was reminded of the adage we were taught at school: "the best wool in the world is English wool, and the best wool in England is Cotswold wool". I looked around and could see no fences to keep the sheep in, but drystone walls all along the side of the road that would later become the A361. In that regard, nothing much would change over the next seven centuries.

My gentle saunter did not take me long and when I reached the flat top I stopped to view my surroundings. I looked down upon the town of Burford, and although the few side streets were a little shorter than in the 21st century, the town was virtually the same, with its beautiful church of St John the Baptist, the bridge and the one main street with buildings from the river to the top of the hill but no further. To the west of the town I could see strip fields along the river banks with almost ripe crops in them. I could even just about make out the parts that had been trampled down the previous night by the marauding Bishop's men. I hoped the crops would recover by harvest time rather than add to the misery caused by the Church. There were no yellow fields of rape, nor the blue of linseed.

Below me I could see the road going through the village of Fulbrook and the few houses of Swinbrook near to Burford. To the east I could not see Charlbury or Witney, but I did not know if this was because they were too far away or because they were still very undeveloped, so too small to see. Neither could I see the villages of Shipton, Milton or Ascot-Under-Wychwood, which were in the next valley. I paused for a while and sat on the grass soaking up the last rays of the setting sun to the west.

I thought it must be about 9:30 pm, as we were not long past the summer solstice, but then I realised that in the 21st century it would be British Summer Time, so an hour ahead of the sun's natural time. So in the 14th century it was 8:30 pm.

As I sat motionless the sheep slowly gathered around me to have a look. I kept pretty still and eventually a couple of them got close enough to sniff me. This was fine, but when one started to lick my face I twitched and began to stand up, and the sheep ran away.

I felt refreshed. I had seen my local area from a viewpoint I would probably never would have seen in the age of the motor car. Now it was time to go back to Burford House. Of course the journey down the hill was much shorter than going up and I was soon approaching the back of the house and saw Henry coming out to meet me.

"Good day, Edmund," he shouted.

"Good day, Henry," I replied and soon we were together as Henry sat on a garden bench and I sat next to him.

"Where have you been?"

"Just for walk to gather my thoughts."

"I see, your thoughts on what?"

I paused before replying and Henry did not interrupt the silence. "I think my purpose here has been fulfilled." As these words left my lips I became aware of how pretentious they sounded. Henry's face reflected his lack of surprise at my thoughts and he said nothing. "Perhaps it's time I left and did not return."

"Perhaps it is, Edmund. Though I will be sad to lose you, as will the whole town. You must go back to your own country." Country? What did he mean, my own country? Perhaps he still couldn't get his head around the fact that I came from a different time, and it was easier to think I came from a different country.

"Your country has so many good things such as the fast carriages, the picture wall and all the fat people, but, er..." he trailed off.

"But? Henry, come along, spit it out."

"Well, it is all very wonderful but, er..." I looked at him to say 'get on with it' and he went on. "Well, no one seems to have any respect for their betters". I reminded myself that he was a product of his time and very open minded for that.

"Yes, you are entirely right," I replied. What else could I say? He gave me a satisfied smile. "So I had better get ready to leave."

"But before you go, Cook has something of yours. Come along." He got up, so I followed him into the house and kitchen."

"Cook, you have found something of Sir Henry's I believe."

"Oh, yes, sirs. It is over here." She turned to pick up my backpack, which I had not seen, or thought about, since I had arrived the first time. "I'm afraid we had to open it, sir, as there was a terrible stink coming from it. We found rotten eggs and bread in it."

"Yes, I had completely forgotten it. I'm sorry about the smell."

"That's all right, sir, we have washed it for you."

"Oh, thank you, Cook." As we left the kitchen I was thinking it would be useful for me to take things back in. Also, it would not do to leave it there to confuse the archaeologists in a few centuries.

We both went upstairs, and I realised I didn't have anything to take back with me. All the medical things needed to stay there, and they might as well play with the left-over fireworks. In my room I stood for a while and looked around, tempted to say, "Bye, bye room", as I would have as a child. Then I took a a deep breath, looked at Henry and we both left the room and walked downstairs.

At the bottom Megan was strategically doing something and I walked towards her and said, "Goodb... Good to see you, Megan. I am very happy to see your new status in the town." She grinned from ear to ear and I casually waved to her as

Henry and I walked towards the horse yard. At the door I took one last look back at her, feeling guilty that I would never see her again and was not going to say goodbye.

In the yard Henry confided in me. "She has been going around the town introducing herself to people who have known her for many years as Megan Freeman," he said, and I realised this must be the origin of the surname Freeman.

As we were mounting the horses I said, "Henry, it must have been you who persuaded your father to free Megan and to give her the chance to read and write."

"Not to free her, no, that was his idea. He is fully aware of what she has done for the town, the countryside and, most of all for our family. It was just my idea to teach her to read and write, and he did not need much persuading."

"Which reminds me. How is your sister Anne?"

"Oh, she is much better and well on the mend."

"Good." We rode off, through the town and up to the barrier, which opened for us as we approached with little or no ceremony. The guards were getting used to us coming and going.

I was not sure if we would find the blue windmill, but once again it was easy to distinguish the hoof prints of last time made by us, the town guards and the Bishop's men, even after the torrential rain. Soon the windmill came into sight and we dismounted to get the laptop out from under the bush. We both sat on the ground as I opened it and watched the icons populate. This time Henry did not grasp the other side as I tapped in, "bbc.co.uk/cricke..." I looked at Henry as I tapped the final letter "t", and we both smiled as the mist gathered...

There was a gentle bump, and I realised I had arrived back in the 21st century without really saying goodbye to Henry. Too late now, I told myself, and reinforced it with the thought that never again would I go back to the 14th century.

I was filled with an overwhelming sense of loss and loneliness that did not make sense. I was safe back home and had survived an amazing adventure that would never be repeated – I hoped. I realised that the fact that I could never tell anybody about this without risking getting sent to the asylum was the reason I felt so lonely. To distract myself I found my phone, which I had left on charge, and opened it. Absent-mindedly I went into Google and tapped in "The battle of Burford".

"The battle of Burford is said to have taken place in the 14th century when a strange young man arrived in the town to defend it from the Church, which was trying to control the town and arrest any who objected. The young man rallied the town and helped fight off the attacking church soldiers with magical lights in the sky and ear-bursting explosions.

"There is no written or archaeological evidence for this story and it is generally regarded as apocryphal, rather like the story of Robin Hood or the Pied Piper."

The end